Published by
Viva Djinn (Horde) Pub
Norwich, UK

www.vivadjinn.com

ISBN: 978-1-913873-02-8

CW00660155

Copyright © 2020 David Viner.

All rights reserved. No part of this publication may be reproduced, stored in a retrieval system, or transmitted, in any form or by any means without the prior permission in writing of the publisher.

All characters in this book are fictitious, and any resemblance to actual persons, living or dead, is purely coincidental. Well, apart from Robert Kett, of course!

This book is sold subject to the condition that it shall not, by way of trade or otherwise, be lent, resold, hired out or otherwise circulated without the publisher's prior consent in any form other than that supplied by the publisher.

British Library Cataloguing in Publication Data available.

Design and layout: David Viner

Printed by PBtisk, Příbram, Czech Republic

Time Portals of Norwich

January 2011

Cassie didn't want to be there. She looked up at her grandad sitting beside her, at the tears in his eyes. She felt his hand shake as it held her own. She thought that maybe he didn't want to be there, either. Cassie also had tears in her eyes and her hands trembled as well. She felt she'd had tears in her eyes for ages. How long had it been? It was a Monday, the last day of January. That meant she'd been crying for a whole week. Every day since January the twenty-fourth.

But it wasn't over yet, and she thought she'd be crying for many more days. Perhaps she'd be crying from now until the end of time.

People were taking it in turns, getting up and saying things about her mum. Some of the things they said were probably even true. But these people hadn't known Mum like Grandad and herself. Nor had they lived in the same house as her Mum. They hadn't seen her mum as she'd seen her: happy, angry, relaxed or stressed, and all the other things she remembered about her mum since the earliest time she could recall seeing her. Very few of them had seen her in pain, or fading to a shadow, or crying with the knowledge that she couldn't hold on much longer.

Then Grandad stood up and made his way to the lectern. Cassie didn't want to look at him. Not because she didn't like looking at him. It was because, behind him, she would see the coffin. And that made her want to cry even more.

Her grandad started speaking, and what he said echoed to Cassie more truthfully than anything that had come from any of the others. He said what she might have said if they'd let her. Or if she wanted. Actually, she did want to say things but she was afraid they'd come out wrong and that people might laugh or tell her she remembered things wrong. But they wouldn't say that to Grandad, so Grandad spoke for her as well as himself. What he talked about was the mum she remembered. The mum she didn't want to forget. The mum she would never see again.

Eventually, the saying of things came to an end and people got to their feet. They all started to file out of the place, this – oh, she didn't want to give it its name. Because she knew what happened here to dead people. She thought of the flames and how they'd burn through the flesh. At least they wouldn't do it while everyone was there. She'd be screaming if they did. She knew how the flames felt – but only her mum had known that Cassie knew about the flames. And now only Cassie knew.

Outside, it was sunny, though cold. She felt it ought to be raining. It always rained on TV when there was a funeral. Why wasn't it raining here? They were standing amongst the flowers that people had brought. There were lots of flowers. Cassie didn't like cut flowers – she knew they'd be dead soon.

People were coming up and talking to Grandad, holding his hand and saying more sad things. Sometimes they talked to her as well, but she merely nodded and wished they'd go away.

The last of the people came out the building. Amongst them were two women, both exactly the same height and looking like they might be mother and daughter. The older one was dressed all in black, the younger one in a faded blue denim jacket and jeans. There was something familiar about them, and not just that their eyes were an intense shade of blue, the same as her own. The younger one looked at her. Her face looked kind but there was also something that made Cassie think the woman was scared. The older one's face was harder, bruised on the forehead and filled with more shadows than just those that sat under her eyes. It reminded Cassie of how her mum had looked near the end. The younger woman lifted a hand slightly and waved to her. Then she gave Cassie a brief smile before they both turned and walked away.

Cassie wondered who they were.

Underground

Grandad

"Told you at breakfast time I was going out!"

"Uh, what, Cassie?" her grandad spluttered. "No, I don't rememb…"

"Yeah, like no change there," she muttered, though not loud enough for him to hear. "Oh, Grandad, it's all you ever do now – forget things, that is. I keep telling you. Write it down. Write everything down."

"Oh, please don't go on, love."

"Sorry, but…"

"No, it's my fault," he sighed. "I know I'm not getting any better. I wish I was. Oh, I wish I could wake up."

"You are awake," she said, hugging him and feeling guilty. He couldn't help it. That was the trouble – no one could help him, not even her. But no one was helping her, either. She held him close – her once great big Grandad. Now he was mostly skin and bone.

"Right," she said, releasing him from her arms. "I'm going out now. Okay?"

His looked at her, his expression blank. "Going out? But didn't you go out last night?"

Cassie's eyes shot ceiling-wards in exasperation.

"Ah, like you remember that all right, don't you?" she shouted.

"Please don't shout, Cass," he whimpered, hanging his head in that way that always made her feel bad.

"Yeah, I did go out," she said eventually, her voice shaking more than a little. "I went up to Aldi to get some things, cos you… well, let's face it, you can't do the shopping anymore. Not if we want to eat properly. Even with a list you forget things. Anyway, shopping don't count as going out. It's Saturday and I'm going down the city to meet friends. I need a break. Is that okay?"

"Friends?"

"Yes, friends from school."

"Oh, I suppose so. You will be back soon, won't you?"

Cassie sighed again. "Sometime this afternoon. Before tea, okay?"

"Where's your mum, Cass?" he suddenly said. "Did she go out as well?"

"Oh, for goodness sake, Grandad. Mum is... Mum is never coming back. Surely, you *must* remember that..."

He looked at her for a long moment, his brows creasing and uncreasing as he struggled to locate the memories. Then his shoulders slumped. Wandering towards the kitchen, he mumbled something that might have been an apology.

How could he forget? His own daughter, seven years ago. She heard him in the kitchen attempting to make another cup of tea. At least he could still manage to do that for himself.

Cassie's phone pinged and her left hand flipped the case open. She read the text. It was from Georgia – she was bringing Mark. Well, she would be, wouldn't she? Like those two weren't already joined at the hip.

From the kitchen she could hear her grandfather rattling a spoon around the sugar bowl.

"One only," she said. "You're supposed to be cutting down. You're diabetic, remember?"

The spoon rattled at least twice more followed by the boiled kettle switching off.

"I give up," Cassie whispered as she opened the front door. "Bye," she called.

"Oh, you going out?" said her grandad. "Is your mum going with you?"

"Gah!" Cassie spat, slamming the door behind her. *How could he be so... so damned...!*

She stepped out into the heat.

"Hell," she said. It had been way cooler in the house. Here they were on the last day of June after a week of burning weather and all the forecasts were promising more of the same. The summer of 2018 was definitely going to be hell.

As she headed towards the Heartsease bus stop, Cassie fumbled in her bag for her sunglasses.

"Nice out, isn't it!" came a voice, which caused Cassie to drop her sunglasses. She looked around – there was no one there.

"Bugger," she said under her breath before hissing, "Go away!"

It was obviously going to be one of those days. She retrieved the sunglasses from the pavement, noting the new scratch across one lens. She wasn't in the mood for this. She was already seeing red over Grandad, and now it looked like she was in for a day of hearing and seeing other things.

Never good things, either.

It wasn't supposed to be this way. After Mum died, Grandad was meant to look after her. But now it was all the other way round. Not her bloody fault he was going senile, was it? These past few weeks he'd got even worse. She'd tried registering as his carer but the paperwork had been so confusing. Citizens Advice was no help, so she'd given up. At least he was getting a full state pension plus a bit extra from a company one. But that, along with the paltry child benefit payment, never seemed quite enough for the two of them to live on.

Another year, after A-Levels, I'll be able to get a job, she told herself. Yeah, and so much for the idea of university. There was no way they could afford the fees and, anyway, he wouldn't be able to cope on his own.

As she stomped up the incline of Heartsease Lane, her phone pinged again. She groaned. Jason had called off, and she'd really wanted him to be there. The time on her phone said just gone eleven.

I'm going to be well early.

On The Bus

At the roundabout she negotiated the Plumstead Road traffic to cross over to the bus stop. She couldn't be bothered to use the pedestrian crossing further up the road. There were several people already waiting and a number 23 arrived a couple of minutes later.

A fat woman wearing far too many clothes for the weather struggled onto the bus in front of her. The woman reeked of sweat but hauled herself inside. To avoid her Cassie went upstairs to the top deck after purchasing a single for Castle Meadow. It was about half full and, despite all the windows being open, stunk nearly as bad as the woman downstairs.

The front seats where the cleanest air was were already occupied. She moved down towards the back past the usual collection of peasant wagon victims. Halfway down, an empty pair of seats on her right weren't quite as empty as she'd initially thought.

"Damn," she muttered, "here we go again."

The man was partially visible. *At least I can see him this time,* she thought. She'd seen him before. He was often on any bus she got on.

He turned empty eye sockets towards her and grinned. "Today's the day, time to play, eh, young Cass or is it old Cass?" His voice, the same as the bodiless one she'd heard earlier, cut like sandpaper across a fresh wound though, of course, no one else noticed. She tried to ignore him and sat near the back but, although his shoulders stayed still, his head rotated 180 degrees to face her. "Hot enough for Hell, such a delightful smell," he cackled, adding, "'specially with sonny Jim Grandad boiling the tea and you as well."

Cassie looked out the window. *Why me? Like, what did I do in a previous life to deserve all this crap?* But she knew if she ever told anyone about the things she saw or heard they'd say she was mental or something. So, only she and her mum ever knew about it – and Mum was no longer in a position to tell anyone.

She kept her gaze firmly out the window trying to ignore the whatever-it-was. It made several more meaningless comments like, "You feeling all elemental, Cassie?" and "There's no time like last week or 1988 or 2010, don't ya know, girl. Tickets please."

Cassie pretended to check her phone. Actually, she did check her phone but neither Snapchat nor Instagram were showing anything important. No more messages had appeared saying who was or wasn't coming today. She even checked Facebook but that was a waste of time, as always.

Two stops further she looked up as several more people got on. Two boys sat where the almost-man had been, though she hadn't noticed when he'd left. There was now no sign of him and Cassie let out a short sigh of relief. The bus trundled down Kett's Hill and, once the traffic cleared, turned left at the roundabout at the bottom. Cassie clamped her teeth together and shut her eyes for a moment – she knew what was coming.

Despite the heat, she suddenly found herself shivering. Out the window she caught a glimpse of Cow Tower. As always, the sensation of being in a crush of dead and dying bodies enclosed her. A few seconds later a second wave of nausea hit her as the bus passed the Lollards Pit pub.

Damn it. I wish I'd never gone on that bloody ghost walk last year.

Even as a nine-year-old, this area of the city had given her the creeps. But the guy running the ghost walk had been quite theatrical. His lurid tales of death and executions had emphasised the sense of revulsion and trepidation she already suffered. How much of it had been true? Especially that bit about a woman who'd been burned to death.

On the bus, Cassie was sure she could feel flames licking at her legs while her top half shivered. It was only by the time they'd passed Pulls Ferry that the sensation finally dissipated.

Castle Falling

Although the bus was five minutes late reaching Castle Meadow, Cassie still had more than half an hour to kill before meeting the others at twelve. She got off, glad to be away from the stench and people. Outside, a relentless sun pounded down. Above her, the stone walls of Norwich Castle gleamed so bright it made her squint, even through her sunglasses. As usual, the ghost of Robert Kett, hanging in his chains from a gibbet mounted high on the castle wall, waved to her as she passed below. She ignored him and headed for the mall entrance. Once inside, she took off her sunglasses and popped them in her bag. She descended the escalator to the lower floor hoping it would be cooler there.

It wasn't.

But there was something else. Not an apparition this time, more of a feeling of collapse, of stuff falling on top of her and burying her alive.

She tried to ignore it.

Maybe I am going mental. Five things in less than half an hour – it's getting downright stupid.

She blamed her grandad for sparking things off and then felt guilty again. *He can't help it,* she told herself. *I wish I could help it, though,* her afterthought added.

Starbucks beckoned. She fancied a coffee before meeting the others. She had enough time – but could she spare the money? She felt a few pound coins in her jeans pocket and was about to go in the shop but stopped dead.

Something was blocking the entrance.

"Wotcha, Cass," the something said, becoming less transparent. "Fancy a ground coffee, with lots of air bubbles? And made from scalding water from a fire that comes straight from hell?"

Cassie let out a grunt of exasperation. That the thing used to be or was supposed to be a man was obvious. It had a body, legs, arms and a head. Some of them were even in the right places in relation to each other. But the body and limbs had seen better days, and had probably seen them on different people – far too many different people. The thing had three legs and at least six arms. Equally obvious to Cassie was that no one else could see the thing – people were casually walking through it as if it wasn't there.

It took a lumbering step towards her and she backed away.

"Hah, you want to watch the sky don't fall on yer head, girl," it laughed, brandishing a smile that would have been far less unpleasant if the thing had possessed a full set of teeth.

There was a rumbling sound. It almost did sound like the sky was falling. None of the other shoppers appeared to take any notice. The thing laughed some more.

A woman who must have been inside Starbucks strode through the apparition to stop directly in front of Cassie. There was something familiar about her. She looked like she was in her late thirties or early forties maybe. Her hair, worn long, was unkempt and frizzy. It acted in a manner that suggested it had a mind of its own – a bit like Cassie's had been until she'd straightened it. The woman's hair was nearly as dark as Cassie's as well. It wasn't her only dark aspect. She was dressed completely in black – boots, jeans, top and a leather jacket that was equipped with more zipped-up pockets than she had ever seen on one garment. The woman must have been boiling in all that.

"Here we go again," the woman sighed. "Okay, Cassie. We need to get out of here. Right now."

The woman grabbed Cassie's elbow.

"Who the hell are you?" Cassie said, pulling her arm from out of the woman's grip and backing away. A few people passing by glanced at her, wearing strange expressions before hurrying on.

"You can call me Kay," the woman said, advancing again on Cassie.

"What do you mean 'call you Kay'? Isn't that your real name?"

"Ah," said the woman who wanted to be called Kay. "Well, that's new. Got a bit more bite this time around, have you?"

"More bite," the thing repeated, laughing.

"Ignore it," Kay said. "This one is relatively harmless."

"What? You can see it as well?" Cassie said, retreating even further. The woman nodded.

The rumbling increased. It came from all around though mostly from above.

"Damn," Kay said, looking up, "the gate is already falling. Quick. This way if you don't want to be crushed. Hold my hand."

"Why?"

"Ah, please yourself. Actually, it doesn't matter with this one. It always goes to the same place. Though," she added, "not always the same time."

Kay took off running in the direction of Boots. Cassie, panicking as the noise got louder, which caused a weird rippling sensation to pass through her body, found herself following. The shoppers around her, in addition to ignoring their apparent impending doom, also seemed to become less substantial. Cassie was sure she ran right through at least two of them. The sunlight, which had been pounding through the glass roof, grew less intense and Cassie looked up. Bad mistake. She saw rocks, bricks and soil crashing through the glass though, after blinking in surprise, she noticed that the glass itself hadn't actually had the decency to shatter.

Her legs pounded after Kay who bore right at the spiral staircase. They headed towards the lifts and escalators that led up to the cinema. Behind them tons of masonry tumbled down turning the main part of the mall dark with its mass. They carried on running towards the lifts but more changes were taking place right beside her.

"What's happening to the shops?" Cassie gasped. She saw their lights flicker out, the glass fronts disappear as they turned into empty, grey shells. Ahead, the lifts disappeared while the walls were stripped of their paintwork.

Then the whole roof was whipped away and the two of them came to a halt in a wide open area. They were alone. Cassie looked upwards and found herself staring at a night sky along with a spattering of stars.

"What on Earth just happened? Who the hell are you?" Cassie shouted. Her breath was not only coming in short bursts but condensing in the air in front of her. It was now cold, very cold.

"Wait," Kay said, standing there, hands on hips. "This could be the one with the fireworks."

"What are you talki–"

"Shut up," Kay barked. "I'm looking for the path out of here. It's not always in the same place."

Cassie jumped as, above them, rockets lanced into the sky. They burst into a spray of colour and delayed noise. Then came the 'oohs' and 'aahs' from a crowd of people that Cassie could hear but couldn't see.

"Ah, there it is," Kay said as another burst above them lit up the wide concrete pit in which they stood. "This way."

The woman started moving again and Cassie felt she had no choice but to follow.

"Where are we?" she asked, catching up.

"Castle Mall, of course," Kay said, picking her way towards a curved ramp that circled up to ground level.

"This ain't Castle Mall," Cassie spat back.

"Yes, it is. But right now it's no longer 2018 – it's the early nineties, 1991 I think. Anyway, it's long before you were born so they haven't finished building it yet."

"What? Are you kidding?"

"Get used to it," Kay said. "We've got a lot more like the last two to get through before we have any hope of getting you home."

"The last two?"

"Yeah, I think the old castle gate came crashing down hundreds of years ago."

Cassie's mouth hung open as she followed Kay up the ramp.

Hot Dogs

"It always starts in Castle Mall with the gate falling," Kay explained, matter-of-factly as they approached a solid fence that was at least a foot taller than either of them. "Then, at the lifts, it branches. We always come out in the early nineties. Sometimes it's winter with the fireworks and other times it's late summer. Always at night, though."

Kay located a door in the fencing and opened it which brought them out at road level. It was packed with people. Peering over the heads, Cassie thought it resembled Farmers Avenue, though it looked nothing like she remembered. Kay pushed Cassie out into the crowd before closing the door behind her, checking that the lock clicked shut.

"How did we get here?" Cassie said. "And why?"

"So many questions," Kay laughed, pushing her way through the throng.

"They don't seem to see us," Cassie said.

"No," Kay agreed. "Stand on someone's foot, though, and they will. We're out of our time. It's like it's hard for them to focus on us so, mostly, they just ignore us. I think they find that easier than dealing with it."

"How does that work?"

Cassie thought she saw Kay shrug as she followed her past the Bell pub.

"Can you feel it, Cassie?"

"Feel what?"

"The next portal," Kay said. "Or crossing point, wormhole, gateway or whatever you want to call it. I prefer portal."

"How should I know?"

"You felt the gate coming down before it happened, didn't you? And the stuff around the Cow Tower?"

"Er, yes. How do you know about that? Just who are you?"

"Who do you think I am?" Kay stopped pushing past people and turned to stand directly in Cassie's path.

"I don't know," Cassie said, shivering and wishing she'd worn something that didn't have short sleeves. Then again, she hadn't expected to come out into 1990s November weather on the same day as experiencing a June 2018 heatwave.

But the woman was far too familiar. They stood inches apart and, as they were pretty much the same height, Cassie stared directly into Kay's face and eyes – eyes that were as blue as her own. She had one of those déjà vu moments. Except this was more like a 'looking in a mirror' moment.

"Are we related?"

"Hah!" Kay shouted. "Come on. I could've sworn you were brighter this time around."

"What do you mean 'This time around'?"

A picture of her mother entered Cassie's head. She remembered that same wild hair. Her mum had never had hers straightened. It had never been straight except, of course, near the end, just before it had all fallen out.

"Are you…"

"Your mother? Nope, close but not close enough."

"How did you know I was thinking that?"

"You always think that first. Well, when you're capable of thinking, that is. I cut you off before you had a chance to mention it this time."

Then Cassie noticed a small scar on Kay's right cheek. Her hand moved to her own right cheek, to the identical scar. She could still remember the fright of toppling off her pushbike at the age of six, falling face downwards onto the sharp stone that had cut deep into her cheek. So no, not a mirror – this was back to front.

"Yeah, now you get it."

"How?"

"Tell you in a while. C'mon, I'm hungry. Let's find a hot dog or fish and chip stall or something. Then maybe something warmer for you to wear."

They stood in front of the library eating the hot dogs Kay had bought from a stand a couple of minutes earlier. Before them, the bulk of the Saint Peter Mancroft church obscured the view of the castle and fireworks. But Cassie was staring at the library.

"It burns down in two or three years time," Kay explained between bites.

"So, how do I become you?"

"By failing to d…, er, to get home."

"But wait, you said 'This time around' earlier on," Cassie said. Her brain was in knots trying to figure things out.

"Yes, I did. Confusing, isn't it!"

"How old are you?"

Kay shrugged. "How old do I look? It sometimes feels like I've been doing this for much longer than the time I was you."

"I– I don't know. Forty-ish, I suppose."

"Well, thanks a lot."

"How come you don't know?"

"It's hard to keep track of birthdays when you keep dodging around in time."

"And you keep on meeting me?"

"Yep, lost count of how many times."

"Why don't I remember that?"

"It's not exactly the same you. There are hundreds, possibly even thousands of you. All slightly different."

"Huh! That doesn't make sense. So, what happens?"

"Well, we often have a conversation very similar to this and then I, well, I try to keep you safe."

"Try? What do you mean try?"

Kay made an expression and stared off into the distance.

"Wait, are you saying that I don't stay safe?"

Kay said nothing but stuffed the rest of the hot dog into her mouth and threw the greasy napkin onto the ground.

Cassie finished her own off but folded her napkin neatly before pushing it into a pocket of her jeans. How could she have turned into Kay? She could see how the woman's face resembled her own, but age had taken the smooth roundness she knew from the mirror and replaced it with lines and hard angles. But that was only the obvious visible changes – she wondered what else had changed inside.

Kay was looking around as if she was expecting company. "We need to move. You feel the next portal yet?"

Cassie certainly felt something, but it had nothing to do with portals. She felt scared and lost, but also that, somehow, this was far less of a surprise than it should have been. It was almost as if she had been expecting something like this to happen for years. It was both new and familiar at the same time. And, while it was definitely scary, she thought she should be far more terrified than she was. How could that possibly be?

But then, something else nagged, and she became conscious of – well, she didn't know what it was or how to explain it. It was something wrong, though what could be more wrong than standing in front of a library that had been destroyed before she was born? But there was a feeling and, also, it had a direction.

"Back that way," she said, pointing past the church. "Maybe off to the right a bit. Not too far away."

"Probably one of the Debenham's portals, then."

"There's more than one?"

"You'll see. Oh, and here they come," Kay said, jabbing a thumb over her shoulder towards the steps of City Hall. Cassie looked in that direction. There were lots of people around, but, between them, something else lurked. Several somethings.

"What are they?" she asked, a squeak of fear tainting her voice. The somethings, numbering around five or six, stopped lurking. Instead, they flowed towards them, their feet gliding above the ground. Their empty faces, containing nothing more than hints of eyes and mouth, peered at each real person they passed.

"Bad things. Nasties. Call them what you want. They're definitely not friendly."

"Yes, but what are they? Ghosts, zombies or something else?"

"Nothing you've ever heard about. Definitely in the 'something else' category, I'd say."

"What are they going to do?"

"If they get hold of you?"

"Yes."

"Kill you, probably."

"What?"

"Get used to it. Right, let's go."

Kay grabbed Cassie's hand and dragged her off running.

Loose Change

"The Debenhams downstairs portal," Kay said. They were standing at the small side entrance in Orford Place. Cassie was gasping – the run from in front of the old library hadn't been far, but she wasn't exactly fit. Kay who, to Cassie's annoyance, wasn't gasping much, peered through the glass of the doors. The shop interior was lit but the doors were locked.

Inside, Cassie could see two staircases – one on the left that led up to the ground floor, the other down to the basement. She frowned – the last time she'd been through that entrance the downstairs one hadn't been there.

"It's shut," Cassie said. She peered behind her, back towards Brigg Street but, so far, there was no sign that the things had followed them.

"Course it's shut," Kay replied. "It's nearly eight o'clock."

"How do you know? I thought you couldn't track time."

"City Hall clock said seven forty-five when we were eating."

"Oh."

"You still feel something's inside there?"

"Yes. Don't know what it is, though."

"Of course not. You'll get the hang of it in time, though. Hah, time! I made a joke."

Cassie, her eyes still scanning the street behind her, didn't laugh.

Kay rattled one of the doors several times and then Cassie saw movement as someone, no wait, not a someone – it was a something – came up the stairs from the basement. Cassie stepped back. It was the guy from the bus, though this time he had eyes – they were dark bottomless staring things that looked mostly pupil but doubtless weren't. He reached the door and came through it as if it wasn't there.

"Hello, Cass and Kay," he said and then, to Kay directly, "Oh wait, am I early or late? Does Cass know Kay is Cass and Cass is Kay?"

"Yes, and even if she didn't, she would now, thanks to you," Kay said. "We need to get inside, please. There's trouble on the way."

"Wombling free?" the man said.

Kay sighed. "Only the first bit at the moment. Ah, one of them has found us."

Cassie squeaked. One of the creatures had come gliding along Brigg Street but turned towards Orford Place and was heading directly for them.

The man thing stared at Cassie. "No curls in the middle of her forehead," he said, waggling a finger at her. "Curls needs curls," he added with a nod as if that made perfect sense.

"Not yet, she's only just started. No time. Mine will have to do," Kay said, pointing at her own hair that did rather more than vaguely curl.

"Suppose so, but she too straight. Straight and narrow, don't get you in the barrow."

Kay tutted and rolled her eyes but then there was a click and one of the doors swung open.

"Quick," Kay said. "In before he changes his mind or that thing gets any closer."

Cassie dodged past the man thing and followed Kay into the shop.

"Mind not changed, entrance gained. Hello nasty, not so fasty," she heard the man say before the door swung shut.

Kay sped down the stairs but Cassie watched, mouth agape as, outside the shop entrance, the man punched his fist through the creature's face. It immediately retaliated, oozing over him in an attempt to enmesh him. His flying arms, punching in all directions, diverted its attention from Kay and Cassie.

"They're fighting," Cassie called to Kay.

"Yeah, they do that. Leave them to it and get down here."

"Are we safe now?" Cassie asked when she reached the basement. She looked around, her heart still pumping in her ears.

"We're never safe."

"That's really reassuring. What about that man?"

"He'll deal with the nasties for us."

"Who is he? And what was all that stuff about hair?"

"No, not hair. This place was called Curls long before it was Debenhams."

"He was on the bus," Cassie said.

"Yes. He's everywhere. Sometimes he's even driving the bus. Now, tell me where that portal is."

"Don't you know?"

"Yes, but do you?"

Cassie frowned. She did know. She could feel it. She looked around trying to locate the source.

"Over there, under the escalator," she finally said, pointing.

"Right," Kay said. "Thought as much."

Cassie frowned. "Did you really?"

Kay grinned. "It's not always there."

Cassie nodded before realising that was no answer.

"So, we going to go through it?"

"Hmm. Not yet, maybe. You still cold?"

"Yeah," Cassie said. "Not so bad in here but…"

"Okay, I reckon we've got enough time," Kay said, walking towards the unmoving steps of the escalator. "Let's see what we can find."

"Wow, everything's so cheap," Cassie said a few minutes later as she went around picking up and comparing jackets.

"Of course it is. It would look expensive to someone from the seventies, though."

"This one," Cassie said, holding up a denim jacket. "It's even cheaper, only eight quid."

Kay shrugged. "If that's what you want. Put it on. Then we can get out of here."

"Hold on, how do I pay for it? The place is shut and none of the tills are working."

"Pay for it? Just take it. No one's going to stop us."

Cassie looked at Kay and frowned. "You mean steal it?"

"What do you think I mean? Anyway, it won't be the first time, will it?"

"Huh?" Cassie's mouth dropped open. "I've never stolen anything in my life!"

"Liar," Kay retorted. "I'm you, remember. I suppose that little matter of getting caught after the shoplifting spree back when we were thirteen has just conveniently slipped from your mind?"

"What shoplifting? I never shoplifted. What are you talking about?"

Kay came close and stared into Cassie's eyes. "I could almost believe you if I didn't know any better."

"Damn you," Cassie screamed, throwing the jacket onto the floor, balling her hands into fists. "I'm not bloody well lying. I have NEVER stolen anything, EVER. If you did when you were thirteen, then you're definitely not me."

It was Kay's turn to take a step back.

"You really don't remember it?"

"No, because it never happened," Cassie spat.

They stared hard at each other for several seconds and it was Kay who had to break off first. "Okay, this is weird. I think I believe you."

"You'd better."

"A few times you've claimed you'd never stolen anything but you were never as convincing as you are right now."

"Are you telling me that you really did steal stuff when you were me?"

"I am still you. But…"

"But what?"

"I don't think I was the same you as you are now."

"That doesn't make any sense."

"No, it doesn't. It makes no sense to me, either. I'm used to the fact that you vary a bit each time we meet – well to be more truthful – are mostly dumb most times we meet, but I always thought we shared the same past. This is new. Damn, I need to think about it. But we can't do that here. The portal may not be around for long. Do you still feel it?"

"Yeah."

"Right, grab the jacket and let's go."

"No, I'm going to pay for it."

"You can't."

"Why not? I've got enough on me." Cassie pulled her wallet out of her jeans pocket.

"What? In legal tender?"

"Huh?"

"How much money have you got?"

"Fifteen pounds in notes – three fives. A handful of change."

"Yeah, right. Fifteen quid in plastic notes that didn't exist before 2016."

"Oh right. Wait, I've got nearly eight quid in change."

"Pound coins?"

"Mostly, and a few fifty-pees."

"So, that will be the twelve sided pound coins and small fifty-pee coins that also haven't been invented yet. It's 1991-ish – what's the value of the coins you've got from that year or earlier?"

Cassie picked through her change. "Thirty-seven pee. Damn."

"Yeah, now you see the problem. Well, that particular problem anyway."

"Wait, how did you pay for the hot dogs earlier?"

Kay reached into one of her many pockets and pulled out four small pouches. Cassie saw there were numbers written on each one. Kay opened the one with 1990 scrawled on it and pulled out an old paper ten pound note. She removed the label from the jacket and placed the money and label on a till.

"Satisfied?" Kay said.

Gentlemen

They were back down in the basement standing next to the portal that Cassie could feel but not see.

"Ok, hold my hand," Kay said. "Let's see where it leads."

"Don't you know?"

"Nope, they change every time."

"Do I have to hold your hand?"

"Yes, if you want to come out at exactly the same place and in the same time as me. Castle Mall is different – the whole place is a giant portal. Actually, I sometimes think it might even be several all mixed up together."

Kay tugged at Cassie's hand and there was a sensation – a feeling that Cassie could only describe to herself as 'shimmying' – a combination of movement, dizziness, a smell of electricity and a buzzing in the ears. It tugged them sideways and down. Then they arrived and the first thing that hit them was the smell.

"Jeez, shit," Cassie coughed.

"Quiet," Kay whispered, placing her hand over Cassie's mouth.

They were in a tiny room, no bigger than a toilet. Then Cassie realised that was exactly where they were, especially as her leg was resting against the pan, one that looked far from hygienic. Pale light filtered through thick glass bricks built into the ceiling above the cubicle. The door, which she noticed was covered in obscene graffiti, was shut but not locked. Kay flipped the lock to engaged as they heard a door slam in a cubicle somewhere to their left. The sound of trousers being dropped, of someone – definitely a man – coughing, was followed by a loud fart and a hefty deposit being made. The smell factor increased in intensity.

"We gotta get out of here," Cassie whispered. "I'm going to throw that hot dog back up if I stay much longer."

There were more footsteps outside the door.

"Not yet," Kay whispered back.

"Why?"

"It's a gents and, obviously, we're not. Also, there's two of us in a single toilet."

"I thought you said they can't see us?"

"Not quite. They don't tend to see us unless we're out of place or doing something unusual or noticeable. And two girls in a gents is asking for trouble."

Several cubicles along, their near neighbour continued with something a lot less solid and accompanied it with several groans. Kay unlocked the door, opening it a couple of inches to peer out while keeping her knee against it to prevent anyone coming in. They heard a chain being pulled, followed by a door banging, water splashing and, a few seconds later, the receding sound of footsteps ascending some steps.

"Now," Kay said, squeezing out the door.

Holding her breath, Cassie inched out after her and, seeing the coast clear, chased after Kay. Her older self was already running up the steps that curved up into daylight and, thankfully, much more breathable air. Halfway up, blocking their exit, they encountered a man wearing a flat cap and a very surprised look on his face.

"Zo zorry," Kay said. "Miztake. We not from Eengaland."

Kay pushed past him and they came out into full sunshine.

"Hah," Cassie laughed. "That was a crap fake accent. Hey, it's warm again. And why is my hair turning frizzy?"

"Portals do that, amongst other interesting things."

Cassie looked around. To one side she could see a market but the stalls were tatty and run down. In the other direction old cars and a red double-decker bus passed in front of them. Beyond the road her eyes recognised the sight of Lloyds Bank even before she saw the words high up on the wall. Her eyes swung round to take in the Guildhall and City Hall.

"It's the Walk."

"Yes, the gents on Gentleman's Walk. Late 1960s I'd say by the look of things. C'mon, there's often several this way," Kay said, pointing towards the Guildhall and setting off at a brisk pace.

"Wait," Cassie said. "Where are we going and why?"

"To look for the next portal. Keep up."

They reached the green in front of the Guildhall when Cassie pulled at Kay's arm.

"Stop," she demanded. "No further until I get some answers. Proper answers. No crap this time."

"We could lose it."

"I don't give a flying monkey's bollocks about that," Cassie shouted. A family of four passing them turned their heads in Cassie's direction. "What the hell are you looking at? Piss off."

"Watch it," Kay hissed. "You're making us visible."

"Well, then. You'd better start telling me what's going on, otherwise I'll give them a damn good reason to start noticing us."

They had a three second staring match. Kay was again the first to back down.

"Okay, okay. But not here. Too much going on. Damn, you really are kicking off early this time." She paused for a second, then added. "Pottergate, the green at Saint Gregory's. That way."

"I know where it is," Cassie snapped back.

She followed Kay without a further word. Much of her silence, though, was more due to taking in the look of a city with which she thought she was familiar. Very few of the shops they passed were still present in 2018. Everything looked so ancient, yet it was also bright and new at the same time.

As they hit Pottergate she got her phone out of her bag to take pictures or even a video.

"Put that away," Kay whispered. "You'll get us noticed again."

"Could be worth a fortune when I get back."

"Don't even think about it. Over to the green. It feels like summer so it should be dry enough to sit on and be far enough away from anyone else."

The Past is Two Different Countries

"Right," Kay said, sitting down on the trimmed lawn. "Well, we both know how this started. After Mum died. When, you know, he began to take an interest in me... us."

"What are you talking about?"

"Four or five years ago, when you were nearly thirteen."

"Yes, I was thirteen four years ago. So? What started then?"

"Grandad. You know."

"Oh, when he started going mental?"

"That's one way of putting it. Wandering hands, I was once naive enough to call it."

"Eh? I meant when he started going senile. What's this 'wandering hands' stuff?"

Kay frowned. "Senile? No, he wasn't senile at all. You mean he didn't start, um, touching you?"

"No, of course not. He would never do that."

"Oh." Kay looked shocked. "Things really were different for you."

"Are you saying…?"

"Yes. I'm saying exactly that. But if it didn't happen to you… Well, that probably explains why you didn't end up shoplifting."

"Are we really the same person?"

Kay stared at Cassie for a moment and then said, "Mum died on the twenty-fourth of January 2011 – correct?"

"Yes."

"Cancer?"

"Yes."

"And you started seeing weird people and things about a year ago?"

"No, a lot longer ago than that."

"What, round about the time your grandad started, um, losing his mind?"

"No. Earlier. A lot earlier – before Mum died."

Kay pursed her lips, digesting the information. Then she slowly said, "My Grandad didn't lose his mind. Sometimes I thought it was me that had."

"Um, what exactly did he do to you?"

Kay's face fell and she swallowed.

"Okay," Cassie said. "I get the picture."

"No, you probably don't if, as you say, it didn't happen to you."

"It didn't."

There was silence for a while. A small flock of sparrows fought for something further across the green – most likely pieces of bread or discarded chips. Cassie had never seen sparrows in such numbers in the city before. The chip shop a few yards away was closed and she wondered what time it was. She stood up so she could see the city hall clock – it said ten-fifteen.

Sitting back down she asked, "What are they? The weird people. That man on the bus and the things that chased us?"

"Some are the ghosts of real people that once lived – as far as I can tell."

"Like Robert Kett?"

"Yeah. You can't avoid him any time you go near the castle. Ones like him are mostly harmless, I think."

"You think?"

Kay shrugged. "Sometimes. A few of them are friendly like the Grey Lady, providing you don't let her chew on your legs. Most aren't. Some seem to be there just to keep an eye on you… well, us. Observers of some kind. Some can even be useful like the bus man."

"Talk crap, though."

"Yeah," Kay smiled. "Though sometimes what they say comes back to you later on and you realise it wasn't quite as crap as you first thought."

"What, like riddles?"

"Hmm, I suppose so. Though often of absolutely no use by the time you understand what they meant. You connect things in retrospect only once you've figured them out for yourself. Totally pointless, mostly."

"Like what?"

Kay frowned again. "Next time it happens, I'll remind you. What they say changes each time. Sometimes there are common themes, like the elements, other times…"

"Yeah, bus man said I was elemental – actually I thought he just meant mental but that's probably true as well. But…"

"But what?"

"But what's the point? Of all this happening, that is?"

Kay shrugged. "I really wish I knew. It's like an endless merry-go-round and there's no way to get off."

"So how many times have you met me, then?"

"Lost count. Hundreds, possibly thousands."

"Really? Thousands? Wow."

"Sometimes, especially at first, I didn't meet you. I just watched to see what happened." Kay lapsed into silence.

"Well? What did happen?"

"Sometimes the falling gateway got you. Sometimes you ran off on your own and something else later on must have got you."

"Oh. And what happens when you do meet me?"

Kay turned her head away as if she was unable to look Cassie directly in the eye.

"Well?" Cassie said.

Kay sighed. "You really want to know?"

"Of course. Why wouldn't I?"

"Yes, but… um, somehow you are never quite as forceful as you feel this time around."

"So?"

"Okay. You're not going to like this but most of the time they get you."

"They? What? Those things that chased us earlier?"

"Yeah. The nasties. The ones that aren't friendly. The things that come up out of the ground or through the walls. The ones that talk just as much crap while they are trying to devour you whole."

"Bloody hell."

"Sometimes I take my eye off you for a moment and you're gone as if you were never there. Other times I just lose you and have no idea what took you. But, usually…"

"What?"

"I've watched you die so many times…"

"That's, um, very reassuring."

"Once I think I saw the one that became me."

"Eh?"

"No one helped me. So I think I must have been the first, or at least the first one to survive all the way through a cycle. There wasn't a Kay to help the Cassie that I used to be. I had to do it all on my own."

"Um, so why did you call yourself Kay?"

"It was what he liked to call me."

"Who?"

"Grandad, of course," Kay snapped and then shut her eyes. "Sorry. But it hurts. It never stops hurting."

"No, I'm sorry. But why stick with 'Kay' when it, um…?"

"Because at first I… well, I wanted to please him, I think. Please him so that he would stop hurting me. So I became Kay, strong Kay who could live a lie and wouldn't tell a soul about what was really going on."

"Oh."

"What a joke," Kay whispered.

"You blame yourself?"

"Yeah, stupid isn't it. Far too common, apparently."

"I… I don't know."

"When I first started hooking up with you, it seemed simpler than having both of us being called Cassie. So, I used Kay. I've been Kay for far longer now than I was ever Cassie."

A few clouds drifted across the sky but didn't come anywhere close to blocking out the sun.

At least it's not as hot as 2018.

"But what I don't understand is how can the same, er, thing, er, no, the same event turn out differently if it's the same thing, I mean, if it's happening at the same time each time? Oh damn, that came out completely wrong."

"Yes, but I know what you're trying to say. Maybe it's different timelines but, as far as I can see, we're the only ones experiencing it differently each time. I used to think that before the castle gate fell our lives were identical. You're not exactly the first to make me think that's not the case, though…"

"Though, what?"

"I don't know. There's something about you. You're different in some way. Stronger possibly. Definitely more argumentative. But why? I really don't know."

"Oh. So, um, what now?"

"All I can do is try to protect you. Maybe this time I can get you through all the portals and transitions. Maybe you will be the one I can get all the way home."

"But how do we do that?" Cassie asked. "And, if I don't become you, then how can we both go home?"

"I sometimes think I can never go home. But I feel – no, *feel* isn't right. It's more like I'm driven to help one of you achieve that. Though, when it comes down to it there's bugger all else for me to do. Even if I don't help you, the nasties eventually start hunting me down – not that they've ever succeeded. It's just easier to find the next portal and get a rest from them."

"Have you ever got close to getting me home?"

Kay shrugged. "I'm not sure – how can I be? If it's only one stop short of home, I'd never know. The paths through the portals are never the same. I just think that if I ever do succeed then maybe all this will… well, um, end. Possibly, I may cease to exist. In fact, I damn well hope so. Because I've had enough. I've really, really had enough. This is not something I'd wish on anyone. So, that's the reason I keep trying."

Cassie felt a shiver go through her.

"Isn't it possible that the ones you lose get to go home?"

"I once hoped that. But, if they do, then why am I still here? And why does another version of you keep coming along?"

Cassie had no answer. They sat in silence for a while longer. Then Kay said,

"We should be on the move. If we stay in one place for too long then the portals change and, worse, the nasties home in on us."

Cassie was about to ask why when some grey looking chips plopped down onto the grass in front of her. They were followed by a smell of rotting fish.

"Feed the birds," came a voice. "Nice birdies wanna chips?"

As Cassie looked up Kay shouted, "Run. Now!"

A shadow that failed to block out the sun reared up out of the ground in front of her. Cassie thought it was manlike until she noticed the extra arms and head.

Okay, so not really manlike.

She pushed herself backwards as a rain of chips fell where she'd sat. They were followed by a couple of metal forks, thrown with force, if little accuracy.

Cassie tried to spring to her feet but something grabbed her ankle and, instead, she fell sideways.

"Kay," she shrieked, but Kay was already pelting down Pottergate back towards the city centre.

For a moment Cassie watched transfixed as a sticky grey hand pulled her foot downwards so that it started sinking beneath the grass. Then she snarled and kicked out at the hand with her other foot. It took three kicks before it let go.

She scrambled to her feet and ran after Kay, taking an occasional momentary glance behind herself. The green was filling with shadows, each a hulking shape that rose straight out of the ground, not that anyone else was taking any interest in them.

"You ran without waiting for me," Cassie gasped as she caught up with Kay. "They nearly got me!"

"Yeah, but you're like buses."

"What?"

"There'll be another one along in a while."

"I thought you said I was different?"

Kay shrugged. "Yeah, but I've just seen too many of you. Anyway, c'mon. We need to find that next portal pretty soon otherwise they'll catch up again."

"They don't move very fast," Cassie said. "They're like stupid zombies in films."

"Yep, but they don't sleep."

"How do you… we sleep?"

"With one eye open," Kay grinned, but without humour.

"You're kidding!"

"Yeah. There are some safe-ish places. Sometimes when you find one of the friendly ones."

"How can you tell which ones are friendly?"

"Simple. They don't try to kill you."

Out of Tune

"Is this place always here?"

"Almost," Kay said. "Sometimes it says 'Established 1835' above the door. There's often a portal downstairs. I don't feel it's there today, though."

"There's definitely one around here somewhere, I think," Cassie said, as eager now as Kay to find the next one. "That way," she said, pointing right. "Quite close."

They rounded the corner of Lobster Lane into Exchange Street and nearly bumped into a man who Cassie thought looked familiar. He was middle-aged, slim and far from unhandsome but wearing a uniform of some sort. He reached into his jacket pocket and pulled out a fob watch on a chain.

"Oh dear, Cass and Cass," he said, his pure blue eyes fixed on Cassie's. "I fear I may be too late."

"Out the way, bus man," Kay snapped and pushed past him. Cassie now recognised him. He was much younger than the version who'd helped them at Debenhams and far removed from the eyeless creature she'd encountered on the bus. But the voice and the shape of his face were almost identical. He seemed to be almost solid this time – the word 'corporeal' popped into her head – words had a habit of doing that to her at the most useless of times.

Then, as she edged past him to catch up with Kay, he started singing, "Rabbits in burrows and bright torches shining, piled high on Alice, she's truly whining. Roadworks and mineshafts. See what a score brings. These are a few of my least favourite things."

Cassie blinked and he was gone, but his disembodied voice added, "I'll keep an eye or two out for you."

"That's what I mean," Kay said. "Any of it make any sense to you?"

"Alice and rabbits. Bit obvious, isn't it?"

"Could be. I've not heard him sing that one before. Okay, located that portal yet?"

"Yeah, it's inside here," Cassie said, staring into the shop window. Inside, there must have been nearly twenty pianos and organs.

"It often is," Kay said. She pushed open a door. Despite the apparent cleanliness of the keyboards around them, there was a distinct smell of stale tobacco.

"Yetch," Cassie whispered. "It stinks. Did everyone smoke back then… or now, or whatever?"

A man appeared from another area of the shop to the left. Cassie could see radios and a couple of TVs through there. "Can I, er, help you?"

He seemed to have a problem focussing on them.

"Just looking," Kay said. "Are the secondhand pianos still downstairs?"

Cassie frowned. What on Earth was Kay asking that for?

"Er, yes, downstairs," the man said. "I'll get the manager. He can show you around and demonstrate them for you."

"It's no bother. Just looking as I said," Kay repeated, heading towards the stairs at the rear of the shop. "C'mon, quickly," she added to Cassie with a whisper.

They descended the stairs while the salesman could be heard stomping up the flight above them to the first floor. The basement was packed with much older pianos, mainly uprights, though there was one baby grand over in the corner. There was hardly any room to move.

"How do they get them all down here?" Cassie asked. "Surely they don't carry grand pianos down these stairs."

Kay had stopped on the bottom step and was peering through a doorway into another smaller room. She pointed to the trap door in the ceiling not far from the stairway. It was supported by a couple of white painted metal bars. "There's a ring in the ceiling on the floor above. I've watched them a couple of times when they haul them up and down with a block and tackle."

"A what?"

"Damn, was I ever actually this ignorant?"

Cassie followed Kay into the side room. It appeared to be a workshop as there were several dismantled pianos in various states of repair. Some had their internal mechanisms missing, which she presumed were the things sitting on the benches along one wall. There was no one else present though the air hung with the smell of coffee.

"It's there, isn't it?" Kay said, pointing towards the far end where a small recess off to the left held a sink. Above it was a wall-mounted, electric water heater and beside the sink, on a separate cabinet, stood several cups, a jar of coffee and a tub of dried milk.

Cassie nodded – the portal was definitely there – she could feel the 'shimmy' from here.

They heard footsteps coming down the upper staircase. Whoever it was stopped to play a short ascending melody on one of the pianos on the ground floor. Then the footsteps resumed and descended the stairs to the basement.

"Right," Kay said. "Hold my hand again."

"Is that really necessary?"

"Yes, I told you before. We might end up in two different places, separated by several years."

Kay hesitated before the invisible portal. The identical melody was played again on one of the pianos in the basement – the sound this time was cheaper and jarred the senses. A single note was hit a few times.

"Hrmph, that C has gone out again," a deep voice grumbled.

Then a square, bespectacled face peered around the doorway, followed by the body of a stocky, middle-aged man in a dark suit and tie. One hand held a burning cigarette.

He stared at them for a moment as if he couldn't make up his mind as to whether or not they were actually there. Then he said, "Ah, excuse me, ladies. You shouldn't be in this–"

"Now," Kay said, grabbing Cassie's hand. And they were off again.

Chalky Breakthrough

It was dark, dusty and cramped. There was also noise above them as if they were underneath a road with traffic passing overhead.

"Oh no," Kay muttered. "Not this one again."

"I can't see anything," Cassie shouted over the rumbling from above.

"Funny I should mention buses a few minutes ago."

"Eh? Where are we?"

"Get your phone out and use the torch."

Cassie pulled her phone from her bag. It complained about the lack of signal and she registered that it only had 48% charge left. She swiped the settings down and switched on the torch.

"Wow," she said, glancing around at her surroundings. She brushed some of her hair away from her face, noticing it was even frizzier than before.

Wish I'd brought a comb.

"Right, quick. This way. We need to get further along these tunnels."

Cassie followed Kay along the low passage. The walls against her fingers were rough, uneven and slightly powdery.

"You didn't answer me. Where is this?"

"I think it's called Discovery Street. I found a map once. Ah, this left turn should be Garden Lane. Damn, it's quite a while since we ended up here. I can never remember which one it fell down."

"What fell down?" Cassie asked as they squeezed along the narrower side passage.

A crashing sound reverberated from behind them and Cassie felt the walls around her shake.

"That," Kay said as Cassie twisted around towards the noise. Her phone's torch picked out the loose tumbling rubble that cascaded past the entrance to the passage they were in. Grey-white dust followed.

"What the hell?"

"You remember seeing pictures of a bus that fell into a chalk mine on Earlham Road?"

"Er, yes. Mum showed me a picture of it."

"Yep, that's right. Well, that's where we are right now. In a chalk mine under Earlham Road in 1988 and that was the bus falling into it."

"How do we get out? Ooh, can you smell gas?"

"Yeah. We need to get away from that pretty quick. Some of it floods as well."

"Floods?" Cassie squeaked.

"Yeah, the bus burst some pipes."

Kay continued on to another junction where they turned right.

"No point turning left," Kay said. "The entrance there was blocked up years ago."

After several more turns that made Cassie feel disorientated, Kay called a halt in a larger chamber and sat down with her back against a wall. "This damned chalk is going to play hell with my jacket," she said, as if that was their only current worry. "At least I can't smell gas any more."

"Phone's down to 44%," Cassie said.

"Turn the torch off, then. There's nowhere here to charge it, anyway."

In the darkness Cassie said, "Now what?"

"We wait and hope the nasties don't find us."

"What are we waiting for?"

"The only way out of here is blocked by a sodding great double decker. They don't drag it out the way until the following day. And then we've got to get out of the hole without anyone noticing or getting drowned from the burst pipes and avoiding caving the rest of it in on top of ourselves. No problem – much!"

"How many times you been here?"

"About a dozen, I'd say – last time feels like about ten years ago, well, as I'm experiencing time anyway."

"How come we don't meet our earlier selves?"

"I am meeting my earlier self – or something similar."

"You know what I mean!" Cassie snapped, getting angry again.

"Yeah, I do. And if I had an answer I'd tell you. So, just assume I haven't, right? But if I ever get my hands on the bastard that's running this show I'll beat the bloody answers out of him, or her, or whatever it is."

"Yeah, me too."

They sat in relative silence for several minutes. There was a faint echo of running water in the distance and Cassie wasn't sure if she could still smell gas or not. There were a number of smells hitting her nostrils: dampness, chalk, sewage, mould and many others she was glad she couldn't identify.

Then her mind jumped and made a connection. "Ah, rabbits in burrows. Shining torches. My phone's the torch. Does that mean we're the rabbits?"

"Yes. You see what I mean now?" Kay said. In the distance they could hear the bus settling further down into the hole. "The information is useless as we're already in the situation he was possibly predicting."

"I'm trying to remember what else was in his song," Cassie replied. "Wasn't it something about whining and a score? But who or what is keeping score?"

"Hmm, a score is also twenty. This is 1988 and that previous one was in the late 1960s. So, it could mean twenty years in this case. Or it might be referencing something completely different. Anyway, I'm tired so I'm going to attempt to get some sleep. Don't know how long ago it's been since I last managed to get some kip but I'm knackered. So, goodnight."

"What, go to sleep? Just like that?"

"You'll get used to it, if you keep alive long enough to get used to it."

"Yeah, thanks, like whatever."

Cassie sat in the dark listening to Kay's breathing get slower until it was obvious she had gone to sleep. *How on earth can Kay sleep in such a place?* Then Cassie wondered how on earth she herself could get some sleep. She wasn't tired – she flipped her phone on and it said 14:25. *About three hours since I met Kay – seems longer. Maybe going through portals is messing the phone's time up like it's messing my hair up.*

She slid down the wall but couldn't get comfortable. The floor and walls were too hard, damp, smelly and several other things that didn't encourage sleep. Every few minutes she tried another position but it didn't help.

What also didn't help was hearing the sound of her heart beating in the almost silence. It was accompanied with the thoughts that constantly bounced around her head.

I wonder what the real time is here in 1988.

Was that noise a rat?

Who is Kay? Is she really a future me?

Maybe this is all just a dream or maybe I'm going completely mad.

Every so often she checked the time again hoping half an hour had passed since the last check only to find it was merely minutes. When it finally said 15:15 she cursed under her breath and resolved not to check her phone again.

There's absolutely no way I'm going to be able to go to sleep.

Tiny Feet

Cassie woke with a start. It took her a couple of seconds to figure out where she was.

Her back ached from lying on the cold floor of the tunnel. But that wasn't what had woken her. She realised she needed to go to the loo. But that wasn't what had disturbed her, either. There was a noise. No, there were several noises and they were coming closer. The noises were squeaking, groaning and slurping. She initially feared the tunnels were beginning to fill with water from the burst pipes but it didn't quite sound like water. She fumbled for her bag and extracted her phone noticing vaguely that it thought the time was now 17:09. She got to the torch setting after a couple of false starts. In its harsh light she saw what the noise was.

"Kay," she screamed.

"Wha–? Oh shit."

Piling out of a smaller side shaft came a multitude of shapes. Some were almost human in outline, others were animal. Many resembled rats. But most undulated and shifted from one indeterminate form to another equally as unrecognisable. In the torchlight they were all an almost uniform murky yellow. There were too many to count and they merged into each other and separated out into new shapes as they spread out into the tunnel. Cassie sprang to her feet and ran in the opposite direction away from the encroaching horde. It was only after several few steps that she realised she'd left her bag behind. At least she still had hold of her phone.

"You can't get out that way," she heard Kay shout.

But Cassie didn't stop. She hated rats and wanted to put as much distance between them and herself as possible. She came to a corner and followed it around to the left. At another junction she carried on straight ahead until a sharp turn to the right took her in a new direction.

"Kay. Help. Where are you?"

But there was no reply apart from the patter of tiny ghostly footfalls accompanied by unearthly squeaking and squelching. The tunnel branched and she turned left again cursing as, after a short while, it came to a dead end. She started back along the way she had come only to find the exit blocked. It was packed from floor to roof with shapes that oozed closer.

One of the shapes formed a mouth. "Come to Daddy, little girl," it screeched. "Custard or custody," said a new mouth that opened in the abdomen of another shape.

"Help," Cassie screamed as she backed away. Then the first of them launched itself at her and she flailed with her arms trying to bat the thing away. Her free hand connected with something, it felt more solid than she expected but not solid enough to grab hold of – like it was made of sponge and jelly.

"Girl light," the mouths of several said in unison as they threw themselves at her.

"Get off me," she screamed, which had absolutely no effect.

"No," she shouted as something grabbed her phone and wrenched it from her fingers. It flew over her head, hitting the roof once to land behind her, the torch still shining.

"Girl heavy."

The smaller rat-sized things were encircling her legs and the larger ones began to wrap arms or tentacles around her chest. She fell backwards and they crashed on top of her, though 'crash' wasn't exactly right, it was more like they sludged on top of her.

"Girl is going nowhere, soon will lose her heady. Empty full, vacant, filled, nice new home for Daddy!"

The phone was right next to her head, the torchlight giving her a detailed view of how revolting the things were. Nightmares about rotting zombie flesh were nothing compared to the way their surfaces oozed and mutated by the second, forming a distorted pigs head here, an eyeless face there, each of which started to repeat the 'Girl' rubbish.

Shit, shit, shit, she thought as she struggled to keep them off her, but their combined weight on top of her was increasing every second. *This is it. I'm going to die. Kay might meet another version of me. But me, I'll be dead.*

A face of sorts pressed itself close to her own and its open mouth drooled mucus onto her forehead.

"Girl li–"

She hit it right in the mouth, but her hand continued until it was buried in the mush of its face squidging its features to one side but doing little to stop it.

Then, suddenly, it was gone to be replaced by a more familiar face.

"Mother, daughter and into the hole she goes," said the bus man as he pummelled the creatures in a whirlwind of arms and kicking feet. "Late as promised," he continued, "but not as too late as too late would'a been way too late."

Cassie felt her back crunch – no wait, it wasn't her back. The floor beneath her was giving way.

"Ahh, Kay. Help me!"

"It shouldn't need explaining with you lying on the floor, but old Cass is entertaining more jelly friends next door," the bus man helpfully replied as he plastered the nasties with kicks and punches, and threw them in all directions. Not that it stopped them for long, as they oozed back into the fight as soon as their oozing allowed.

The bus man ripped the head off one gruesome thing and hurled it into the stomach of another, all while telling her, "Young Cass go south for a while in a while."

The ground beneath Cassie lurched and she started slipping down. There must have been another concealed mineshaft below this one. She tried to grab for her phone as she fell but missed. It remained in the tunnel above illuminating the fight that was still going on. Above her the bus man was being subsumed by all the creatures around him. A tentacle forced itself into one of his blue eyes – it reappeared out the other. He clamped both eyelids shut chopping the tentacle into pieces. But his eyes, when they reopened were no longer blue – they were hollow.

"Cass, Cass. The status quo shouldn't remain status quo," he shouted and then started singing while his arms continued to wrestle with the creatures. "Working down a chalk mine. Going down down deeper and down. Map you later, alligator."

The light went out and Cassie fell further. Then she felt something familiar envelope her as she dropped into the darkness. That shimmying sensation again – it was another portal. Abruptly, her fall backwards reorientated itself sideways and she tumbled out into a room, her hair flashing with static electricity as it clung to her face. She flopped down onto a grubby floor, arms and legs spread wide where they landed. She gasped air back into her lungs, waiting for the things to follow her through the portal but nothing appeared.

After a minute she sat up and brushed her hair away from her face and then realised that her hands were clean of the slime. Did that mean nothing of the nasties could make it through a portal? Was that something useful to know? What was also weird was that the need to use a toilet had also completely gone.

So, where did it go?

She took in her new surroundings. A single dim bulb illuminated the room enough for her to see the graffiti scribbled on the wall in front of her. One piece said 'Lakenham boys', and above it were several names. Around her the graffiti covered what might once have been clean white walls.

"Kay," Cassie shouted. Her voice echoed but there was no reply.

Apparently, she was safe – for the moment anyway. Safe but also completely alone.

Getting to unsteady feet she explored where she was. She left the room – viewed from outside it looked like nothing less than a prison cell.

She found herself in an undercroft of some sort. A couple of chairs stood out amongst some other general junk. There was also a thick wooden door that seemed to be the way out of the whole place. She rattled the handle but the door didn't budge – it was locked. She yelled for help and pressed her ear to the door, listening for a response. There was nothing and no one came to rescue her.

She sat down on the least rickety looking chair and, remembering the loss of her bag, felt in her pocket for her phone.

"Damn," she swore, remembering its fate in the chalk mine.

"At least there's some light here," she muttered to herself exactly three seconds before the place was plunged into darkness.

Underground Map

At first she dared not move a muscle. The darkness felt tangible and oppressive.

"It's only a basement," she tried to tell herself. "No one else is here. No nasties, monsters or bus men."

Unfortunately, there was also no Kay nor anyone else who could get her out of the place. If she'd had her phone she could have used some of its remaining charge to light the place up once in a while. She might have also been able to use it to tell when she was. A phone signal would have at least told her she was close to 2018 and it might have adjusted itself to the local date and time. Without it she felt completely lost.

Panic rose in her chest and she had to clamp her teeth together to prevent herself from screaming her head off. Not that she had ever been a screamer but, in the darkness and after what she'd experienced in the chalk caves, she was getting a lot closer to becoming one.

Her mind flew in all directions. At one point she tried to convince herself that it would be safe to try to get some more sleep, knowing that the likelihood of sleeping remained almost at zero. Not that she was tired – it was more in the hope that, in a few hours or so, someone would come to unlock the place. Of course, if it happened to be a Friday night then she might be stuck there for an entire weekend. And what if it was a bank holiday? Could she survive three days in the darkness? What could she do for food and drink? She tried to remember if there had been a sink or a tap with water here, but she could no longer recall.

The panic rose further and she could do little to suppress it. She was terrified that the nasties from 1988 would find her again in the dark. She still felt amazed that she'd escaped them so quickly. It was extremely lucky she'd happened to be directly above another portal when they'd pounced on her. She fully realised she might have been dead by now had it not appeared when it did.

Then the bus man saying, "Into the hole she goes," came back to her. Had he known the portal was there? And the nasties repeating the, "Girl light, girl heavy," thing – well, she'd lost her light though felt insulted that maybe her weight had made her fall through the floor. She was only a little bit overweight. No more than a few pounds, really.

She sighed, but at least trying to analyse the bus man's nonsense was an escape from thinking about the pervading darkness. She might be connecting random coincidences where no such connection existed. Still, the presence of a portal in exactly the right place at the right time did reek of some sort of… of some sort of what? Words buzzed around her head and she settled on 'external manipulation' wondering where the expression had come from.

She forced her thoughts onto more practical matters. *If no one's coming to rescue me then I need another portal out of here,* she decided. She tried to remember how it felt when she'd detected the portals in Debenhams and the piano shop. Away from Kay she wondered if she could detect them on her own, as it was only by Kay's prompting she'd found them before.

But Kay is a future version of me, well sort of, anyway. So if she could detect them then so can I, she hoped.

But how did it work?

And why wasn't it working now?

Or was it working?

She tried to feel the portal she'd come through. There was something definitely there but she wasn't even 100% sure of its location. She tried to pinpoint its direction in relation to the rickety chair upon which she sat.

"Where are you?" she whispered, attempting to determine the portal's precise location.

She could sense something roughly in the opposite direction. But it appeared muffled, as if separated from her current whereabouts by something solid. Then she found there were other places, possibly other portals. She tried to concentrate on them.

Suddenly, her perception changed and instead of there being the odd sensation in various random directions, everything came together as if she was sitting at the centre of a life-sized three-dimensional map. Not only that, but the map started filling with structures – buildings and roads, all a uniform dark grey on a background of black with the occasional coloured dot that Cassie was sure represented the location of a portal. Each building was partially transparent so that she could see through it to those beyond. And some of those buildings were becoming recognisable. A short distance in front of her, City Hall rose up like a giant grey monolith and, not much further away and to her left, the Saint Peter Mancroft church was unmistakable as was the Forum alongside it.

Cassie tried to remember exactly when the new Forum library had been built. *Does that mean I can't be too far in the past? Maybe I'm even back in 2018.*

She turned her attention to the dots representing the portals themselves, like coloured Christmas tree bulbs, some of them were dim while others were brighter. There was a flash as one portal somewhere in a basement off Upper Saint Giles Street momentarily lit up followed by another down on Saint Benedicts Street. Cassie was sure that those two flashes were briefly connected by a filament of light.

That's probably Kay or someone else moving from one portal to another, she decided. If it was someone else, then she wondered who or what that might be. Did the nasties use the portals in the same way? The lack of slime on her hands suggested they couldn't. *Do they have other ways of getting around?*

She turned her attention to the structure she could feel surrounding her. And at that moment she knew exactly where she was. Above her the solid flint and crenelations of the Guildhall became apparent. She was underneath it, in its basement. To her left the portal in the toilet at the front of the market was an extremely dim red. Was that because, in this time, the portal was buried and unusable? Or maybe it was dim because she'd used it recently.

She shook her head. She was only guessing at how all this worked.

Turning her attention to the brighter portals, she saw one flare up and, a moment later, another corresponded somewhere to the north across the River Wensum, a short distance off Duke Street. Seconds later, there was a flash westwards – it looked like it was in the underpass beneath the Saint Stephen's Street roundabout. Its destination was somewhere out east, miles from the city centre.

Cassie drew her attention to the portals directly surrounding her. She felt she could navigate her way through the darkness to the one she'd arrived by. However, it was dim. That other one she'd detected not far away a few minutes ago appeared to be brighter now. Then she saw, if 'seeing' was the right term, one that was even closer. In fact, it appeared to be at the other end of the undercroft in which she was sitting. She watched as the portal appeared to grow in strength, as did the one a short way through the solid earth to her right.

She stood up and approached it slowly, hands outstretched in front of her, feet feeling for obstacles on the ground. Up close, she encountered the shimmering, hair tingling sensation once again.

Swallowing hard, she said quietly, "Okay, here we go."

She stepped through and stumbled into a pile of boxes, which promptly fell over.

Stack 'em high, sell 'em cheap

"You again? Where the bloody hell are you all coming from?" said a surprised looking man, his moustache wobbling with indignation. He was hardly taller than herself but his bare arms showed he either worked out a lot or had a manual job that involved a heck of a lot of lifting.

"Sorry," Cassie said, looking about herself. They were in a basement of some sort that was stacked with boxes everywhere, with identical packages grouped together. Well, that explained his muscles if he was shifting these things around all day. Images of hi-fi, radios, TVs and old ghetto-blasters adorned each box. The ground beneath her feet appeared be just that – earth but dusty, dry and solid from lack of water. It inclined slightly towards a desk about twenty feet away, alongside which stood a wooden stairway leading upwards.

A younger man, not much more than a boy in appearance, looked up from the desk. He dropped his pen on the pad of paper upon which he'd been writing and said, "What? Another strange woman down here? What's going on? That's the third one."

"Third one?" Cassie said. "Wait! Was one of the other two dressed all in black, jeans and leather jacket?"

"Yeah," the first man said. "About two minutes ago. Come to think of it, the other one looked exactly like you."

"Where did they go?"

"Ran for the stairs," the boy said.

"Thanks," Cassie said.

"Hold on, not so fast," the body-builder said.

Then a third man appeared, coming down the stairs. Unlike the other two, he was attired in a neatly trimmed dark suit. "Get me a Philips D8134 Radio-Cassette," he ordered in a tone that suggested he expected to be obeyed. Then he noticed Cassie. "Who's this? Are you storing women down here as well?"

Body-builder turned to answer boss-man so Cassie made a run for the stairs. The boy came towards her and tried to block her way. She swung to her right and pulled down some bulky and badly stacked boxes.

"Watch it!" boss-man shouted. "Those TVs are fragile."

The boxes tumbled as she dodged around them. There was a crunch and a bang from a box as it hit the ground. The boy tried to prevent the rest falling and Cassie used the diversion to reach the stairs. But boss-man successfully made a grab for her arm and tried to drag her back. She bit his free hand and he let out a yelp of surprise and pain, causing his grip to loosen. It was enough to allow her to escape.

She rushed up the stairs two steps at a time and found herself in a small crowded shop. Its shelves were packed with old-style TVs, radios, cassette machines and other stuff that looked ancient to her. The exit door was only a few feet away. She pushed through the throng of startled customers, interrupting those who were rummaging through the contents of the jewellery counter. It was filled with ridiculously cheap items, each with its own bright red price label. She wondered if she was hallucinating – why on earth would a hi-fi and TV shop also be selling jewellery? Her thoughts were punctuated by the boss-man shouting from the stairs at the back of the shop.

Sod this, she thought and ran out of the door where, once again, she stood in the shadow of the Guildhall. The pavement was crowded with people. It was even more packed than her experience of a Christmas Saturday. In her time, Guildhall Hill had been pedestrianised and only Gaol Hill, on the far side of the Guildhall, was used for traffic. Here Guildhall Hill itself pulsed with vehicles, forcing pedestrians to jostle for space on the narrow pavement.

"Kay," she shouted. People around her stopped and stared, but no one close by resembled her future self. She stood on tiptoe, trying to peer over their heads. She spotted a woman, further up the hill in front of the Guildhall itself who had the requisite dark, wild hair and was dressed all in black. While the woman closely resembled Kay from the back, she appeared somewhat skinnier as she trotted across the road towards the market. Cassie wasn't absolutely sure it was Kay and debated if she should call out to her again. Then she noticed a girl following several yards behind the woman and let out a squeak. Apart from the jacket she wore, the girl appeared identical to herself.

Cassie's mouth dropped open as she stared at her clone. The woman turned to chastise or beckon the girl to keep up – it was unquestionably Kay. Despite the prompting, the girl continued to dawdle across the road between the traffic.

And then Cassie let out a larger squeak, before clamping her hand over her mouth. A stream of around ten ghostly figures erupted from somewhere to the right and overwhelmed the girl. Each grey-white and partially transparent, the things were substantial enough to grab and pull the girl to the ground. Cassie heard her own voice screaming though the noise didn't originate from her own mouth.

Kay took one look and ran off into the market, leaving the hapless girl to fend for herself, much as Cassie had been left on her own on the green on Pottergate. Cassie gasped as the creatures dropped through the tarmac, dragging her clone through the surface of the road until nothing remained above ground. A second later traffic passed over the spot where the girl had been. Throughout all this, no alarm had been raised and all the other people milling about acted as if they had seen nothing out of the ordinary.

Cassie's heart pumped in her chest as she glanced up and down Guildhall Hill on the lookout for any more of the creatures. Seeing none, she ran through the traffic, oblivious of the car horns that blared, and plunged into the market shouting Kay's name.

The stalls were different again. Not the ones she was familiar with in her own time but far from the state of those she had seen when they'd come out of the gents toilet. She tore along, still calling, but failed to spot any sign of Kay. One of the stalls had some music playing, it was an old song she remembered her mother liking – Ghost Town. She guessed she was now somewhere around the early 1980s. She continued her dash through the market – up and down the aisles, colliding with people. A few shouted back at her in annoyance, especially the woman whose bag of chips she managed to up-end all over the ground.

After several minutes without any success, she ran up the steps to the memorial gardens that overlooked the market. Kay wasn't there, either. Exhausted, she leant on one of the stone walls and scanned the crowd for any sign of her.

Nothing. But at least there was also no hint of nasties.

To her left a bench became free. She claimed it, slumping down and spreading herself out, deterring anyone else from joining her.

Below her within the market the music now playing was "It's My Party and I'll Cry If I Want To" – not the original, but some 1980's remake. Cassie definitely felt like crying. She rested her elbows on her knees, and lowered her head. But she felt no respite – her hands were shaking and blood pumped loudly in her ears.

"What am I supposed to do now?" she whispered to herself. She'd now lost Kay twice in a row and had also seen the result of becoming caught by the creatures.

Cassie felt the bench move. She opened her eyes and straightened up to see a bag of chips drop down beside her.

"Want some chips?"

Reunion Chips

Remembering what had happened last time chips had been dropped in front of her, she was about to make a run for it when Kay sat down beside her. Cassie gasped in surprise, then grabbed and hugged her tightly.

"Whoa," said Kay. "Anyone would think you were glad to see me. Eat some chips before they go cold."

Cassie devoured the chips but then stopped and looked at Kay properly. She was different. There was now some grey in her hair – only the occasional strand or two, but it was also more curly and her face looked slightly older and more lined. But, that wasn't all. Kay was definitely leaner than before, even skinnier than the version she'd seen a few minutes before. There wasn't an ounce of fat on her.

"Okay," Kay said. "So which version of Cassie are you, then?"

"What do you mean?"

"I mean what I say. I've lost thousands of you over the years but this is the first time I've ever found one again. I just want to know which one you are."

"How did you find me?"

"I heard you calling my name. Actually, I've heard you several times over the past few years when I've been here on the market in 1982. This was the first time you were clear enough to track down. So, which one are you?"

"How can I know?"

"Well, how about telling me what we were doing when you last saw me?"

"The bus and the caves under Earlham Road."

"We've done that one about fifty times. Be more specific."

Cassie frowned. "You said you'd only been there about a dozen times before."

"And we got out the hole after they pulled the bus out?"

"No, I didn't get out the hole. We were attacked by the nasties and I fell down a new hole. Bus man helped me with the nasties."

"Oh, that one," Kay said, and then frowned. "Weren't you the volatile one?"

"Volatile?"

"Yeah, the one who claimed she'd never stolen anything? Got really narked when I told her about the shoplifting."

"Her? Well, yes, that was me."

"Blimey, that was ages ago. I thought you'd been killed by the nasties. I think I've still got your phone." Kay rummaged around in various pockets for several seconds before pulling out what looked like Cassie's phone. But it was severely battered and the screen was cracked. Cassie tried to turn it on. "Don't bother, it's been dead for years apart from that one time it fired up on its own. I did try to recharge it but it's busted."

"On its own? What happened?"

"I was up on top of the castle talking to Robert Kett when your phone pinged. Must've been about a week after you disappeared."

"What did it say?"

"It just showed a map of the market and a pin located in the memorial gardens, right here where we're sitting. Then it died. I never threw it away just in case it ever did it again."

"Is that how you found me?"

"Sort of. As I said, I heard you calling from within the market several times when I was around here but could never locate exactly where you were. This time I just happened to be buying some chips when you shot past the next row. So, I followed you up here."

"Wait, you kept my phone – but what happened to yours?"

"I didn't have one. Never wanted Grandad to be able to track me down if I didn't want to be found."

"Oh, but you got into my phone without problem?"

"Duh, yeah! You'd set up the fingerprint recognition so it worked for me."

"Ah yes, of course."

Cassie was quiet for a moment before asking, "So, exactly how long ago did you last see me?"

"What? You you or any you?"

"This me!"

"Hard to say. Certainly the last 'any you' I saw was about half an hour ago. We popped out in an undercroft down Bedford Street. That you was a right dumbo. I immediately spotted the nasty with the big mouth hiding in the shadows but dumb you didn't."

"What happened?"

"Bit your head clean off. So, I thought, sod it I fancy some chips."

Cassie's mouth hung open. "You watched one of me die and that made you fancy some chips?"

Kay shrugged. "Well, it was a particularly dumb version of you. A real lights on, no one at home job!"

Cassie shook her head in disbelief. "You didn't answer the question about when you last saw me."

"Hmm. How old did I think I was back then?"

"Forty-ish, maybe?"

"You sure?"

"No, maybe I thought you were forty but you might have been younger."

"Well, right now I feel more like fifty. Maybe I am. No real idea. I did try watches, you know."

"Huh?"

"Wearing a watch – one of those old wind up things with a date. They'd last two or three portals and then break. By the time I'd realised they'd broken I had no idea how much time had passed."

"Oh, I see. Um, another thing. I, um, I needed the loo when I was in the caves, and…"

"Oh yeah, that's well convenient. You're dying for a pee, you go through a portal and then you no longer need to go."

"What happens to it?"

Kay laughed. "Well, those caves did smell a bit, didn't they!"

"Ugh!"

"Hah, I'm only guessing – there might be a different reason. Anyway, it could be worse. It only works for pee, you know."

Cassie looked at Kay askew – she wasn't sure if she was kidding or not.

Kay changed the subject. "So, how long has it been for you since the caves?"

"About an hour, tops, I'd say."

"Wow, that was a heck of a short cut! And how many portals have you been through since then?"

"Erm, two – the one in the caves that ended up under the Guildhall and the one that came out in the basement of that hi-fi shop on the other side of the market. I think you must have just come out the same place as I missed you by a couple of minutes and then saw you go into the market."

"No, not been in there for a year or two."

"But I just saw you. And I also saw me."

"Which you? Real you or a dumb one?"

"Must have been a dumb one as she got dragged under the road by a lot of grey ghosts. It was just over there," Cassie said, pointing.

"What, in front of the Guildhall?"

"Yes!"

"I vaguely remember it. Must have been at least five years ago when I saw that. Didn't realise it was today again."

"Hell, this is too damned confusing."

"You going to finish those chips?"

"Yeah, definitely."

Cassie munched on the chips. They were greasy, tangy and extremely delicious.

"I saw the map – all dark and shadowy, with the portals on it," Cassie said, between mouthfuls. "Sometimes they lit up and flashed from one to another and I wondered if that was you. Was it?"

"You saw what?"

"The map. I was under the Guildhall in the dark and I saw the map."

"A map?"

"Yes, the map of the portals."

"Describe it again, in detail."

Cassie did so, telling Kay all she remembered. Kay looked hard at Cassie, then her eyes lost their focus and she gazed out over the colours of the market stalls, towards the castle.

"I've never seen or imagined a map like that. None of the other Cassies have, either, as far as I know. They've certainly never mentioned it." Kay looked at her younger self again. "Maybe there really is something different about you. It was you I thought might have been different, wasn't it?"

"Yes, but I– oh, I don't know."

"Well, I'd say yes. Just lately I've had a complete rash of useless ones. I recently lost one in Castle Mall. That version of you was a complete dork – even worse than the last one. Hadn't even got started before she fell over her own feet and ended up with a ton of castle gateway embedded in the top of her skull. Talk about stupid. But you? Well, maybe you really are something special… Shit."

"What?"

"Grandad used to tell me I was… special."

"Oh?"

"Yeah, and then he'd climb into bed with me."

Cassie shuddered.

Transition

"Can you see the map any time you want?" Kay asked. They were walking towards Saint Giles Street as Cassie had felt the strongest portal was in that direction.

Cassie slowed her pace and shut her eyes. "No," she said. "I can't concentrate here. Maybe I need quiet and total darkness. I can still imagine it, though. All those portals under the ground."

"Ah," Kay said, halting. "You only saw the underground ones then."

"Oh, are there others?"

"Yep, like the one on top of the castle and the top floor of Debenhams. I think there's one at the top of City Hall as well – in the clock tower," Kay said, peering up at the tower in question. "I've felt it but never used it. There's often an observer up there."

"A what?"

"A not-so-nasty nasty."

"Oh."

"I don't think there's one at the moment. You sure you didn't see any overground portals on the map?"

"No, I'm pretty sure the ones I saw were all underground."

"Interesting. Maybe you'll see those once we transition."

"Transition? Oh wait, I think you mentioned that once before."

"Did I? Well, maybe I did. Anyway, they go in a sequence. First the underground ones, then the overground ones higher up."

"Wombling free," Cassie murmured. "Underground, overground, Wombling free. Grandad used to sing that song."

"Yeah. Don't remind me."

"But the bus man said it at Debenhams, didn't he?"

"I can't remember. Sometimes he does. Look, it may have only been a couple of hours ago for you but it's been years for me."

"Sorry… You were talking about the transitions."

"Yeah. As I was saying, we seem to have to do the underground ones first, and then there's a transition and we do the higher ones."

"And then what?"

"I don't know. Once I had one come out on the Lord Nelson. You know, that boat that used to be parked on the river near the railway station – it belonged to the Sea Scouts or whatever they were. Actually, as this is 1982, it's probably still there. I think that was one where I lost you soon after we arrived. Once I lose you then any portal I go through takes me back to Castle Mall again to hook me up with the next victim. It all gets ridiculously boring. I was expecting that to happen after I lost the last idiot. But, now you're here, maybe that won't happen. Seems a bit too soon for you to do a transition, though. There's usually about ten underground portals first. You haven't been through ten, have you?"

"No, um, five, I think."

"That's more than most Cassies manage."

"Found it. It's here," Cassie said, halting.

"Ah, the car park. Let's hope no one's parked where the portal is. I once came out of a portal here and found myself inside the back of a locked van. Confused the hell out of the guy who tried to drive it off a few hours later. Still I did get a good sleep that time. Of course, the best one was coming out the portal here when it was still the old Hippodrome."

"The what?"

"The theatre that was here before they replaced it with this monstrosity. Laurel and Hardy were playing there that day. Mid fifties I think it was."

"What, a film?"

"No, the real them. They were well old by then."

The portal, when they found it, was on the lowest floor stuck in between two closely parked cars. It was a squeeze to get both of them into position.

"Right, here we go again," Kay said holding her hand out for Cassie.

The shimmying happened again except that, upon exit, they were lying down on their sides and forced together into a very small, cramped space. It was so tight that they were almost wrapped around each other, with Kay partially on top of Cassie and both tangled up in each other's frizzed hair. Also, it had that smell like open roadworks; earthy, pungent and unpleasant. Even worse, it was almost completely dark apart from a small sliver of light coming through a crack to one side of whatever was above them.

"Hell," Kay said. "I wasn't expecting this so soon. This one is a right bugger to get out of. But it *is* a transition one – well, it is, normally. Which is weird this soon."

"Where are we?"

"Okay, try to get to one side of me and stay on your back. Can you feel the slab of stone above us?"

"Feel it? It's almost in my face."

Kay wriggled one way and Cassie went the other. Then Cassie felt Kay contorting herself so that she, too, was laying on her back with her knees almost on her chest.

"Now, all we've got to do is push a whacking great big huge stone slab off of us. Hands and knees together."

"I can feel something like writing or letters in the stone," Cassie said.

"Not surprising. You'll see what it is once we've got this thing out of the way. Right, start shoving now!"

Cassie pushed against the stone above her. She had trouble getting leverage with her knees. At first nothing happened. Kay was grunting and swearing beside her. Then, the sliver of light became marginally brighter and Cassie could feel the slab moving.

"Hold it there while I get a foot positioned against this end," Kay ordered.

After more grunting and effort the stone began to lift and a shower of loose dry sandy soil fell on them as the slab rose. The light, not daylight, but an artificial fluorescent coming from the building next to them, revealed what the worn lettering on the stone signified. Cassie could make out the words 'Died 18th August' followed by a year that was mostly unreadable apart from the 1 at the beginning. Above their heads, a cloudy night sky was illuminated from below by the orange glow of street lamps.

"Ugh! It's a gravestone! Are we in a graveyard."

"Probably was once," Kay said, pulling herself out the hole and holding the gravestone vertical so that Cassie could get out. "Either that or whoever did the paving here nicked them from a local church, like that one over there across Duke Street."

There was a crump sound as Kay dropped the gravestone. It caught on one edge and refused to reseat itself even when both of them kicked it.

"Oh, leave it," Kay said. "I'm sure someone – human or otherwise – will put it back. It's always back in place whenever I arrive."

"Where are we, then?"

They were in a small yard with old buildings all around them. On one side was an archway underneath one of the buildings, the far end of which was blocked by a tall and solid double gate. The arch looked big enough for a small lorry to come through.

"Muspole Street," Kay said as she peered in the doorway from where the light came. "It's up there, isn't it?" she said pointing up to the second floor level of one of the buildings.

"Yes," Cassie agreed, after concentrating for a moment. "Upstairs somewhere."

"Yep. We're about to transition from the underground ones. Goodbye undercrofts and caves and buses falling on our heads, thank goodness. You know something?"

"What?"

"Congratulations."

"Eh?"

"I reckon I only manage to get about one in seventy of you through a transition. But I think you must have talked it up and taken a short cut."

Baker Boy

Cassie was about to try the door.

"Don't bother, it's locked," Kay told her.

"How we gonna get in, then?"

"I've got them somewhere," Kay said, rummaging around again in her jacket.

"How many pockets does that thing have?"

Kay grinned. "Plenty and, damn, do I fill them up!" There was a jingle and she produced a bunch of keys which she inspected one by one. "Ah, this one, I think." She slid the key into the lock and it turned. Kay grinned again and opened the door.

"Where did you get that?"

"Not the first time I've been here. I had to break in the first time and found a spare. Right, now be as quiet as you can. There's sometimes people still around. Often there's something else as well."

"Nasty?"

"Nah."

"What is this place?" Cassie whispered as they ascended the staircase to the floor above.

"They make printed circuit boards – you know, the things inside TVs and computers and whatever."

"Why?"

"Well, someone's got to make them, I suppose."

"No, I meant, why this place? Why are the portals in particular places and not just where we need them to be when we need them?"

"Don't know. Though the ones between transitions are often only a short distance apart."

"Why's that?"

Kay shrugged – she had a habit of doing that. Cassie wondered if she did it herself.

At the top of the stairs they passed an office door – the glass panel showed that it was empty, its interior quite dark. Ahead of them another door opened up into a larger room. Kay peered in cautiously before slipping sideways along the wall to the left with Cassie following. One section in the middle was curtained off but to its right a smaller room whose own lights were off was lit dimly by something brighter beyond. They could hear the sound of machinery, a high-pitched whining.

"This way," Kay whispered as she led Cassie around the middle section. "It's a bit of a maze – I think several buildings got knocked through into one at some point."

The noise was louder here. Whatever it came from was in the next part of the building, beyond a double door.

"Ah, I think we have a visitor," Kay said. "How you doing, baker boy?"

Ahead of them there was something partially transparent standing or hovering in front of the doorway.

The ghost solidified a bit and Cassie took a step back.

"It's okay. He won't hurt you. Actually, he's got quite a sense of humour."

"For real?" Cassie said, unbelieving.

"Oh, is that Kay and Cassie?" the ghost said. "Haven't we done this already?"

"Yep," Kay said. "But around us, time does get rather screwed up. We keep coming back to the same places and sometimes at the same time but different things happen each time."

"Why is that?" the ghost asked and then frowned. "And, not only why, but how is that even possible?"

"Well, I'm always the same, but older each time. And Cassie is always different."

Cassie could see the ghost's face a little clearer now. He looked as confused as she felt – Kay's explanations always seemed to result in more questions than answers. She could see that the ghost did resemble a boy, in life he would hardly have been any older than herself. He was attired in a white coat and grey trousers. He had the smell of yeast and baking about him, and there was a dark line around his neck.

"Part of this place used to be a bakery," Kay explained. "Is the portal still upstairs?"

"Portal? Oh, yes, I believe so," the ghost said, adding, "but I was about to do a bit of official haunting."

"Oh great," Kay chuckled briefly. "Can we watch?"

The ghost nodded. "There are two people in there – a man and a woman. I tried to scare the man a few weeks back by appearing to him in the daytime while he was working. He looked up at me for a second without any surprise and then looked down to turn his drill off. Of course, when he looked up again, I'd made myself invisible. He looked confused but then went on working. I think he must have thought I was someone else who worked there who was having fun with him."

"A bit of a waste of time, then."

"Yes," the ghost said with a sigh. "But tonight there's two of them working overtime on their drills and they're completely on their own. The place is empty otherwise. Or it was until you two showed up."

"Well, don't mind us. Anyway, we'll probably help spook them as we're out of our time which often means people can't focus on us properly."

"All right. Follow me," the ghost said, walking through the closed doors and fading almost to invisibility.

Kay opened one door slowly and, crouching down, crept into a larger room with Cassie following behind doing likewise. Inside, there were sheets of something stacked on edge. These provided adequate cover to hide from anyone down the far end of the room. The place was about three times longer than it was wide. Apart from the door they'd come through, there didn't appear to be any other exit except a flight of stairs opposite which gave access to the floor above.

Cassie peered out cautiously. At the far end she could make out the two people working at machines. The man, seated at his drilling device, which was no bigger than a school desk, stared into a small horizontal tube mounted on top of the desk. If it was a drill then it looked like nothing Cassie had ever imagined before. The machine the woman sat behind was larger, more the size of a small dining table. Her fingers held a handle by which she slowly guided a free-moving framework above the table surface. Upon the framework were four vertically mounted drills arranged in a square about two feet on a side. Each time she released her grip on the handle, the drills dropped down and made their holes before rising again, barely a second later.

Cassie didn't understand how the woman knew when and where to release the handle.

So this is how printed circuit boards get their holes drilled into them. Not exactly information I'm likely to find useful in the future. She shrugged, and then thought, *Okay, so I do actually do the shrug thing. It's not just Kay.*

Neither the man nor the woman appeared to have noticed them. They certainly couldn't have heard them as both wore headphones – not surprising given the noise the drilling machines were making.

The ghost indicated that they should move across to the staircase. Kay and Cassie crawled across the floor and ascended a few stairs. Then the ghost became more corporeal, standing up tall to rattle a few of the sheets. Then he faded to invisibility again. Peering over the bannisters, Cassie saw movement as both heads shot up at the far end of the room, their fear emblazoned across their faces. Without speaking, the two caught each other's eyes, pulled off their headphones and switched off their drills. The woman grabbed her bag and coat, and they both hurried towards the doorway, glancing back and forth, their wide eyes filled with horror.

"Boo!" Kay shouted as they passed. The baker boy tugged at the woman's coat making her scream and run all the faster. The two dashed through the door and ran out the building, turning the lights off as they went. They heard the distant sound of the front door being slammed and then locked.

The ghost appeared again and gave off enough light by which Kay and Cassie could see.

"I wanted to shout 'boo' as well, but I was so busy laughing I couldn't," Cassie said, giggling.

"Well, that will certainly give them something to talk about tomorrow," Kay added.

"If they actually dare come back," the boy chuckled.

"So, you remember how long you've been haunting this place now?" Kay asked.

"I'm not sure. What year is it?"

"Ah, well that's something I'm not at all sure about, either," Kay said. "Nineteen seventies or eighties, I'd guess. When did you, erm, well, pass away?"

It was the ghost's turn to look confused. "Do you know, I don't think I remember that myself any more now. It's funny what you forget, isn't it?"

Kay shrugged. "Maybe it's time for you to move on. Or whatever happens next."

The ghost nodded solemnly.

"What does happen next?" Cassie asked.

This time both Kay and the ghost shrugged.

"Well, that was a waste of breath," Cassie mumbled to herself.

The ghost scratched at the mark on his neck. "Hmm, I think you should go and find your portal. I feel we're due for a different sort of visitation."

"Oh, I don't like the sound of that," Kay said.

"Nasties?" Cassie asked.

"If so then, yes, they're rather enthusiastic this time. Most times they don't bother to put in an appearance here whether or not baker boy is around. Right, Cassie. Time to move. Hunt out that portal."

"Hey, I'm not some kind of sniffer dog, you know!"

Calamari Chaos

They ran up the stairs leaving the ghost of the baker boy to fade away. At the top they entered a room that was built into the roof space. Regular street light filtering in through a low window made it possible to just about make out the interior. It was obvious this area was only around half the length of the room below.

"Did you see that mark around his neck?" Kay said.

"Oh yes, what was that?"

"He hung himself from the bannisters of the stairs we came up."

"Eew! Why?"

"That's another thing he's forgotten. I've asked him a few times in the past. Sometimes he remembers more than other times. Poor sod. Anyway, there's nothing we can do about it now. The portal is usually in the other half."

"What, through this door?"

"Yes."

Cassie pushed it open. Inside, to the left, there was something resembling a shower. From a wooden frame, a plastic sheet hung around a large tub inside of which stood a wooden rectangle that had a silk mesh stretched across it. A hand-held spray attached to a pipe dangled into the tub. There was a chemical smell about the place. A white-surfaced table took up the centre of the room. Upon it sat a solid metal thing with a door.

"Some kind of oven, I think. They do screen printing up here," Kay explained, pointing out a screen printing table that stood against the far wall. To its right was a black curtain running half the length of the room. On its left were more rectangular wooden frames of various sizes, stacked against each other. As they got closer Cassie could see the silk mesh stretched across them though a few had tears and other damage. Several had patterned masks stuck to the mesh showing circuit layouts in some cases and lines, letters and numbers in others. Cassie assumed these were the screens used for the printing process.

Then there was a sound of something, not quite footsteps, coming up the stairs from below.

"Right, no time to waste. We're about to get company. Where is that portal?"

Cassie looked around. "Oh, where's it gone? I can't sense it now."

"What?"

"It was definitely up here when we were down in the courtyard."

"Yes, it was. Concentrate. It must be here. You look while I see if I can do something about the door to give us a bit of breathing space."

Cassie searched around the area of the screen printing table. Kay picked the screen frame from the tub and jammed it under the door handle.

"Will that stop it?"

"Only for a short while – these things can often get through the walls anyway. Oh, and here it comes," Kay said backing away from the door to join Cassie at the other end of the room.

"What is it?" Cassie said, pointing to the dozen thin tentacles that oozed through the gap between the frame and the door. Once enough of their length was inside the room they ranged about, probing and testing anything they touched. Cassie had a pretty good idea what they were after.

"Not good," Kay said. "That type tend to wrap you up and then squeeze the life out of you."

"You've had that happen to you?"

"No, but you have. Well, not you specifically, of course."

"What happened?"

"Shall we just say it didn't end well."

"Oh, great. What are those tentacle things attached to?"

"You don't want to know. Well, maybe you do, but you'll regret it. Nearest thing would be a giant squid or octopus. At least jamming the door was the right thing to do. Hmm."

"Hmm, what?"

"I have a theory," Kay said, her eyes following the tentacle movements. "Move over towards that curtain."

"Why?"

"Just do it," Kay demanded as she picked up something resembling an artist's palette knife from the centre table. She then jumped onto the table avoiding the waving tentacles that swept through the air. "Yes, they're ignoring me and heading for you."

"Why?"

"You might be more tasty."

"Uh. What do I do?"

"Keep out of their reach."

A couple of tentacles edged closer to Cassie but as they stretched out Kay sliced at them with the palette knife. It was far too blunt to do much damage but must have inflicted some sort of pain as one tentacle snapped back towards the door and the other flopped down on the floor and writhed.

The door itself started shaking.

"It's breaking in," Kay shouted. "Have you found that damned portal yet?"

"No. Maybe it's behind this curtain," Cassie said, pulling it to one side. The sloping roof restricted the height so that there was hardly room to stand upright. But opening the curtain revealed a long, narrow table upon which some sort of machine rested. That wasn't all. Cassie's eyes spotted a hefty pair of pointed scissors beside the machine and she grabbed them.

Kay swiped at another tentacle that was getting too close and then jumped from the table towards Cassie. The creature must have detected the movement as one rubbery tentacle hurled itself at them, wrapping itself around both of their necks. It began dragging them towards the door.

Kay tried to slash at it without success. Another tentacle encircled both their bodies, trapping them against each other, pinning both of Kay's arms to her sides along with one of Cassie's. There was a crack as the frame Kay had jammed up against the door shot across the room. Cassie screamed as the door sprung open to reveal the huge body of the creature, both wider and taller than the door frame. As it squeezed itself into the room Cassie could see that it was some sort of octopus-squid hybrid. A single, huge eye focused on them and its beak-like mouth snapped open and shut as it sent a dozen more tentacles towards them.

Cassie transferred the scissors to her free hand and stabbed hard into the tentacle that pinned them together. The thing emitted an ear-splitting screech from its beak and the tentacles loosened enough for her to free her other arm. She managed to grab hold of the frame of the screen printing table with one hand whilst attacking the tentacles with the scissors in the other. While doing so, she became aware of the portal, sensing that it was located to the right of the screen printing table near the back wall. Then, as the noise from the creature died down, the portal started to fade again.

"It's hiding the portal," she shouted.

"What?" Kay shouted back.

Cassie could see that Kay had also freed one arm and was slicing at tentacles with the palette knife, doing very little real damage.

Cassie realised it was taking the creature's full attention away from her. She saw a chance and, taking the open scissors in both hands, lunged forward to slice the end of a tentacle completely off. An even worse screech erupted from the creature and its tentacles unwrapped from around both of them to flail wildly about the room – both Cassie and Kay ducked to avoid them. But, that wasn't all that happened, the face was changing. The one eye morphed into two, and the face grew a nose above the beak, which was widening and becoming more like a human mouth.

"I've never seen that before," Kay gasped as the face became that of a man.

But Cassie was concentrating on the portal. The sensations emitting from it had become stronger again.

"This way," Cassie shouted as she grabbed Kay's arm and dragged her towards the familiar shimmer.

The octopus-man thing opened its hideous mouth and screeched, "No!" as another tentacle was flung towards them.

It hit home, wrapping itself around them. Cassie screamed again but they were already falling into the portal. She felt the electricity buzz through her body and then her scream was whipped away by a gust of wind accompanied with a dose of cold, sleety rain.

Overground

Upon High

Cassie fell flat on her back, gasping as her shaking knees gave way.

"Oh, hell," Kay said, unwrapping the remainder of the truncated tentacle from around herself. Cassie watched as Kay's eyes rapidly scanned the horizon. "Ah, I reckon we're up on top of Ranworth Church. Better than being an octopus meal, I suppose."

Cassie also remembered this place – her mum had brought her here one warm sunny day, many years ago. She tried to sit up but, despite the metal railings surrounding them, the strength of the wind felt enough to blow her over the side. Her legs felt like jelly and there was no way she was going to attempt to stand up.

"How do we get down?" she gasped.

"Well, not the quick way," Kay said, slinging the tentacle over the side of the tower. Instead of falling, the wind caught it and tossed it further up into the air. It spun around and then disintegrated into a fine mist that mixed with the almost horizontal rain.

"Right," Kay said, hands on her hips, the wind whipping her hair around. "Where's that trap door? Oh, I'm standing on it. Hopefully, it's not locked from the inside or we'll be right up shit creek given the state of the weather."

Kay pulled at the trap door in the slightly angled roof and it came up without resistance. "You want to go down first or shall I?"

Cassie looked at the ladder that descended into the darkness inside and couldn't decide which was worse – staying on the roof in the rain or tackling the ladder. At least the rain was taming her hair.

"Come on. I'm not staying up here all day," Kay said and started climbing down leaving the trap door propped open. Cassie swallowed and crawled towards it and, with a struggle, swung herself into the hole.

It took her a couple of minutes to inch down first the short ladder and then the longer one.

"The rain's still coming in. Did you shut the trap door?" Kay shouted from below.

"Oh, sorry, no."

"Well, go up and do it."

Cassie shook her head. Her knees still felt like jelly and she could not stop shaking. All she could see in her mind was that octopus eye transforming into a man's face. It was worse than the things in the chalk cave. She'd be having nightmares for a month, if she survived that long.

Kay swore but waited until Cassie had descended the second ladder down to the solid stone floor.

"Can't you leave it open?" Cassie said.

"What, and be responsible for flooding the church tower?"

Kay tutted but climbed back up both ladders and shut it herself.

Cassie frowned as she dripped cold rain onto the floor. This version of Kay seemed to be more conscientious than the younger one who had thrown her hot dog wrapper onto the ground. To Cassie that occurred only a few hours earlier, though she knew this Kay was around ten years older than the first version she'd met.

"Right, let's get down to ground level," Kay said, indicating the spiral staircase.

"Not yet," Cassie gasped. "I need time to recover from that... that thing."

"You'll get used to it."

"What was it anyway? That face..."

"Yeah, that was definitely a new one on me. I've seen that type before, though, and that one was particularly aggressive, I must say."

"And what was it doing to the portal? It was only when we hurt it that I could sense where it was."

"Now that's interesting. I've sometimes met a Cassie or two who claimed the nasties were hiding portals. Didn't really believe them at the time as they were the dumbo type and got eaten or killed quickly."

"Good job I found those scissors."

"Yeah, it was getting pretty terminal in there. I was expecting it to finish you off and then lose interest in me. They often do, you know."

"Um..."

"What?"

"Do you, er, sometimes let them kill the copies of me so you can get away?"

Kay looked away.

"Oh, so you do, then," Cassie pressed.

"Only when there's no choice."

"Oh, right. I see," Cassie said, making a mental note not to place as much trust in her older self as she had been doing. "Okay, let's get down these damn stairs before you leave me to be eaten by something else."

Kay raised her eyebrows and led the way.

The eighty-nine steps of the spiral staircase that wound their way down the tower were hardly any better than the ladders as far as Cassie was concerned. In several places the stone was worn and uneven. Twice, where the light on the staircase was almost absent, Cassie missed her step, jarring her back on surfaces that were an inch or two lower than expected. She had to stop several times and rest, which annoyed Kay but, still angry at Kay's earlier response, Cassie refused to rush. By the time they reached the door at the bottom, Cassie's legs ached.

Kay pushed the door open and they stepped out into the church proper. Cassie leaned on the stone font to reassure herself that her feet were definitely back on solid ground. She wasn't normally this bad with heights but fighting octopus monsters wasn't anywhere near normal, either.

"Now what?" Cassie asked.

Kay didn't answer but opened the main church door instead. Outside, the sleet was shooting past almost horizontally.

"Bloody hell, don't open that. It's freezing enough in here as it is!"

Kay shut the door. "It's miles back to Norwich. There's a pub about five minutes walk away. If it's open, of course. I have no idea of the time."

"We'd be drowned in a minute, let alone five."

"Yes, it's obviously winter here and–"

"Winter! You're not kidding!" Cassie shouted.

Kay smirked but then said, "Hold on." She opened the door again and ran out into the sleet. Cassie saw her peer up at the tower and then move first to one side and then the other. Then she returned, closing the door firmly behind her.

"Nearly three o'clock," Kay said. "The clock's not above the door. It's above the roof. What a stupid place to put it. If the wind drops for a moment we'd better make a run to that pub."

Cassie nodded. She couldn't think of any alternative. "Any idea what year this is?"

Kay looked around at various crumpled leaflets sitting in a rack near the door. Cassie joined her but none of the pieces of paper held a clue as to the year.

"Can I help?" said a faint voice beside Cassie, making her jump. There was a smell of sweat and straw, and something snuffled at her ankle.

For a moment nothing was visible. Then a short man appeared. He was dressed simply in a one-piece robe of rough, woven material. His hand clasped a length of ragged rope to which was attached a small mongrel dog.

"Is he a nasty?" Cassie whispered, her teeth chattering.

"Okay, right," Kay sighed. "Not met you before, I think. You some kind of monk or something?"

"That would be my calling," the man said with a smile. "Brother Pacificus at your humble service," he added with a small bow.

"Well, at least you're not talking in riddles. Do you know what year it is?"

"It is the year of Our Lord fifteen hundred and thirty-seven."

"Really?" Cassie said, wide eyed. "Wow, that's the furthest back we've ever been."

"No, it isn't," Kay said. "Those leaflets may be useless as far as giving us the exact year but they were definitely printed on a laser. So, probably no earlier than the nineteen nineties. I reckon Mr Ghostly Monk here just happens to have come from the fifteen hundreds."

"Oh, you are from the future time, are you?" the monk said, tugging at the rope but failing to stop his dog from dribbling over Cassie's leg. For a ghost the dog dribble had a distinctly non-ghostly and sticky presence.

"Yeah, and do you know which future time this happens to be?"

"Oh no, not at all. Though I expect a motorised coach will be along in a moment and the coachman in command usually knows when it is."

Kay and Cassie looked at each other. "Okay, so that's weird," Kay said. "How come a sixteenth century monk knows anything about motorised coaches?"

The sound of a horn came from outside.

"What was that?" Cassie asked.

"Ah," Kay said, running for the door. "I see. Come on."

"Sorry," Cassie said to the ghost monk. "I think we've got to leave now."

"Bless you and your journey," the monk said, starting to fade away. "At least you could see me and talk for a moment. It's so rare nowadays and, even more regretful, those that do see me tend to leave in rather more haste than you."

"Yeah, I'm sorry," Cassie said, urging her still trembling legs to run out the door and into the sleet.

Kay was already on the bus, waving to Cassie to hurry up. It was a single decker of, to Cassie's eyes, ancient vintage. Bright red with Eastern Counties splashed down the side in yellow. The destination board at the front sported HEMPNALL in capital letters. Beside it was the service number, 18.

"Cass and Cass, bus and bus, jump on quick, don't make no fuss," shouted the bus man from the driver's seat.

No Place Like

"Him again?" Cassie shouted over the rumble of the engine as she got on. This version was as substantial as the one they'd seen outside the piano shop, though he looked older. Appropriately enough, he was still wearing a driver's uniform and cap. He was, at least, far preferable to an octopus monster any day of the week.

"Don't look the proverbial in the mouth," Kay said. Cassie had no issues with looking at his mouth, it was his eyes that were the problem – this time around they were merely shadows. Kay continued, "Anyway, I'm sure I must have told you once or twice he not only appears on buses but also drives them on occasion."

"Yeah, I think you did, must have been all of several hours ago. How did he know we were here?"

"When time is right, it's the right time for the time for collecting Cass and also Cass," the bus man said.

Ignoring him, Cassie said, "Where are we going? It said Hempnall on the front."

"City centre, big adventure, spinning up and down, and round and round," the bus man helpfully told them as he wrestled the vehicle into first gear with a crunch. "Elemental child cursed to roam, magic toy might take you home."

"He still talks crap, though," Kay added.

Cassie grunted and sat several seats away from Kay.

With more than a few rattles, they trundled off into the rain, sleet and early evening.

As the bus wound through the darkened lanes Cassie pressed her face to the window partly trying to make out where they were going. Her mind, though, was mainly on the situation with Kay.

How can I trust Kay to look after me? Can I stop her running off to safety if something's about to kill me?

She vaguely took in that they passed a sign saying Woodbastwick. A little while later she recognised the entrance to the Salhouse Broad car park.

Then again, I survived being separated from her once, so I can do it again if she buggers off deliberately.

She wondered if she was fooling herself. Just how much was Kay dependent upon her as a reason to exist, and how much did she depend on Kay in order to survive? She sighed.

"You okay?" Kay asked.

Cassie shrugged but said nothing.

After another ten minutes the street lights of New Rackheath punctuated the darkness for a short period before the night enveloped them again.

There was little other traffic on the road.

"Any idea of the year, bus man?" Kay risked asking.

"Paper boy got very stroppy when his girly nicked a copy," came the reply. It was accompanied by a gesture of his head that indicated something behind him. Cassie looked back and then noticed a newspaper on the floor near the rear of the bus. She was sure it hadn't been there earlier but went and picked it up.

"Sunday the seventh of February, 2010," she said. Kay held out her hand and Cassie reluctantly passed it over.

The bus man burst briefly into song. "All my papers seemed so far away."

"That probably means it's yesterday's paper," Kay said, flicking through the pages but finding nothing of any real interest.

Cassie was about to sit back down but then gasped as they shot through a set of red traffic lights without stopping. "Bloody hell!" she shrieked.

"Yeah, he does that," Kay said. "I pretty much crapped myself the first time, too."

At the next main set of traffic lights, where they hit the ring road, the bus did slow down but that was only so they could turn left onto Heartsease Lane.

Despite the cold, Cassie found her hands suddenly sticky with sweat. She also had an overpowering urge to get off the bus. "Stop, stop!" she shouted, running to the front.

"No," Kay said. "Not here. We daren't."

"Why not?"

"*He* might be there."

"Don't care. Stop, bus man, stop right here!" Cassie ordered.

"Wishes, commands, does as girly demands," said the bus man, bringing the bus to an abrupt halt with a squeal of brakes.

"Don't listen to her," Kay shouted but the bus man merely grinned. Then he pressed the button that opened the doors. Kay groaned as Cassie jumped off.

"More flights and heights for girlies two…"

"Shut up," Kay snapped, following Cassie off the bus and into what was now only rain.

"Cassie," she shouted. "This is madness. We can't go there."

"I absolutely have to. Don't stop me."

"But–"

Cassie spun around and snapped, "But what? Don't tell me you never wanted to."

Kay said nothing. *Damn her, I bet she did,* Cassie thought to herself. She stomped up the incline so fast that Kay was forced to break into a run to catch up.

Less than a minute later Cassie was standing outside her own front door. The curtains were drawn but there were lights on inside.

"No," Kay hissed. "We can't do this. What if one of them sees us? It's 2010 – we could really screw things up."

"Isn't it all screwed up anyway?" Cassie shouted.

"That's not the point."

"Why not?"

"Keep your voice down," Kay hissed.

"Shan't! What's the point, anyway? You don't know why all this is happening. And I don't know if I can trust you anymore. Maybe this will help us find out."

"Yeah, but think how freaked out they might get if they realise who we are."

There was a click of a lock and Kay gasped.

"Too late now," Cassie said as the door swung open and she found herself staring straight into the eyes of her mother. A moment ago she thought she had been prepared for this, but now she knew she wasn't. The lump that was caught in her throat prevented any further words escaping her mouth. Her heart felt as if it was about to burst.

No Surprise

"Well, I wondered what all the noise was," Rebecca said, inspecting them closely. "Ah, two of you. Hmm, must admit I wasn't quite expecting two at once. You'd better come in, Cassie. Both Cassies, that is."

"You recognise us?" said Kay.

"Of course, don't they say a mother always recognises her daughter? Even if two different aged versions of her have the nerve to turn up simultaneously? Also, you both having that scar in exactly the same place on your right cheek is a bit of a giveaway."

"Yeah, but…"

"I'll explain inside. Come on in out of the rain," Rebecca said, beckoning them into a house that, to Cassie, felt both strange and familiar at the same time.

Rebecca wore a headscarf. It hid the state of her hair, or lack of it. Cassie did a quick calculation. This was February 2010 so Mum was already well into the chemotherapy.

Cassie followed her into the lounge. Most things like the furniture and TV were in the same place as they'd been when she'd left the house in 2018. But that version of the house lacked her mother's touch and presence. This felt more like the warm nest of a home. The one she'd left was only a house, a place she happened to live. Until she'd seen how it used to be, she hadn't realised how much that subtle change meant to her. There was no comparison and Cassie ached to come back here permanently. She felt herself fighting hard to suppress the tears.

"Mum, I…"

She lost.

Suddenly her mum's arms were around her and her dam burst.

"There, there, there," Rebecca whispered, holding her close. After a couple of minutes her embrace loosened but she didn't let go, and guided Cassie down onto the sofa to sit beside her.

"Is Grandad here?" Kay asked from the other side of the room, her voice cold and hard.

"No, he's already spent all afternoon up at the bowling. They've got a big match on this evening so he probably won't be back until late. You know what he's like when he gets in with his bowling pals."

"Yeah," Kay said, sitting herself down in Grandad's armchair. "I know *exactly* what he's like."

"What do you mean?" Rebecca said.

"I don't want to say. It's not happened yet. Not here in 2010, it hasn't."

Kay and Rebecca locked eyes for a couple of seconds.

"Oh no. Oh, dear God, no," Rebecca said. "I'm so sorry."

"And where is, um…," Cassie, wanting to change the subject, asked through her sniffles.

"Your younger self?" Rebecca asked. Cassie nodded.

"Round at Georgia's having tea. It's Monday, if you hadn't already realised – so her mum picked you both up from school. I've got to go round and collect you at seven as usual."

Cassie glanced at the clock on the mantelpiece. It said the time was just gone half-past three. It felt a lot later.

"Okay," Kay said. "First, let me say that I didn't want to do this. Come here, that is. She made me. But it's like you were expecting us. How the hell did you know? I thought us being here would freak you out completely, especially with two of us being here at the same time. And, also, while I'm full of questions, why on Earth are there some bloody great big oily bolt cutters sitting on the coffee table?"

Cassie looked to where Kay pointed. She was right. She had a vague recollection of the cutters from when she was young. Hadn't they always been out in the shed caked in rust? Then, one day, she remembered noticing that they'd gone.

"I had the urge to get them out earlier on," Rebecca said. "At the time I didn't know why but now I suspect I need to give them to you two for some reason. And the strength of that compulsion earlier on is why I thought you might be on your way. As for the oil, well, they needed oiling."

"That doesn't make any sense," Cassie said.

"No, it doesn't," Kay said. "Add it to the list."

Their mum sighed and rubbed the back of her neck. "I think before I try and explain things to you, you'd better tell me what you've experienced and discovered for yourself. I need to know how many blanks I need to fill in."

"Are you saying you know what's happened to us? You know why we've been trapped in this merry-go-round of portals and nasties and things?" Kay said, her voice getting louder.

"Ah, portals? So, that's what they are. I've sensed them appearing and disappearing for years but never got close enough to one to see it for myself. So, you've been going through portals between places and times?"

"Yes, different places and times," Cassie said. "What are they and why me… us?"

"Right. Well, I didn't know he would make it take this form exactly but…"

"He?" said both Kay and Cassie in unison.

Rebecca nodded. "Yes, he." She sighed again. "Sorry, but it's probably about time you found out a few things about your father."

This time it was Cassie's turn to shout. "What? You told me he died before I was born."

"Yes and no. It wasn't a lie. I was pregnant with you the last time I saw him. However, as you've discovered for yourselves, time has this sort of habit of not exactly being linear where our family is concerned."

"You've experienced it as well?" Kay asked.

"Not quite as I suspect you have. As I said, I've never been through a portal myself – maybe it takes your father's genes to achieve that."

"Oh, my God," Cassie said. "You mean like all this is something we've sort of inherited?"

"Yes, and now I need to know all that's happened to you. Both of you. In detail. Tell me as much as you remember and then I'll fill in the missing details where I can."

Kay and Cassie exchanged a brief glance. "Okay," they both said.

"Before you do, though, I want to know something else first. Don't be afraid to tell me as I know it's going to happen anyway."

"What's that?" Cassie asked. But Kay was way ahead of her and was already shaking her head with the word 'No' forming on her lips.

"Tell me – when do I die?"

Family Spirit

Silence hung in the air for several long seconds. Rebecca looked from Kay to Cassie.

Finally, Kay said in almost a whisper, "Surely you don't want to know that?"

"Yes, I do. It lets me know how much time I've got left in order to try and sort this out, if I can."

"Sort it out?" Kay asked. "How do you mean?"

"Look, I've known something has been going on for years. I could sense the portals, though I wasn't sure exactly what they were. It's like I could also sense you out there flitting around. Not only that, but I could tell it was you in the way I can sense your younger self, even though, right now, she's at Georgia's. The fact that you and your younger self appear to me as aspects of the same person made me realise a long time ago that something was fundamentally wrong. Not only that, but I figured out that it probably affected your older self in a way that was projecting you back into your own past. I had no way of pinpointing exactly where you'd be, so I had to hope that, one day, you would actually come for a visit. Then, about half an hour ago, I could feel you were near and getting even closer. And here you are!"

"Yes, but what can you actually do about it?"

"Well, I might be able to figure out a way to get you back home properly. Back to whenever it first started for you."

"2018. Last day of June 2018," Cassie whispered.

"I live that long? Really?"

"Oh no, sorry. That's when it all started for us," Kay said. "I'm afraid you were... well, you were long gone by then."

"The date of my death, then. Please?"

"Oh hell, Mum," Cassie whimpered, but then she forced some inner strength to the surface. "This is February 2010, isn't it?" Rebecca nodded. "Slightly less than a year. Next January. The twenty-fourth. Oh, Mummy, I'm so sorry."

Cassie burst into tears again and Kay closed her eyes and bit her lip as Rebecca pulled Cassie close.

"It's okay, love. I've known it would come to this. Your father made sure of it. Though I thought I might have had rather a bit longer than that. Still, it does give me the best part of a year. Maybe that's enough time for me to do something, if I can figure out what. Now, your stories, please. I need to know what to plan for. Older Cassie first."

"Call me Kay, it's simpler than having two of us by the same name."

Rebecca frowned. "Why Kay?"

Kay made a face and then said, "That will become obvious." Then she started to tell her tale.

After a few minutes Rebecca looked aghast when Kay described what their Grandad had done when she was thirteen.

"Oh, he will pay for this," Rebecca whispered.

"No! My version of Grandad didn't do any of that," Cassie cried.

"It's okay, Cass. It's not your grandad's fault. I meant your father. He's the one who's to blame."

"How?"

"Ca..., er, Kay. Please finish telling me everything first."

Kay took about forty minutes to describe how she'd managed to survive on her own without any help apart from the occasional friendly spirit or whatever they were, especially the bus man. It took that long to tell because Rebecca interrupted constantly, wanting to know more detail about the portals, what dates they led to, who Kay met, how the nasties manifested themselves and how she managed to evade them so often. But she wanted to know a lot more about the bus man in particular.

"Right, I think I know who he might be. Hold on a moment."

With effort, she stood and went over to the chest of drawers in the corner of the lounge. Opening a drawer she pulled out some old photo albums and started thumbing through them. Cassie remembered idly flicking through them herself on many occasions. There had been several pictures in it of unnamed people she had no memory of ever meeting.

"Is this him?" Cassie and Kay looked over her shoulder to inspect an old black and white photo. It showed a man in a bus driver's uniform standing beside a bus. Even though his eyes couldn't be made out, shaded as they were by the brim of his driver's cap, the profile of his face matched and the smile was a dead giveaway.

"Yes," Kay said. "He was actually a bus driver then?"

"Yes, though I never met him when he was alive. Properly alive, that is. Anyway, meet Charlie, your great grandfather. Grandad's dad."

"Oh, wow," Cassie said. "Is that the only photo?"

"Only one I've got left. There were others but I have no idea where they went. He died relatively young in the late 1960s. Mysterious circumstances some said. Dad said he was found dead in the driving seat of his bus. It had been his last shift of the day and he'd been on a run out into the countryside but was on his way back to the bus station. There was no damage to the bus. Also, when the bus was found the engine was switched off and the handbrake was on. It was like he'd felt too ill to drive any further and had pulled over to rest."

"So, what were the mysterious circumstances?" Kay asked.

"Well, there were two things but Dad said he could never find out for certain. First of all, the bus wasn't actually on the route it should have taken and then a rumour went round saying that when he was found his eyes were missing. Neither of us really believed that last one."

"Oh, shit," Cassie said. "Every time I saw him his eyes were different. Sometimes blue, sometimes brown, sometimes they couldn't be seen and other times they were completely empty. I saw them getting poked out by nasties when we were under Earlham Road."

"Yetch," Kay said. "You didn't tell me about that."

"I didn't want to remember it."

Rebecca said, "As you see him so often maybe you could ask him how he died."

Kay snorted. "Yeah, but pretty much everything he says is gibberish. Rhyming nonsense. Or it seems that way."

Rebecca grimaced. "Ah yes, I think your father must have got to him and scrambled his brain somehow. The only thing he ever said to me was mostly rubbish."

Kay frowned. "I thought you said you never met him?"

"Not quite – I never met him when he was properly alive."

Cassie butted in. "I thought that was what you said – I wondered if I'd heard you right."

Kay grunted. "Anyway, it's just as likely he doesn't know how he died. Remember how the baker boy didn't know how long he'd been a ghost? It took me several encounters to figure out he'd hanged himself as he'd pretty much forgotten. And *he* wasn't talking crap all the time."

"What number bus was he driving when he died?" Cassie asked. "The one he drove us here in had a number 18 on the front."

"Yes, it would have been," Rebecca said. "I think the bus was found somewhere south of Norwich. Saxlingham or Stoke Holy Cross. Somewhere around there."

"Aren't those on the way to Hempnall?" Cassie said.

"Yes, exactly."

"The bus also said Hempnall on the front," Kay added.

Rebecca nodded.

"Wait a minute," Cassie said. "Does that mean, like, we were travelling on a ghost bus? Ew!"

"It felt real to me," Kay said. "Also, what would a ghost bus be doing with yesterday's paper on it?"

The Lie of the Land

Cassie took only a few minutes to tell her side of the story. Rebecca questioned her on the map that had appeared to her.

"Can you see it now?" Rebecca asked.

"I don't know. I was completely on my own in the dark when it happened."

Kay stood up and switched off the lounge light. "Try again. We'll keep quiet if that's what's needed. I think it's important as no other version of you – or me for that matter – ever saw such a thing."

Although the room was dark, Cassie couldn't help being aware that there were two others in there with her and, despite trying for several minutes, she couldn't conjure anything.

"Sorry, it doesn't feel the same."

Kay turned the light back on.

"How about my bedroom," Rebecca said. "Being upstairs at the back you will have less to distract you."

Cassie nodded, standing up. "I know the way."

She did indeed for, by 2018, what used to be her mother's bedroom had become her own. Entering the room in 2010 emphasised all that had changed in eight years. It initially felt like a stranger's room, but the relationship between the bed and window was the same, so familiarity won out and the original sensation faded after a moment.

One of the few luxuries that had remained was the double bed. It would be the same bed she'd take over in a few years. It held memories of nights as a young child when illness or a nightmare had meant her mum allowed her in with her, enfolding her in the protection of her arms for the rest of the night. Even in 2018 she had sometimes imagined her mum still being there at night holding her safe.

She had never considered the possibility that her mum's arms would ever physically hold her again. She felt tears welling up once more.

She swallowed as she shut the door and, in almost complete darkness, stepped across to the bed. After resting her hands on it for a moment she lay down, absorbing the atmosphere, aware of the softness of the quilt underneath her. The room smelt of Mum in a way that it no longer would in 2018. It felt cosy, safe and warm, despite the temperature being lower up here than down in the lounge.

Cassie tried to remember how the map had come to her underneath the Guildhall. She also tried to figure out how long ago that had been. It felt like only a few hours had passed since then but she had no way of making sure.

It's no wonder Kay has no idea how old she is if I'm losing track after only a few hours. She was pretty certain that the local time bore no resemblance to the number of hours and minutes that had passed since Castle Mall. She sighed and tried again to see the map. After several more minutes there was still nothing.

Maybe I'm using the wrong approach.

When she'd been trapped under the Guildhall she'd been desperate to find a way out after fearing she might be stuck there for days. She remembered she'd been trying to sense a portal – at that point any portal would have done. The map had come later once she'd detected several of them. So, she tried again, seeking out any indication of local portals.

After a few minutes of nothing she found herself yawning. The bed was far too familiar and comfortable, and she needed to sleep anyway. Even though the real time was probably around five o'clock, her personal body clock was telling her it was between nine and eleven at night. The short and uncomfortable doze she'd managed in that chalk mine had been far from enough.

To hell with the map, she thought as her body started to relax. She needed a snooze and there might still be time to take one. But a noise at the window made her jump back to wakefulness. Her immediate thought was that the nasties had found her but after a few seconds of listening decided that it was more likely to be sleety rain pattering on the glass. But, the urge to make sure got the better of her so she got off the bed and, with not a small amount of trepidation, opened the curtain an inch or two. She felt relief that the noise really was the weather.

Flopping back onto the bed she decided to give the map one more go.

Portals. There must be some around here somewhere.

She imagined again the tiny coloured shimmers they'd made on the map before the outline of the buildings had formed and grounded the portals in familiarity.

And then she realised there was something directly below her – she imagined it was no more than a few feet away. But it didn't feel like the pinprick of a portal, more like the presence of a familiar friend, or an old memory. Something that was definitely here in the house of 2010 but missing in 2018. It wasn't her mum, though – this was something separate. But it was slippery and she couldn't pinpoint it exactly.

She sighed. This wasn't getting her anywhere at all so she tried to ignore it.

After a while she became aware of a dim yellow point somewhere to the south. Her senses, sure they could detect it through the ground, was countered by the impression that it was elevated. Then another almost directly west impinged on her consciousness. Again, it felt partially hidden. Feeling her way to it she became aware of others, some underground and others elevated. More and more appeared, as if clouds were parting on a bright starry night.

Then she saw dozens of them. A multitude of colours and intensities all around her.

She gasped. *I've found them again.*

Folly

As Cassie explored further, the dark grey shadows of the land and buildings became clearer against the black of the map. The first portal she'd seen glowed slightly brighter and she felt drawn to it. She homed in as if flying above the map.

Oh, I know this. It's that old folly on the grounds of what used to be a sports club. Her memory dredged up the name – Pinebanks. It had closed years ago and, later on, had been vandalised and burnt down. She remembered visiting it with Mum several years ago. *When was that?* The memory suggested she would have been about eight or nine, which meant around 2010 – i.e. now! Had they already been or had her mum still to take her younger self there? She tried to remember details but little came back except the view of a spiral staircase behind a metal grill.

She examined the view of the folly within the map. The portal was near the top of the tower. The more she examined it, the more she felt it calling to her. It must be where they needed to go next but she had a feeling it wasn't ready yet – though it was getting stronger by the moment. There was also a sense that something was trying to hide it, which was worrying. She didn't relish another run in with yet another tentacled, octopus monster.

But, at least, she knew where the portal was.

I've done it. I wanted to see the map and it finally happened.

She opened her eyes and, despite the fact that she was still in darkness, the map disappeared. She closed her eyes again and sought out the portals. It took a few moments but they appeared once more. She repeated the sequence three more times – opening her eyes to banish the map and then willing it to appear again. Each time it seemed to get easier and the portal at the folly became marginally clearer.

"Yay!" she shouted.

"Are you okay?" came her mum's voice a few seconds later from downstairs.

"Yes, I found the map again," she shouted, wishing now that she'd kept quiet for longer and had that snooze she knew she needed.

She heard two pairs of footsteps on the stairs followed by the door opening. The light from the hallway beyond spilled into the room. Cassie covered her eyes with an arm as Rebecca turned on the bedroom light.

"Oh, sorry," Rebecca said.

Cassie sat up and yawned. "This bed is way too comfy."

"Was the map the same as before?" Kay asked, looking concerned. Cassie glanced at her elder self's face. Was Kay realising she needed Cassie more than vice versa? Hopefully, that meant that Kay might be less inclined to run out on her should they both be in danger. But Cassie decided she would definitely not depend on it.

"No," Cassie said. "I was seeing the above ground portals this time as well as, I don't know, maybe something else quite close. But I think the next portal is at that tower at Pinebanks."

"Oh, I remember going there," Kay said.

"When?" Rebecca asked. "I don't think I've ever been."

"In that case I reckon you should take younger me there pretty soon," Cassie said. "I remember it too. It was all shut up with a metal grill across the entrance."

"Yes, a metal grill. Wasn't it damaged?" Kay said.

"Oh yes, that's right."

Kay's face lit up with a wide grin. "Aha, and I bet it was vandalised by someone with bolt cutters."

"I knew it!" Rebecca laughed.

Cassie stood, yawned again and stretched. "I wonder – can we wait a few hours – I'm feeling whacked out and I don't think that portal's quite ready yet."

"Yeah, you're not the only one," Kay said. "But I don't want to stay here any longer than necessary and make this place a target for the nasties to find."

"Oh, I don't think your father would dare."

"Why not?"

"This place is protected."

"What? How?" Kay asked.

"I'll tell you later. Right now, I think you could both do with a meal and a good sleep. You can't use your own room as younger you will be back in a couple of hours. So, you'll have to share," she said, nodding at the bed.

"We've always shared, if you think about it," Kay said, with a wry look on her face.

Cassie frowned. She hadn't thought about that. Then she caught her own reflection in the full height mirror on the wardrobe door.

"Oh," she said, her hand going to her mouth.

"What is it?" Kay said.

"I just realised something. Come and stand here next to me."

Kay raised her eyebrows but did so. Then, as they were both looking at their reflections, Kay all in black and Cassie in her denim jacket and jeans, Cassie raised her right hand and did a little wave to the reflection with her fingers.

"Oh, my God," Kay said. "That was us."

"You remember it, too?"

"Absolutely."

"What are you talking about?" Rebecca said.

Cassie sighed and said, "Sorry Mum. But at your, um, well…"

"Your funeral," Kay said.

"Yes, sorry."

"Go on," Rebecca said.

Cassie sighed and continued, "Well, I remember seeing two women who kept to themselves. I think they sat right at the back during it all – I only noticed them once the service was over. Afterwards, when we all went outside, when everyone else was coming up and talking to Grandad, these two stayed back and didn't speak to anyone else. Then they caught my eye and the younger one waved to me like I did just now."

"Oh, I see," Rebecca said. "So, you were there three times in all. Interesting, and possibly useful."

Cassie frowned and looked at Kay.

"What?" Kay said.

"Didn't you have a bruise or a cut on your head or something?"

Kay shrugged. "Don't remember."

Then the doorbell chimed, which made Cassie jump. "Who is it?" she whispered.

"Ah, that'll be the pizzas we ordered about twenty minutes ago," Kay said.

Rebecca added, "It was easier than cooking and won't leave any dirty plates around for your younger self or Grandad to comment on. Not that either would notice."

The Fly Trap

"Laurence seemed kind of old fashioned when I first met him," Rebecca said, between chewing on a slice of pizza. "It was around November 1998, my last year at Essex Uni in Colchester and I was twenty two. He started turning up to the same art history lectures I was attending. At first he didn't seem to notice me. I later concluded that that was a deliberate deception – he was homing in on me, though at first he gave the impression he was checking out other girls as well. There was something about him, dark and mysterious sounds totally clichéd but it did make him stand out against the usual jeans and t-shirts crowd. I was put off at first by the beard and constant dark suit he wore – basically, I didn't find him at all attractive. But, we occasionally found ourselves next to each other – only once in a while at first and then it got a lot more common."

"What, you were going to sit near him?" Kay asked.

"No, him sitting near me. Well, certainly that at first. He started asking me questions about some of the stuff covered before he'd arrived, claiming he'd had to miss the start of the year. Said he'd been travelling abroad. He said he'd had a gap year in 97/98 which is why we'd never seen each other before. I later checked up and found he'd never attended Essex before 98. Another one of the stories he made up."

"So, you started going out?"

"No, not at first. We were well into 1999 and I was finishing up my dissertation when it happened. And it happened quickly, so much so that, much later on, I questioned how willingly I had gone into the relationship. Just after the exams finished it was as if he flipped a switch and suddenly we were a couple. Though, at that point, it wasn't physical. But he was completely in the driving seat and I was swept up. No, 'swept up' isn't quite right. Looking back now it feels like I wasn't in control of myself at all – like I didn't have a choice. It was as if he was pulling strings inside my head that I had no idea existed. The weirdest thing was that, as uni ended and I returned to Norwich to start job hunting, I really didn't mind that he went off to Europe and then Asia for several months. Travelling again, apparently. Austria, Hungary, Turkey, Nepal, Indonesia, Taiwan, Japan – you name it. All over the place. I got the occasional post card and phone call. It felt like I was in love and care free, but without having a partner actually present. Dad thought I was mad or possessed. He was right."

"He didn't like Laurence, then," Cassie said.

"They met only the once. When uni had finished, Dad had driven down to Essex to move all my junk back up to Norwich. My intention was to lodge here only for a short time until I found a job and could afford to rent somewhere else. After spending three years away from home, I'd done a lot of growing up and wanted to spread my wings, as they say."

"So, what happened when Grandad met him?" Cassie pressed.

"It was nuts. Laurence was helping me pack. Then your grandad turned up and within minutes they were arguing – though about what, I had no idea at the time. Later on when I questioned Dad about it, he didn't seem to recall either. And he wouldn't remember for about a year and a half. Apparently, they'd shaken hands and then it had kicked off. He was in a foul mood all the way back to

Norwich."

"So, what made him remember?" Kay said.

"Your father dying, I think. It seemed to release both of us. Although Dad had completely forgotten the reason for the argument at the time, he seethed about it for days afterwards."

"Why did you never tell me any of this before?" Cassie asked.

"Well, for a start, right now the real you is only eight – what I'm telling you isn't exactly suitable for younger you to hear back then or now – damn, this is all rather confusing. Anyway, it all kicked off the following summer. After uni I'd managed to get some rubbish jobs – shop work mainly. Definitely not what I'd done a degree for but, at the time, I didn't appear to care and, to be honest, the whole period is like a dream to me now."

"Grandad was right then. You were possessed," Kay stated. "And maybe he was as well for a while."

"Yes, absolutely. I was drifting until Laurence summoned me. A letter arrived around the middle of June 2000. He asked me to come out to Bucharest to help him on some project he'd got involved in. The letter said it was something to do with cataloguing some recently discovered Ottoman Empire art and sculptures. Apparently, his finances were enough to cover the employment of an assistant and was I interested. Well, given the hold he had over me, I couldn't resist. Dad was against it, of course. But, by the end of July, I was on my way. I was still young enough to be rebellious."

Kay grunted. "That's something I never got the chance to be. I'm obviously far older than you but I have no accurate way of telling exactly what age I am. Maybe I've already hit fifty – I have absolutely no way of knowing."

Cassie watched as Rebecca looked at Kay, as if seeing her properly for the first time.

"It's been hell for you, hasn't it?" Rebecca said, in almost a whisper.

Kay nodded. "I've described it sometimes as a merry-go-round that I can't get off from."

Rebecca shook her head. "He had a thing, a device – like a tiny machine but not really – that tapped into all this… this, whatever it was. Back then I can only vaguely remember seeing it once or twice. When I first got to Romania he whisked me off north to an isolated place in the mountains. It looked like some sort of research facility and he appeared to be in charge of it. The pretence of there being a job soon evaporated but I still didn't suspect what was really going on. I was still in the dream. He set me up in a furnished flat not far from his own. A couple of days in I found him at my door and that was when he set the ball rolling properly, if you excuse the pun."

Both Kay and Cassie frowned.

Rebecca sighed, "It went something like this…"

A Nice Romantic Interlude

"I'm in love with you," Laurence said, leaning on the doorpost, holding a small metal object in one hand. "We should get married."

"What?" Rebecca said. "Don't be silly."

"It will be wonderful," Laurence replied, matter of factly while stroking the object. "You are happy."

"Yes," Rebecca concluded. "It will be. I'm so happy."

"That's right," Laurence said, placing the object in his pocket. "You are happy and I am, too. We'll celebrate over dinner."

"What, right now?"

"Yes, right now."

"Oh, okay. That'll be nice."

"That was really nice," Rebecca said, a few hours later. "What was it?"

"Oh, just some local stuff. Salată de icre, sarmale and muschi poiana – that sort of thing. You feeling tired?"

Rebecca yawned. "Yes, the wine was nice as well. I should probably be getting back. Is it late?"

"You will stay the night."

"Yes, that would be nice."

"Yes, it would. Get undressed. We will make love."

"Of course. That will be really nice."

Laurence smiled. "Yes, you have perfect genes."

"What? But I'm wearing a skirt. Oh, you mean…"

"Yes," Laurence said.

"I feel a bit funny," Rebecca said a few days later.

"In what way?" Laurence asked.

"Sick, not nice."

Laurence took Rebecca's face in his hands and stared into her eyes. "No, you feel fine. There is no sickness."

"Oh yes, it must have been my imagination."

"The baby will stay with me," Laurence stated.

"What baby?"

Laurence smiled. "You will go home soon. We will, um, get married when it's time for you to return."

"Oh, okay. That will be nice."

Power Source

"By late August I was back home again and apparently still deliriously happy. I was also completely unaware that I was pregnant."

"Bloody hell," Kay snorted. "You sounded as dumb as some of the Cassies that get inflicted on me. What was it? Hypnosis?"

"More complex than that, as far as I can tell. Somehow he'd totally suppressed the memory of the chance that I might be pregnant. A bit like he suppressed Dad's memory of that argument."

"So, how did he do it?" Kay persisted.

"That machine, device."

"What, like a computer or something?" Kay said.

"Oh no, definitely nothing like a computer. He could tune it to lock onto people's brain waves, make them do or believe whatever he wanted. And that's how it was at first with me. But, later on, the process became more of a two-way thing."

Rebecca stood up slowly with a barely suppressed wince. *She's weaker than she makes out,* Cassie thought. Her mother went back to the chest of drawers from which the photo albums had been taken. She pulled one of the drawers out – it had to be twisted slightly before it released itself. Attached to the back was a small wooden box, which came free after a couple of clips were undone. Leaving the drawer on the floor she returned to the sofa and opened the box. Inside was a metallic device – no more than five inches in length, two in breadth and barely half an inch thick. Carved into its surface were randomly-shaped markings.

Rebecca stared at it, stroked it with one hand and it clicked open, hinged along one of the longer sides. The inside glowed green.

"Wow, is that it?" Cassie asked. "And it was here all the time I was?"

"Yes. Can you feel it with your mind? Either of you?"

Kay frowned and concentrated. Cassie did the same.

"No," Kay said. "Nothing."

"Yes," Cassie said. "Oh, it's what I was feeling earlier on upstairs – when I was trying to see the map."

"Interesting," Rebecca whispered. "I can feel the connection between the device and Cassie but there's nothing similar for you, Kay."

"What do you sense, Cassie?" Kay asked.

"It's a bit like the portals. I'm aware of it. Actually, it's more sort of familiar than the portals, like it's something that was always around when I was a kid."

"Well, that's because it has been," Rebecca said. "Maybe Kay can't feel it because she's been too many years away from it."

"No, it's like I've never had anything to do with it," Kay said, her frown deepening. "What does it do? And how did you get it?"

"Well, it's what is protecting us but how I got it goes back to when your father died. Around late October Dad was starting to ask about my bump. At first I was in denial but then Laurence sent another letter – seems primitive now but we weren't on the internet back then. I think Laurence was, but this place wasn't – we didn't even have dial-up."

"What's that?" Kay and Cassie said in unison.

"It's not important. Anyway, Laurence wanted me to go back to Bucharest. Dad insisted that I should not go and, deep down, I knew I agreed with him.

Perhaps I was beginning to fight back – I don't know. Anyway, I said it would have to wait as I had appointments at the hospital. Actually, I didn't, but I was forced to admit that the bump – you, that is, Cass and Kay – did actually exist and decided there and then to get it checked out."

"Laurence wrote back in November saying he would come back to England in December to see me. That news made me deliriously happy as well as scared. It was as if there were two people in my head fighting for dominance."

"Which one was winning?"

"If your father hadn't died then I'm not so sure. It's obvious to me now that you were something he'd wanted created and had sought me out as the method by which that creation would occur."

"Are you saying he had me – us – made for some specific purpose?" Kay said.

Rebecca nodded. "You won't remember this but when you were about a year old he tried to get custody of you. I had to fight him through the courts in order to keep you."

"Something else you never told us," Kay said.

"And neither did Grandad," Cassie added only to hear Kay snort.

"I swore him to secrecy," Rebecca said. "I told him I'd let you know everything when you were old enough. Well, it looks like that bit is coming true, though not in the way I expected. Of course, back then I hadn't expected to be dying quite so soon."

"Mum. Did he cause the cancer?" Cassie's voice shook on that last word.

Rebecca nodded again. "I'll get to that in a while. First let me tell you what happened the day I saw him die."

"Okay," Kay said.

"Right. Well, I'd been for a scan the day Laurence was due to turn up. I was around eighteen weeks pregnant and apparently everything was normal. I'd left the hospital and was walking along the pavement to a bus stop when I heard my name being called. And, suddenly, there he was. Interestingly, he looked a lot older, fatter even. Also, unusually for him, he looked unsure of himself, as if he was no longer fully in control. Actually, at first sight, I wasn't even sure it really was him but the voice, mannerisms and the inevitable dark suit finally convinced me it was."

Out of Mind

"Rebecca," Laurence called.

"Oh, Laurence," Rebecca replied, seeing a man who was both familiar and unfamiliar at the same time. "You've, er, um…"

"Don't worry about it. It's all perfectly normal."

"Oh yes, perfectly normal," Rebecca answered. Her head experienced a moment of gooiness as if her thought processes were slowing down. She tried to fight it. This definitely isn't 'perfectly normal' said a growing niggle at the back of her mind.

"How's the baby? The boy. It is a boy, I presume?"

"I forgot to ask," Rebecca said, frowning. But that was a lie – she had remembered. The baby was a girl. Why was she lying and why was she like this around Laurence? And, for that matter, what was wrong with Laurence? He looked, well… old – as if it wasn't him but his own father. There was a hint of grey around his temples and his suit looked scuffed in places. It definitely didn't fit his waist as well as it should. He stood with his back to the road – too close. It was around two-thirty and the early afternoon traffic was passing by quite fast only a foot or two behind him. She was scared for him but also felt a momentary urge to push him into the road. Could she do it? She glanced around at the other pedestrians – too many witnesses.

"Well, not to worry," Laurence's face contorted into a forced smile. It was unnatural and broke Rebecca's train of thought. "It doesn't really matter, does it?" he added, his eyes darting around as if he was trying to look in several directions at once. Rebecca noticed that his attention was primarily focussed along the road to his left, as if something in that direction was more important than their conversation.

Rebecca suspected that, to Laurence, it did matter – he obviously wanted the child to be male.

"No, it doesn't matter, I suppose. How did you know I was going to be here?" she asked. The urge to push him into the road grew stronger. Could she do it?

"You told me in the letter you had the appointment."

"Did I? Oh yes, I must have done."

There was a pause in the traffic and Rebecca glanced up the road to where an old bus was holding things up. Behind it came the impatient revving of a motorcycle. She turned her attention back to Laurence who had said something, though his eyes were also fixed on the bus.

"Pardon?" Rebecca said.

"I said that you can come out to Bucharest for Christmas and stay until the baby has been born."

"What do you mean 'until the baby has been born'? Then what?"

"Well, you then become somewhat insignificant," Laurence grinned, his eyes leaving the bus and boring into her own.

"I do what?"

"Redundant, of no use to anyone. Superfluous. Dispensable." Laurence's grin widened and his stare became more intense. "That's what you will be, isn't it?"

She felt an overpowering urge to agree but something stronger was fighting it. It was almost as if his closeness was giving her the power to stand up to him.

"No," she said. "You're not taking her."

"Her?" Laurence's smile dropped away and his face turned purple. "No, wait! I already knew that, didn't I? What's happening? Someone is playing games."

Despite wanting to hit him, Rebecca instead took a step backwards. Then Laurence's outline flickered momentarily as if, for a moment, he wasn't there.

"Damn," he said, his form flickering again. "Locked. This changes everything. I should take her now," he hissed. His eyes dropped from hers and he stared at her abdomen, his hands reaching towards her. "You will…"

The sound of the motorcycle screeching past the bus drowned out the rest of what Laurence said. He stopped and swore, annoyed at the interruption, and then turned to look at the bike, which roared towards them. The rider was… well, he was rather odd looking. A skinny, gangly shape that was way too small for the size of bike he was riding. Whatever he was dressed in was ragged, shredded almost. It looked as if it had been in a fire. That wasn't all – his hands and what she could see of his face were also tattered and burnt. Only the helmet looked undamaged. A few wispy strands of white hair protruded from the back of it – it seemed to be the only part of him that wasn't burnt. She thought the motorcyclist would zoom straight past but, in one fluid movement, he skidded to a halt and reached over his shoulder to pull a long thin sword from a scabbard. He swung the sword in an arc, the blade hissing through the air until it connected with Laurence's neck, slicing his head clean off his body.

"Oh dear," Rebecca said. Her eyes followed the path that Laurence's head took. It bounced once on the pavement before rolling off into the road. The rather surprised expression set on its face came to rest staring upwards from the gutter.

The motorcyclist dropped the sword and gunned the throttle, racing off as quickly as he had come. Laurence's body remained standing for a couple of seconds more. Then it collapsed backwards to hit the tarmac with a squelch, the neck pumping blood onto the road in metronome-timed spurts.

For a moment part of Rebecca's mind found the whole situation absurd as well as amusing. Well, her wish had come true and she hadn't needed to do anything herself. Then the air filled with screams as other people took in what had just happened. Accompanying the screams, a squeal of brakes announced the bus coming to a juddering halt about a yard from Laurence's body. It hadn't stopped quickly enough and Rebecca watched as the front tyre rolled Laurence's head half a turn before squishing his expression face down into a drain.

She looked up at the bus. It was an ancient looking single decker. Rebecca noted the bus number and destination and frowned. He was well off course. Around her the screaming rose in pitch.

The bus driver jumped down from the bus and nodded at her. Then he ran to Laurence's body, his feet avoiding the growing red puddle that surrounded the upper torso.

"Is he dead?" said a girl's voice from somewhere. Rebecca looked at the voice's owner. The girl was hardly any younger than herself. Of course he's dead, you stupid idiot, Rebecca wanted to tell her.

"No head for heights," said the bus driver, grinning. That was definitely unexpected. It wasn't all – there was something odd about his eyes. He rummaged in Laurence's pockets and retrieved a small wooden box, holding it as if it was fragile. He approached Rebecca and placed the box in her hands.

"Oh, minty," she said as her hands touched the box. A fresh, tangy sensation washed through her body and mind.

Then the bus driver put his face close to her ear and said, "With great power comes great headache. Let the blood run free. Tickets please. Mindless becomes mindful. All change here. Isn't it?"

"Oh yes, definitely. Thank you," Rebecca said, holding the wooden box for a second before slipping it into her handbag. She sat down on a nearby wall while others milled around the body. After a while the milling was interrupted by the arrival of a police car, with an ambulance following only a few seconds behind. She looked up and noted that the bus, along with its driver, was nowhere to be seen.

The police closed half the road causing traffic to build up in both directions. Then they helped the ambulance crew erect sheeting to hide Laurence's body from onlookers. Once that was complete, they began taking statements from witnesses. Rebecca heard several say it had been a crazy motorcyclist who had sliced Laurence's head off. Others concurred, pointing to the abandoned sword still lying in the road. A couple also pointed in Rebecca's direction saying she was the one who had been talking to the victim moments before.

So, she was taken to a police station and asked to make a statement. Throughout all this she felt as if she was awakening from some sort of dream but she gave the police answers to everything they asked about. In her increasingly rational opinion, she realised they never actually asked the questions that should have been asked. She did voluntarily reveal she was pregnant, after which the police's manner seemed to soften, especially when they were informed that the deceased was the father.

After convincing the police she didn't need any counselling, they released her but, given the knowledge of her condition, called for a taxi to get her back home – though they did leave her to pay for it.

A few hours later a policewoman phoned to report that they'd found the motorbike in Earlham Road Cemetery. Apparently, it had crashed into a tree and then caught fire. The driver had either been killed by the crash or the fire that accompanied it – there was very little left of the body that would allow for identification. The sword, which had been taken away for examination, contained a number of fingerprints which hadn't, as yet, matched any on file. Rebecca asked about the bus driver but the woman sounded confused and said that no one had reported any buses being anywhere near the scene of the crime.

"Oh, that's right. My mistake," Rebecca said. "Sorry, not thinking straight."

"Are you sure you don't want to be referred for counselling?" the policewoman asked. Rebecca said she'd keep it in mind.

That evening, sitting at home, Rebecca's head felt a lot clearer. Funnily enough, so was her Dad's.

"I can remember what he said now," he told her. "He glared at me while he said, 'Your daughter is mine and there's nothing you can do about it.' He made me hate him there and then, even as I forgot every single word he'd said to me."

"Hell," Rebecca said. "What did he do to me? To both of us?"

She moved her hands over the swelling of her belly. Indeed, just what had Laurence done to her? And, of course, that wasn't all. She retrieved the wooden box out of her handbag.

"You have any idea what this thing is the bus driver took from Laurence?" Rebecca said, opening it up and examining the metallic contraption it contained.

"No idea. What bus driver?"

"I thought I told you about the bus and the driver."

"Wait, yes, I think you did. I remember now. But it's like a slippery eel. I can't seem to hold onto the thought. Tell me again."

Rebecca did, adding, "The bus looked very old. Oh, and it was a number 18 and had Hempnall on the front."

"What? Hell!" he said. He stood up and came to sit next to Rebecca. "Right, can you tell me exactly what the bus driver looked like and what he said?"

Her Dad had turned as white as a sheet by the time she'd finished the description. Then he located a photo album and a particular photograph. As she stared at the picture of the man standing beside a bus, Rebecca felt the blood drain from her face.

Revelations

Cassie and Kay sat there stunned as Rebecca finished that part of her story.

"Well," Kay said after a while. "So Great Grandad pops up everywhere. He's been looking out for you as well as us."

"And this is the thing he gave you?" Cassie said, running a finger over the device that Rebecca held. "And it's been here ever since?"

"Yes."

"What exactly does it do?" Cassie asked.

"Well, apart from give you cancer…"

Both Cassie and Kay gasped at that revelation, and Cassie snatched her hand back from the device.

Rebecca continued, "…it enables you to, well, shall we say, it allows you to manipulate things that probably shouldn't be manipulated. The cancer seems to be the cost of using it."

"So why use it?" Kay said.

"Because, without it, your father would have been able to abduct you so he could use you for the purpose for which you were, um – well – created."

"Which was?" Kay said.

"To prolong his life."

"How did you find out?"

"This thing. Ask it the right questions and the answers appear in your head, as if someone is directly talking to your thoughts. Well, when it actually answers, that is. Some of the time, it's like it refuses to acknowledge me."

"It looks sort of ancient."

"It is – though I could never find out exactly how old it is. Anyway, that was why Laurence was checking out the girls at uni. He needed to find someone with compatible DNA in order to create the next body which he would take over and inhabit."

"Hell!" Kay said.

"So, he was trying to abduct me even after he was dead?" Cassie gasped.

"You're still thinking in linear terms," Rebecca said. "Just because I saw him die in 2000 doesn't mean that, here in 2010, we can't come across an earlier strand of his timeline. You already know that he can create time portals."

"So, he can still come and get us?"

"Wait," Kay said. "If an earlier version of him knows he died in 2000 then what's to stop him going back to that date and preventing his own death?"

"Yes, that's what I thought as well. Once I possessed this device I suspect my own DNA was compatible enough to make an automatic connection to it. It probed me and some sort of learning mode kicked in, which enabled me to figure out how to use it. Like I said – ask it the right questions, etcetera. Anyway, it also showed me what he was up to and how to throw up some sort of protection which can be both location and time related. I still don't understand it but that protection is why he can't attack us here, not that he hasn't tried, and why he can't return to 2000 and prevent his own death. But that wasn't all I learned. Let's just say that 'Laurence' was far from being the first body he'd appropriated and, if we don't stop him, yours won't be the last. There have possibly been tens or maybe even hundreds going back, oh, God knows how many years."

Kay whistled out loud.

"As far as I can tell, all of his previous bodies have been male. He must have made some sort of mistake with you. Hopefully, it's costing him dearly."

"He's not the only one it's costing," Kay murmured.

"So, what exactly is he?" Cassie said.

Rebecca shook her head. "Now that was something I couldn't find out. Whether I wasn't asking the right questions or whether the device itself didn't contain that information, I genuinely have no idea. Maybe I'm not quite compatible enough."

"Okay, so what do we do now?" Kay said.

"Don't let him get you."

"But he has," Kay shouted. "Thousands of times. I've lost all the other Cassies to the creatures that he sends after us. What does he do with them?"

"Now that bit puzzles me completely," Rebecca said.

"And why the multitude of Cassies? And why are most of them – no offence, Cass – so completely dumb? Not only that, but the things he sends after us are sometimes almost as stupid. In some cases they are really easy to get away from."

Rebecca frowned. "That doesn't make any sense at all. He's created this network of portals that you are using but they don't seem to be actually helping him get to you. It's more like they are helping you get away, Kay. Even if the Cassie you are with doesn't."

Cassie grunted.

"What?" Rebecca said.

"Nothing," Cassie replied but, for a moment, she and Kay locked eyes. Kay was the one to glance away after a brief second. Cassie wondered if she was feeling guilty.

Kay changed the subject. "What was that about him trying to get custody of me when I was one?"

"Oh yes. That was definitely fun," Rebecca said, her expression indicating it was the exact opposite. "One day I got a letter from him claiming that, as your father and as someone who had more disposable income in his possession, he was in a far more suitable situation to raise you than I was. As you can imagine that was a little bit of a surprise given that he'd died more than a year earlier."

"What did you do?"

"Well, nothing for a while – I thought it was some sort of hoax – but, apparently, he'd already started custody proceedings. So, when more formal letters started arriving, I passed all of it on to a solicitor. Mind you, he was rather confused when I told him that I'd seen Laurence killed in public, along with witnesses and police evidence. But, soon after, Laurence's own solicitor appeared and managed to prove to my solicitor that he was far from dead. I heard that Laurence was calling me a deluded liar and even visited my solicitor to prove he was still alive. My solicitor showed me a picture that Laurence had got him to take of them both standing next to each other. It was definitely Laurence, though he looked years younger than the one I'd seen die, which I sort of let slip. Everything went a bit haywire for a while as they tried to say I was losing my mind by assuming that the older person I'd seen killed was Laurence when, evidently, he didn't fit Laurence's current description."

"Bloody hell," Kay said. "Obviously you won. But how?"

"Well, your grandad was a rock and pretty shrewd as his evidence centred on Laurence's manipulation of me, which helped give the court grounds to start swinging the case against him. Also, by this point, I had started to figure out more about the device and how it could be used to influence others. I must admit I used it on all those I met to do with the case to bias them against Laurence in any way I could."

"Neat," Cassie said. "And he couldn't do anything about it?"

"Yes, but remember that, although I had this one, I think he still had at least one more."

"Did he realise you had it?"

"I don't think he did but I also made sure I took you with me when I did go to court so that they could see that I was looking after you properly. And also having this thing with me meant I could reinforce that impression. I made sure they felt guilty if they even contemplated the idea that you should be taken from me."

"Did you meet Laurence in the court?"

"No, I managed to avoid him completely. Using the device I exaggerated and spread the fear I felt so that it infected the others. I wanted to give the impression that it wasn't safe for me to be in the same country as him, let alone the same room. I think everyone felt that way about him by the time I'd finished. So, he lost, which I think was far more of a surprise to him than it was to me."

"Um," Cassie started. "Is that thing still in the house in my time – 2018, I mean?"

"I suppose so. I'm not sure how I can tell. Why do you ask?"

"Well," Cassie said, screwing her face up. "Even given the good it can do, I don't want it around. Especially if it causes cancer. And is that all it does? Maybe that's what was affecting Grandad – making him senile. And, if it was, then what the hell was it doing to me as well?"

"Could you feel its presence in 2018?"

"I don't remember. But, if it had always been here, then maybe I wasn't noticing it as it was too familiar."

"Hmm." Rebecca's face took on a faraway expression. Then she wrapped her hands around the device and closed her eyes. After half a minute her eyes opened again and they looked bloodshot. "No, I don't think so. I asked it some new questions and it answered, eventually. It's like it never really wants to reveal anything unless I push it. Oh, it's all rather exhausting."

"Mum, don't make it worse for yourself."

"The questions needed asking."

"What were the answers?" Kay said.

"I, er, I need time to think about what they mean. However, I got the impression that it's not present in the house after I die. So, I need to determine what happens to it – and, more importantly, whether or not your father manages to get it back. As I said, it can't have been the only one he had. It might have been part of a set." Then Rebecca glanced at the clock. "Right, it will soon be time for me to go and get younger Cassie – I'd better get myself presentable."

Rebecca struggled to her feet. Cassie helped her mother steady herself.

"It's okay, Cass. Using the device always wears me down for a bit. It will fade. But, while I'm gone, you two could have a shower or something, especially you, Kay," she said, wrinkling her nose. "Then use my bedroom. Shut the door and wedge a chair up against it just in case younger Cassie or your grandad decide to investigate for any reason. Once Grandad has gone to bed then, sometime gone midnight, I'll come and let you know the coast is clear. You should be able to get at least six hours rest. I expect you're going to need it."

Pinebanks

It was cold, frosty and nearly two in the morning as their feet crunched along the grass verges of Henby Way. Cassie had only managed to get around two hours of sleep before her mum had woken them at around one o'clock. While trying to get to sleep she had heard both her younger self's voice and that of her grandad. What would they do if they suspected that older versions of Cassie were hiding in the house? Kay, accustomed to grabbing sleep any time she could, had dropped off almost immediately and her heavy breathing had kept Cassie awake for quite a while. Well, that and the way Cassie's mind kept returning to picking over whether Kay could be trusted. Finally, though, exhaustion had kicked in.

Kay swung the bolt cutters as they marched past houses where only the occasional window showed a light. Cassie pulled the thick scarf – a parting gift from her mother – around her neck and face, and wondered if anyone watched them as they passed by. What would they think they were up to at such an hour, especially Kay with the bolt cutters?

"It really would have been a lot quicker to go down Harvey Lane," Kay muttered.

Cassie said nothing. That was the route they were going to take until, having reached the Heartsease roundabout, she'd felt something wrong. Unbidden, the map had suddenly flashed across her vision plotting out a path that turned left along Saint William's Way, right into Pilling Road, Gordon Avenue and then onto Henby Way. That wasn't all as, along Harvey Lane, the map contained something green and wide, ominously suggesting it was quite huge. Kay had initially insisted on taking their original route, dismissing Cassie's fears, until Cassie had sworn at her and stomped off down Saint William's Way ignoring Kay's protests.

They reached the cut through from Henby Way to White Farm Road and saw the row of trees that hid the tennis courts. Somewhere up ahead on the left would be the turning they'd need to take into School Lane. But there was something moving in the distance further down White Farm Road and Cassie couldn't make out if it was before or beyond the turning.

"Still think I was wrong to avoid that way?" Cassie said, trying to focus on the object. It looked more like a shifting cloud that, like the vision on the map, was glowing green.

Kay shrugged. "No idea what it is from here, though I have seen that shade of green before."

"What was it?"

"I didn't get close enough to see, but…"

"But what?"

"You did."

"Ah, and did it, um, end badly?" Cassie said, remembering the term Kay had used back when they'd faced the octopus monster.

"Come on, let's avoid it completely and cut across the field," Kay said, ignoring the question and pointing left. "It's shorter and safer than going along the road, anyway."

Kay chucked the bolt cutters over the fence that bordered the field and then climbed over it. Cassie followed. One thing was certain, her older incarnation was far fitter and used to this sort of stuff than she was. By the time she finished struggling over the fence Kay was running diagonally across the field. As Cassie wheezed her way to the other end, Kay had already jumped the fence there and was eyeing up the gate that prevented access to the old Pinebanks grounds.

There was a clunk as the bolt cutters chopped through a chain and a noisy rattle as it slithered to the ground.

"Damn," Kay said. "Don't want to wake up the neighbours."

Cassie looked back along School Lane. "The green stuff is following us."

"Come on then," Kay said, pushing past the gate. "Now where's that damned tower?"

Cassie closed her eyes for a second and willed the map to reappear. Knowing that the green whatever-it-was was getting closer by the second put her off for a moment, but then it appeared.

"Over there," she said, pointing into the darkness.

"Where?"

Cassie grabbed Kay's hand and pulled her along. She was now sensing the portal directly but realised after a few seconds that it was hidden by something.

"Not this way," Kay hissed. "There's a building or something in the way."

"Ah. Okay, we need to veer to the right and around it."

They passed the ruins of Pinebanks to their left and then they saw it, higher than the trees. Its black outline silhouetted against the barely lighter night sky – the tower of the folly.

"The entrance with the stairs is on the left hand side," Cassie said.

"Yes, I remember," Kay replied, racing ahead again, leaving Cassie puffing after her.

The entrance was blocked by a grill, the right hand part of which was a gate. Two padlocks and a chain prevented the gate from opening. Kay chopped through the chain bypassing the first padlock completely but suitable access to the second padlock was impossible for the thick bolt cutters.

"It's getting closer," Cassie said as the green shape oozed past the gate and continued its relentless path towards them. "Come on – I don't want to become another of your statistics."

Kay grunted and snapped, "Going as fast as I can."

Kay cut above and below where the latch fitted into the frame and there was a solid crunch as the section of frame fell away. Kay swung the gate open and they started up the spiral staircase. Inside, they were in almost complete darkness. Cassie could hardly see Kay directly in front of her as she felt her way upwards. She wanted to close her eyes and let her view of the map guide her but was too scared and the map wouldn't materialise.

They had reached and passed the first floor when a glow from below was accompanied by a voice. "How dare you invade my tower. I, Queen Kapiolani, command you to descend."

"Ignore it," Kay whispered. "Concentrate on the portal. Where is it?"

"Fourth floor, I reckon," Cassie said as they passed the second.

Kay stopped at the third. The boards covering the windows on three sides had circular peep holes but an ominous greenish light could be made out coming closer to one of them. The damned thing was attempting to climb the outside as well as the inside.

"It's trying to cover the entire tower," Kay said. "We need to get up the last flight before it does."

Kay sprinted up the last set of stairs with Cassie, her legs getting weaker, following.

"Right, where is it?" Kay shouted.

"Over there, in that little side room. Can't you tell?"

Kay shook her head. "I can't register it at all. You sure?"

"Sort of," Cassie shouted. "It's a bit like the octopus again – it keeps fading in and out. Oh, watch out – it's getting in!"

The room started to glow green from two sources – the stuff oozing up from the spiral staircase was joined by gunk seeping through the holes in the window boards from outside.

Cassie grabbed Kay's hand and dragged her into the annex. Behind them, the room filled with the green presence which coalesced into a human-like figure, a woman of ample proportions that dominated the centre of the room. It drew itself up to a more than realistic height as its mouth opened.

"I am the Queen of Hawaii – and you are my prisoners."

"No, you're not. You're Laurence – and we know all about you," Kay shouted back.

The shape halted and changed, shrinking slightly in stature. Now it resembled a man, one who was a bit bulky around the middle but was immaculately attired in a green glowing suit and tie.

"It's him, octopus features, again," Cassie whispered, realising she'd seen that face before.

"An interesting development," the man-figure said. It stared directly at Kay as Cassie tried to hide behind her older self. "I can only conclude you have made contact with Rebecca. So, exactly what are you? You are more real than the others – those decoys sent to tempt me. Just like the one behind you."

Cassie gasped. Decoy? She was a decoy? What did that mean?

The creature that might have been Laurence continued, "Ah, but wait. That isn't a decoy. It may look like the others. But now, as I get closer, it feels even less of a construct than you, older decoy!"

Then the creature's mouth widened into a grin and it started towards them. "At last," it shouted, "after all the endless misdirections, you can't get away this time."

"Where's that damned portal?" Kay shouted.

"It's gone – I have banished it," the glowing green Laurence shrieked as it advanced. "You are trapped here."

"No," Kay shouted.

"No," Cassie echoed. "He's definitely attempting to hide it. But it's here, I can feel it. It's still behind us somewhere."

"Get us into it, then!" Kay screamed.

The man-shape hurled globs of slime that spread around their bodies as soon as they hit. The impact flung Kay against Cassie and threatened to envelope them completely. Cassie grabbed a lungful of air before her nose and mouth were covered, but the gunk stopped at her mouth, leaving her free to breathe. In front of her Kay wasn't so lucky.

"Hah," it screeched, "you can hardly move, can you? Now the old decoy will be disposed of and, you, Cassie my dear daughter, will finally serve the purpose for which you were constructed."

Laurence's face no longer resembled anything human – his ever-widening grin was in danger of splitting his head in half.

Panicking, Cassie struggled to think how they could escape. Kay's squirming was doing nothing to free her head from the suffocating slime. Laurence would succeed in killing her unless Cassie did something in the next few seconds. But what? Her right hand was barely touching Kay but she couldn't move it any higher.

"Bye, bye, decoy," the thing cackled. Cassie wondered if it actually was Laurence or just something he'd sent after them. But it didn't matter – either way, the thing was killing Kay and Cassie could think of nothing she could do that would help.

Then she felt a tingle in her rear and knew exactly what it was. With Laurence's attention fully dedicated to killing Kay, she found her own ability to move increase slightly. She forced her left hand behind her, pushing her fingers through the ooze towards the portal, guiding her fingertips to where the tingle was strongest. As she thrust back with one hand the resistance pushed her other hand forward.

And then she felt it fully, another half an inch and her hand would start to cross the portal. Her right hand was now touching Kay's waist, her fingers seeking out anything to grip. For a moment, she considered letting go and leaving Kay to her fate. It would serve her right, given the number of times she'd sacrificed the other Cassies in order to escape. But Cassie knew she'd feel guilty for the rest of her life, however long or short that might be, if she did abandon her older self.

She hooked her fingers into the top of Kay's trousers. Then she forced her left hand into the portal and felt it fighting the slime to pull at her. At first she thought she wasn't going to be able to hold on to Kay but, two seconds later, with a squelching sound, the portal won and sucked them both away.

Heading For Trouble

Suddenly free of the slime, they flew sideways several feet and crashed into a railing. But Kay's forehead also connected hard against something metallic and it did so with a loud clunk that made Cassie wince. The impact caused Kay to pitch backwards into Cassie, knocking them both to the floor, which shook with the force of their fall. Extricating herself from beneath her older self, the wan light was enough for Cassie to see that Kay's eyes were shut and there was a cut above the right one. For a moment Cassie feared the worst. Then Kay groaned, her eyes flickering a few times as she gasped for breath.

Cassie was quite breathless, too, though more from the dual relief of escaping Laurence and knowing Kay hadn't been badly injured. Still feeling a bit guilty for her earlier thoughts of abandoning Kay, Cassie grabbed the metal handrail and pulled herself back to her feet, checking for any immediate danger. They were up high again and it was night, though not exactly dark. Street lights dotted the landscape but in one direction the sky was decidedly lighter. Maybe the sun had just set or was about to rise – she had no idea which. They were on a platform at the top of a tower, except that this tower was no brick-built folly – it was an open metal framework and they were more than fifteen feet up in the air. On one side, a metal ladder descended to ground level. Down below she could make out a few parked cars.

At her feet Kay opened her eyes properly and looked up at Cassie. She raised a hand and Cassie reached down to help Kay to rather unsteady feet.

Leaning against the railing, Kay felt around her skull and grimaced as her fingers found the cut.

"Ow! Damn," Kay groaned. "That thing, I presume?" she said, pointing at the metal contraption she'd crashed into. It was mounted on one side above the railing and looked like a large camera.

"Yes," Cassie said, nodding. "I thought we'd had it for good that time."

"Yeah, me too," Kay said and then fell silent for a moment before adding, "Um, thanks. You obviously found the portal."

Cassie nodded.

"He really was going to kill me," Kay said.

Cassie nodded again.

"You could have left me."

"Yes," Cassie said.

"Maybe you should have done."

"No, couldn't do that," Cassie said, realising as the words fell out of her mouth that her answer might be construed as being somewhat ambiguous – as in 'didn't want to' and 'wasn't able to'. She wondered if Kay picked up on it.

But Kay merely nodded. Neither of them said anything for the best part of a minute.

"I'm just an ungrateful bitch who's lived far too long without hope," Kay finally whispered.

Cassie reached out and gave Kay's arm a brief squeeze.

"Thanks," Kay said. "I mean that. Really."

Cassie flashed a quick smile, and then looked away and out towards where the sun was beginning to rise.

Kay let out a sigh. "That thing did raise some rather interesting points, though."

Yes, Cassie thought. *The creature mentioned 'decoys' – exactly what had it meant by that? It said I was a decoy at first and then it changed its mind.* But she wanted to think through things for herself first and so changed the subject, saying instead, "Where are we? There are cars down there. That camera is pointing down to look at them."

To Cassie's eye the cars looked positively ancient. So, that meant they were back in the past again.

Kay rubbed her temple.

"You're bleeding."

"I know. Bloody hurts like hell," Kay said, hunting in various pockets and pulling out a tissue. She dabbed at the injury and then stared at the tissue which had come away red. "Damn thing's a health and safety hazard," she added, with a nod to the camera. "But it does explain you remembering me having a bruise at the funeral."

Cassie scanned the horizon and recognised a few of the landmarks that were coming clearer as the light grew. "Oh look. That's the river. The castle is over there and isn't that the spire of the cathedral?" she said, pointing out each in turn.

Kay agreed. "Yeah. This is Riverside – the old version."

Cassie frowned. She recognised none of the buildings close by. What surrounded them looked more like a factory. It was also warmer so she unwound the scarf from her neck and scrunched it into a pocket in her jacket. Amazingly, neither the scarf nor her jacket or any other item of her clothing had any hint of slime of them. That reinforced the nagging question that, if Laurence had made the portals, then why couldn't he or his creatures use them?

"Look, down there," Kay pointed in the direction from which the sun was rising. "Railway lines. This is the old Boulton and Paul factory – and it's still up and running. So we're back as far as the seventies or even the sixties. Going by those cars down there I'd say seventies. I bet you've never seen Riverside like this, have you?"

Cassie shook her head – she had never really thought about what might had been here before the redevelopment of the 1990s.

"Right," Kay said, starting down the ladder, "we'd better get out of here before someone decides to…"

"Oi, what you doing up there?" came a gruff voice from some distance away.

"Too late," Cassie said, following Kay down.

A man in a flat cap came running towards them. "Git orf there," he shouted as they reached the ground.

"We're just leaving," Kay said but added, pointing to the growing bruise and cut on her forehead, "You're lucky I won't sue you for that dangerous camera up there."

"What the hell you talking about?"

"We're really sorry, we got lost," Cassie said. "We only climbed up there to see if we could find the way out. Can you tell us how we get out of here?"

"Same way you got in probably!"

"Nope, that's not going to happen," Kay mumbled.

"Please?"

"Don't waste your time, Cass," Kay hissed.

But the man was pointing so Cassie started running in the direction indicated without waiting to see if Kay followed.

A minute later they found the factory entrance and came out onto the original Riverside Road. Kay crossed over to the River Wensum.

"Well, he was friendly. Not!" Kay dabbed at her head. "Am I still bleeding?"

"Don't think so, though you're going to end up with a huge bruise," Cassie said, squinting in the still poor light.

"Oh well, I expect I'll live. Unfortunately."

Cassie looked at Kay askance.

"Yeah, I know," Kay said, seeing Cassie's expression. "Right, do you feel anything about the river?"

"No, why should I?"

"Probably means we're not ready for the next transition. Pity, I thought you were taking short cuts."

"Are the transitions important?"

"I don't know. I think the next ones are around the river but I've only had a couple that have got that far so it might just be coincidence. Anyway, with you not feeling anything special about it I suppose we'd better find the next up-in-the-air one. Might be the knock on the head but I can't detect anything. You?"

"Nothing so far. I'll try for the map again."

Kay shrugged. "If nothing else works."

They leant on a solid metal bar that made up part of a railing that did little to prevent access to the river. It was probably more to do with stopping cars driving off the road. Cassie shut her eyes and tried to see the map. A couple of early morning lorries rattled past, pumping out fumes as they went, which disturbed her concentration. But, slowly, the map appeared in her mind. There were several portals showing quite brightly but one a long way behind her outshone all the others. She turned around and pointed in the general direction of Kett's Hill.

"It's up there somewhere. That look out point where you can see all over Norwich."

"Saint James Hill?"

"Yeah, I think so."

"Let's hope we can get there before Laurence rustles up more of his minions."

Cop a Load of This

"Oh no," Cassie said about twenty minutes later. "I'd forgotten we had to come past that place."

"What? Oh, Lollards?"

"Yes, doesn't it affect you?"

"I feel something – though obviously not at the same level you do," Kay said.

Cassie momentarily wondered why that was but then the sense of burning overwhelmed her and she stopped walking.

"I-I'm not sure I can get past it."

"You must have been past it loads of times."

"Yeah, on a bus I have. It's bad enough then but at least we go past quite quickly."

"Hold my hand," Kay ordered, grabbing Cassie's own. "Shut your eyes if it helps."

It didn't, but Cassie kept her eyes tightly shut until the feeling subsided as Kay had guided past the pub. A few seconds later she was getting the echoes from Cow Tower but it was further away and, with a bit of effort, she ignored them.

"Why those two places?" Kay asked as they reached the bottom of Kett's Hill. Dawn had fully broken and the day was getting brighter by the second.

"They're not the only ones. I get a feeling of suffocation around Chapelfield Mall – you know, near where they found those bodies down a well. And sometimes on Castle Meadow as well."

"Oh yes, weren't there a bunch of hangings there at some point?"

"No idea," Cassie shrugged.

"Hmm, I think Robert Kett told me about them once."

They reached the roundabout and Kay said, "Talking of Kett – which way? Up Kett's Hill or cross over to whatever that road opposite's called?"

"Um. Cross over – I think the portal is closer that way."

They strolled across the road – there was absolutely no traffic about. It felt quite mild so Cassie assumed it was summer. All the trees she could see were adorned with thick foliage and everywhere echoed to the sound of bird song. The air here felt cleaner and she breathed deep, taking it in, attempting to wash away the images that still lingered in her mind.

Kay, watching her, said with a smirk, "There's still lead in the petrol in this time, you know."

There was a movement as a door opened in a small building they were passing. A man in a police uniform stepped out.

"'allo, 'allo, 'allo," he said.

"What?" Kay shouted. "You've got to be kidding me! No one actually says that for real."

Cassie hesitated. The single storey block really was a tiny police station with lettering above the door that said 'City Police'.

"I'm going to have to take you down the… down the… d-d- strattle, gwawk, crit," the policeman said. Then he made a face as if he was trying to say something more, but was unable to.

The door opened again and another policeman joined him. "What's goin' on 'ere, then?" the new one said and followed it up with, "'allo, 'allo, oooollooo, grackle snork!" His expression then took on one of confusion.

"They've started talking crap," Cassie said.

"And they're identical, clones," Kay said. "That often means there's going to be loads of them. Run!"

Cassie gasped and then tore after Kay as several more spilled out of the tiny building. As usual Kay had taken off on her own leaving Cassie yards behind.

"Wait for me!" Cassie shouted.

Around the corner the road curved to the right and lost its pavement. Trees arched over their heads as they ran while, behind them, the sharp staccato of dozens of hobnail boots on tarmac drowned out the bird song.

"There's more of them in the trees," Cassie shouted, noticing shadows moving between the trunks. She could see there was a distinct chance they'd be cut off, which was reinforced when Kay came to a sudden stop.

"They're lining the road up ahead," Kay said.

There was a gap in the trees to their right. Beyond it Cassie could see the slope that led up to Saint James Hill.

"It's up there," Cassie panted, "I can feel it."

"You run for it," Kay said, picking up a broken piece of branch.

Cassie grabbed a smaller branch and ran for the summit. *Kay is actually looking out for me for a change. Will it last, I wonder?*

There was a shout behind her as Kay swung the branch at two of the pseudo-police. Cassie turned around in time to see one's head come off and roll on the ground. The body casually strolled over to the head, picked it up and placed it back on its shoulders at the wrong angle and carried on as if nothing had happened. Seeing that, Kay abandoned her attack and ran to join her.

Cassie's legs ached as she forced herself to tackle the incline. She'd been here on several occasions but had never been forced to climb it via this particular route. It was far more overgrown than it would be in her time. She used the branch to smack a path through the plant life in her way.

Finally she reached the top and turned to see how Kay was getting on. Most of the police were making their individual ways up the hill towards her but three were converging on Kay. Cassie gasped as they reached her at the same time. But, like the zombie creatures they'd encountered on the green on Pottergate, these police seemed slowed down and unable to coordinate themselves properly. Cassie wondered if it was because Laurence was stretching himself trying to control so many at a time. Getting several to do the same thing – such as running after them – seemed to work. Here, where each clone had to pick its own path through the low foliage, was possibly causing Laurence problems. Kay knocked the head off one of the three and drop-kicked it back down the hill. The headless body stumbled around, arms outstretched, trying to locate its missing cranium. The other two police wrenched the branch from her hands, holding one end each. Instead of backing away as Cassie expected, Kay instead pushed at the branch sending both creatures tumbling back down the incline. Then she turned and sprinted up the rest of the hill.

Cassie spun around trying to locate the portal. It was definitely here somewhere but she couldn't quite pin it down. Was Laurence hiding it again? She was next to the edge of a sharp drop on the eastern side of the hill. Kay reached her side.

"Where is it?" she shouted.

"I- I can't tell," Cassie spluttered. "It's like we're almost on top of it."

Then her senses pinpointed it.

"Oh hell. It's about ten feet over there," she said, pointing out over the drop whose edge was only four feet away.

"Shit," Kay said. "One of those. Damn, I really am getting too old for this."

Many of the police clones were stumbling their way to the top. Some had started lumbering towards them while uttering their inane nonsense chatter interspersed with the occasional 'allo'.

"You come across this type before?"

"A few times. What they lack in coordination, they make up for in numbers."

"At least there's no sign of Laurence's face on any of them – they all look the same."

"Yeah, that's an interesting point. Annoying as they are, this lot don't feel anywhere near as dangerous as our last two encounters. Okay, I think I can sense the portal myself now. Grab my hand. We're going to have to jump at it."

"What? It's like a sheer drop down there!"

"No more than sixty degrees – piece of cake."

With the clones little more than twenty feet away, Kay pulled Cassie back from the drop so that they had a ten foot run up.

"Ready?"

"No!"

"Three, two, one. Go!"

Cassie pumped her legs as hard as she could as Kay dragged her towards the precipice.

"Jump!" Kay shouted.

Cassie screamed as they flew out over open space. Their momentum tailed off and they started to drop. But then she felt the shimmy of the portal followed by the usual bodily wrench. Accompanying it was the customary sensation of her hair bushing up with electricity.

Observers

Their feet hit concrete. Cassie crashed into Kay smacking her into a car and, yet again, they collapsed into a heap on the ground, their arms half wrapped around each other.

"Not again," Kay groaned. "Stop falling on me!"

There was a sudden ear-splitting screech right next to them. The car, its wing showing a distinct dent, had set off its alarm in protest.

"Damn," Kay panted, rubbing her arm. "That's all we need. I really could do with a rest. No time, come on.”

She pulled Cassie to her feet. That they were at the top of a multi-storey car park was obvious. But which one? And when? The cars looked quite modern.

After trying and failing to calm down her well-frizzed hair, Cassie pointed out across the skyline. “Look, it’s that spiral thingy on top of Chapelfield.”

“City Hall over there,” Kay pointed at the clock tower and, after a quick glance over the parapet, added, “Right, Saint Stephen’s roundabout down below. We’d better get out of here before someone comes to investigate that car alarm.”

Still out of breath they trotted for the exit.

“Cold again. Feels like winter. Bright day, though.” Cassie felt that much of Kay’s running commentary was unnecessary. She retrieved the scarf from its pocket and wound it around her neck again.

“I’m so totally unfit,” Cassie said between breaths as they sped down the stairs.

Kay nodded. “Yes, you are. I was, too. Not quite so bad now but, hell, I’m really starting to feel the aches and pains of growing old, especially when unfit versions of myself smash me into cars or knock me into cameras.”

“Sorry,” Cassie whispered.

“Don’t be. Better a bruised arm than being caught by copper clones. Hell. I don’t know how long I can keep doing this. Sometimes, I don’t even know why I bother.”

“Because there’s no alternative?”

“Yeah, probably.”

“Those police were really dumb though, weren’t they?”

“There are a number like that. I sometimes wonder if Laurence sets these things up in anticipation of finding us but leaves them on autopilot or something. Then – well, I don’t know – maybe they go wrong or hit a situation they can’t handle. Sometimes they are ridiculously easy to escape from.”

Cassie couldn’t stop herself from saying, “What, just you escaping, you mean?” She regretted it a second later.

Kay stopped suddenly, swivelled around and, hands on hips, stared hard at Cassie. “For crying out loud. Stop it. You try and do this time after time, day after day for years and years and years.”

“Okay, sorry, but…”

"But nothing. Most versions of you that I have traipsing after me are dumber than a cucumber and have as much chance of surviving as a mayfly. Yeah, so I leave a few to get eaten, dissected or whatever. But I still come back so that maybe, just maybe, one day I'll achieve something like get one of you safely back home. You may be the least dumb one I've come across but you still act like a complete jerk a lot of the time. Right now being one such."

"Oh yeah! So how do you think it makes me feel knowing you could bow out at any time things are getting too hot and leave me to face Laurence's creatures on my own?"

"I only do it to the thick ones."

"Really?"

"Yes!"

"What, like on that green on Pottergate? You ran off then. I almost got pulled underground."

Kay's brow furrowed. "Which time was that? We've been there hundreds of times."

"Well, what about the time we got separated in those chalk caves then?"

Kay grunted, turned around and carried on stomping down the stairs. After a few seconds she said, more quietly, "If I remember correctly, I didn't abandon you at all. You ran off on your own. It was the only time I didn't get one of you out of those caves. I did look for you afterwards but you'd gone so I assumed you'd been eaten or captured."

Cassie had to admit to herself it was true that she'd panicked and run off without waiting for Kay. The bus man had said Kay had also been fighting the creatures.

"It's… well, it's all getting to me," Cassie said. "I don't know how much more of this I can take."

"Try doing it for thirty years," Kay said.

"Okay, sorry," Cassie whispered, to which Kay grunted yet again.

By the time they reached the ground floor and the pedestrian car park exit, they were down to a slow walk. The sun was low but going by the traffic and number of people around it felt like the middle of the day.

"How can we find out when we are?" Cassie asked, wondering if Kay was still speaking to her.

Kay made a face and then said, "Easiest way is find a newspaper. Smiths is round the corner."

A minute later they'd reached Saint Stephen's Street. Apart from the big Co-op on the opposite corner, all the shops were open so it felt like a weekday.

"Pretty recent, I'd say," Kay said. "I can't remember exactly when the Co-op closed. Looks like it's only been a short while."

It took them a few minutes to get through the crowds and reach the W H Smith store. Inside, Cassie picked up a newspaper and froze.

"What's up?"

Cassie pointed to the date – it read: 31 January 2011.

"Oh shit," Kay whispered.

"Yeah, shit indeed. We're wearing the right clothes and I remember you having the bruise on your face so we need to get to the crematorium. What's the time?"

"Just gone one according to the City Hall clock when we were up on the multi-storey."

"The service started at two-thirty, didn't it?"

"Yes, that's right."

"Well, that gives us around an hour to get there," Cassie said.

"And hopefully avoid all the nasties until then."

"Right. But I'm hungry from all that running and… stuff. I don't want to go to Mum's funeral with my stomach rumbling. It must have been hours since we had that pizza."

Kay nodded in agreement.

"What is it with you and fish and chips?" Cassie said, tucking into her portion. "And why the market again?"

"It's quite quick to get served and easier to get away from in case anything nasty turns up."

Cassie couldn't fault her older self on either of those two points and, at least, the tension between them from earlier on had mostly dissipated. In spite of the sun shining brightly, it was far from warm and the food was already getting cold, as was the bench they were seated upon. Cassie's rear was feeling distinctly numb, despite using the scarf as a temporary cushion. She shovelled a few more lukewarm chips into her mouth before they became inedible.

After sharing a can of fizz to wash the remains of the fish and chips down, they left the pigeons and gulls to fight over the last of the cold chips. Several minutes later found them walking up Saint Giles Street towards Earlham Road and the crematorium.

"We don't want to be too early," Cassie said as they crossed the pedestrian bridge over Grapes Hill.

"We've got to get there in one piece first," was Kay's reply.

"Any sign of anything?"

"Yeah, down there – on the centre green. Hadn't you seen it?" Kay pointed at the strip of grass between the traffic lanes. Cassie squinted at the scarcely discernible shape. It was translucent but, at times, resembled a man made out of assorted parts.

"Yetch," Cassie said. "Is that the same thing that was outside Starbucks in Castle Mall?"

"Similar, I'd say. Probably not the same one, though. They are observers as far as I can tell. They don't chase you, just keep tabs on where you're going. Talk complete bollocks, of course. I usually ignore them."

"Like you did in the Mall."

"Did I? Can't remember. I didn't at first until I figured out they were harmless as far as any immediate violence was concerned. Of course, seeing them often means that others are going to be along soon after."

"Oh, at least it's the first one we've seen."

"Ah, so you missed the others."

"What others?"

"That's the third one I've seen since the market. Also, there was one in front of the railway station – he could have been the reason the police clones turned up. You really didn't see any of them?"

"No," Cassie said, feeling both guilty and inadequate.

"Maybe I should try to train you properly," Kay said.

"Why didn't you tell me about them?"

"Dunno. I'm so used to seeing them. I just assumed you'd seen them as well."

"Where were the others?"

"There was one in the Saint Giles churchyard and another inside City Hall staring out of one of the windows."

Cassie shuddered. "Okay, please point them out next time. Can you sense them? Or is it just by chance that you see them?"

Kay shrugged. "Bit of each, I suppose. You know that feeling that someone's watching you?"

"Oh great! Now I'm going to think there's one behind every tree and windowpane."

Kay grinned. "Get used to it."

As they reached the end of the bridge Kay pointed upwards. "Look. Up there on the roof of the Roman Catholic Cathedral."

Cassie squinted and could almost make out the fuzzy shape of something against the sky.

"I can barely see it."

"You can sense them, though, can't you?"

"No, I don't think I can. I probably wouldn't have even noticed it if you hadn't pointed it out. You must be more used to them."

"Weird. I could always see and sense them. Then again, now that I think about it, none of the dumb Cassies ever seemed to mention them, either."

"You never told the others about them?"

"Most of them didn't stay alive long enough for me to get around to it. After about a hundred of you I didn't even bother to start explaining things unless you survived to get through the first couple of portals."

"So, what is it that makes me different from the rest? And you as well? You're the only one to survive. And what did the Laurence thing mean about decoys?"

"Yeah, I've been wondering that, too. Especially as, according to him, I'm one as well."

Cassie kept an eye on the shape on top of the cathedral but it didn't make any movement towards them.

"Oh, I'm feeling something weird again. Like darkness and corridors or something," Cassie said a few moments later.

"That'll be the chalk caves below us," Kay said. She pointed a short way ahead to a junction with a side road on the right. "That's the place where the bus fell through in 1988."

"Oh yes, I recognise them now – the caves and passages," Cassie said. "Not the horrors I always felt going past Cow Tower or Lollards Pit. It's like, I don't know, just a sense that I'm above something of, well… of significance, I suppose."

"Hmm, that's interesting. You feel that but can't sense the observers properly. It's like we're tuned to different things."

After a few more minutes the cathedral was behind them and Kay didn't point out any new observers. But the respite didn't last long.

Freaked Freaks

"Uh oh," Kay mumbled a short while later, pointing to a building about twenty yards ahead of them on the right. "Here it comes. The Mitre pub is crawling with something."

As they passed the pub Cassie couldn't see anything untoward about it at first. Then she noticed movement at one of the pub's many windows – faces and arms writhing behind the glass.

Kay broke into a trot as they put the building behind them, crossing Edinburgh Road to pass Saint Thomas' church. Cassie glanced back to see several grey, translucent creatures pop through the windows and land on the pavement where they milled around in confusion.

"What are they doing?" she asked.

"Probably trying to figure out where we are."

"Why are they always different?"

"Oh, I've seen these ones several times. They seem to get quite disorientated in daylight – you wouldn't want to meet them at night, though. We might not have been so lucky to get away if those things had been after us at Pinebanks."

"I wonder why he sent those ones after us when it's daytime, then? Doesn't he realise?"

"Yeah, that's something I've asked myself many times. But, as I said earlier, it may be that he stations them around at random in the hope that the right type are in the right place at the right time."

"Could be, I suppose," Cassie said. "But something else has been bugging me."

"What's that?" Kay said. Behind them the creatures all started turning in their direction as if finally realising where their prey had got to. "Right, they're on to us. Better start running. So, what was bugging you?"

As they ran Cassie said, "Mum said Laurence made the portals but I've started wondering if she was right about that. Have you ever had anything other than us come through a portal?"

"Go on," Kay said.

"Well, nothing followed me from the chalk caves to the Guildhall and the slime didn't get through from the folly to that tower at Riverside."

"A bit of tentacle came with us to Ranworth."

"Oh yes, I'd forgotten about that. Damn, every time I thought I'd figured out some sort of rule then we find something that breaks it."

"Anyway, I agree. I decided a long time ago that the portals are mainly for our benefit and not there to actually kill us."

"Yeah. It's almost like we're being forced to do the running around for some other purpose. But what?"

"Hmm, not quite thought of it like that before. But, yes, you could be right. Also, sometimes I think it's not only us against Laurence – it's like there's something or somebody else involved as well."

Kay dodged around a group of smartly dressed people walking the same way as the two of them were running. They were about the same age her mum would have been when she died and their faces were vaguely familiar. Cassie suspected they might have been Mum's friends from Essex University though, if they were, she wouldn't have seen them since she was around nine.

"Here's the entrance," Kay said, turning right into the lane that led up to the crematorium. Before following, Cassie glanced back along Earlham Road. The grey creatures were about twenty-five yards behind them and gaining. They were passing the group of people – actually, in some cases they appeared to be passing through them, not that the people had any inkling of that.

Cassie ran up the lane towards the crematorium and caught up with Kay.

Another glance back showed that the creatures were putting on a late spurt and were only yards behind. There were even more people around and some of them were beginning to notice them, especially as they were running.

Then Kay glanced back and stopped. "Look," she said.

Cassie turned around. The creatures had come only a little way up the lane and then halted, milling about in confusion.

"Something's freaking them out," Kay whispered. Indeed, it was as if the creatures had hit some sort of invisible barrier through which they couldn't pass.

"Right, let's carry on at a more normal pace," Kay whispered. "Don't want to attract too much attention."

They joined in with several other groups of people all heading towards the crematorium building. Many were dressed in their finest. With her denim jacket and jeans, Cassie felt completely out of place – even Kay, all in black, was attired more suitably. There were cars parked along the roadway and more were arriving, a queue building up as each one slowed to look for somewhere to park. She wondered if her grandad and younger self were already here or in one of the queuing cars.

They reached the crematorium but Kay, after a quick glance in the waiting room, which was already quite full, continued around to the other side. Obviously, the service for her mum hadn't yet started.

"I need the loo," Kay said once they were out of earshot of any others. "I think it's round the back here."

"Don't the portals deal with that for you, then?"

"Yeah, but number two!" Kay laughed nervously, leaving Cassie on her own.

The Gift

Cassie leant on a wall away from all the other people. She was feeling quite jittery. Images of people burning slunk through her head. She remembered feeling that the only other time she'd been here. It wasn't quite the intensity she felt at Lollards Pit, but it unnerved her all the same. What she couldn't recall, however, was where the images came from – she had no definite recollection of ever seeing people burning.

A couple glanced in her direction and she wasn't sure if they saw her or not. But she didn't want to get into a situation where others asked who she was and how she knew her mum, so she kept her distance, though with an eye trained on the entrance to the waiting room. There were now several people standing outside as there was so little spare room inside. A memory flashed into her mind – she remembered the overwhelming claustrophobia of that room and of being continuously close to tears, especially when her grandad had gone off for a few minutes. He'd left her on her own in the middle of a crowd of people who, although many were vaguely known to her, felt like total strangers.

Cassie watched the crowd – the way they milled around reminded her of the grey man-like creatures she knew were waiting for her back on Earlham Road. Then two figures caused her breath to catch in her throat and Cassie watched as her grandad ushered her younger self into the waiting room whilst greeting some of those present. There were several bowed heads, reassuring hands on shoulders and other solemn gestures going on.

He suddenly glanced her way and a brief smile crossed his lips. He nodded once and then extricated himself from the others, motioning with his hand that they shouldn't follow him. Then, he purposely strode towards her.

Cassie's heart was in her mouth. How had he recognised her?

She felt the urge to run and took a couple of steps in the opposite direction.

"Please wait," he said, slowing his pace. "I have something for you."

He reached in a pocket and retrieved a brown envelope that, judging by its thickness, contained something more substantial than just paper. Holding it in one hand he halted about six feet away from her.

"Did you arrive with a woman all in black? Name of Kay?"

Cassie nodded but said nothing.

"Is she around?"

Cassie glanced over to where the toilets were.

"In the loo," Cassie said.

"Good, this is for you."

He took a few more steps towards her and held the envelope out so that she could see the writing on the front. Cassie gasped recognising her own name written clearly in handwriting that looked a lot like her mum's.

"Hello, older Cassie," he said. "Yes, I know who you are. I could see the resemblance, even from back there. Your mum did explain some of it to me but I don't profess to understand more than a tenth of it. Just before she, um… she passed she told me you'd be here and had already prepared this for you." He sighed before continuing. "Okay, please listen carefully. Take the envelope and put it straight inside your jacket. Under no circumstances let Kay see it or know that you've got it. That bit is extremely important – your mum was concerned that your life may depend on Kay not knowing you have it."

He held the envelope before her and, with a hand that shook, she reached out and took it.

"Hide it," he said, with urgency. "The fight with Laurence is far from over and I get the impression my life might also be dependent upon how successful you are. Remember, not a word of this to Kay. Be safe – if such things are still possible. And good luck."

Then he turned and walked back to the waiting room.

Cassie slipped the package into an inside pocket but as she did so she realised she knew exactly what the envelope contained. Not only could she feel the heaviness of it, she also sensed it as she'd done only a few hours previously in her own timeline, but nearly a year ago in real time. It was the device her mum had shown her. The one she'd used to fight Laurence.

The one that had caused her cancer.

And now it was in her possession. What on Earth was she supposed to do with it? And why couldn't she tell Kay? Was Kay an ally or dangerous somehow? She felt her ambivalence towards Kay slide again towards the negative. There were far too many questions and precious few answers.

She glanced back towards the waiting room and watched her grandad enter. So, now she knew why he had left her younger self for a while.

She felt her heart pumping so loud it echoed in her ears but continued to watch the crematorium from a distance. But nothing much seemed to be happening and there was no sign yet of Kay. Could she have encountered some nasties in the toilets? Cassie began to panic again, her hands and legs trembling, her breathing rapid and shallow. Needing to be on her own for a while to get time to think about what had just happened, she started walking down the path that led to one of the alternative crematorium entrances.

Then she stopped, seeing the way blocked by another horde of the grey creatures. She was about to turn around in case they came after her when she realised that, instead of getting any closer, they appeared to be retreating. She took two more steps towards them and they retreated by the same amount. She repeated the exercise with the same result. Then a brief smile flickered momentarily across her lips.

Was it the device?

Well, Mum had said it was what had kept the house safe back in 2010 and, now that she had it, was it protecting her from the nasties as well? But did that mean that her younger self was no longer protected? Maybe but, then again, she herself was proof she'd made it as far as seventeen.

She stepped forward another two paces and watched as the creatures milled about, repositioning themselves further back.

Then she became aware that something was going on back at the crematorium. The exit had opened and those attending the previous service were leaving the hall to go to the gardens. She started to make her way back but stopped when she saw Kay coming out of the toilet.

Kay, after glancing around, spotted her and came to join her.

"You okay," Kay said. "You look a bit pale."

"Grandad's here. And so is ten-year-old us."

"Not quite – our younger self will still be nine unless our birthday is no longer in April."

"Yeah, sorry. Maths never was our best subject, was it?"

"You look even more spooked than when we saw Mum."

"Well, there's that lot behind us," Cassie said with a tilt of her head.

Kay looked down the path towards the other entrance. "Ah, more of the sods. Still keeping their distance though, aren't they?"

Cassie nodded but knew she couldn't offer any explanation.

"Something's holding them at bay," Kay continued. "Good job. It'll be real embarrassing if the damned things try to attack us during the service."

"That didn't happen, though, did it?"

"No, not if memory serves. Ah, the funeral car's arriving."

Cassie swallowed. This had been bad enough the first time around. Could she handle it again?

The back of the hearse was opened and the pallbearers slid the coffin out gently before raising it onto their shoulders. They watched as Grandad and young Cassie followed it into the hall. Neither looked their way.

"We'll wait until everyone else has gone in," Kay said.

Cassie nodded.

"Damn, my hands are shaking," Kay whispered as the last of the party approached the door to the hall. She looked at Cassie.

"Mine too."

"C'mon, we don't want to be shut out."

They walked towards the hall and entered.

All Too Quiet

"Well, that was even worse the second time round," Kay said as they left the cemetery. They had used one of the alternative gates that came out onto Bowthorpe Road. It kept them away from the other mourners. The grey creatures were nowhere in sight. "At least no one recognised us. I was sure Grandad was going to at one point. Made me really shiver, that did."

Cassie said nothing. The tissue she'd been carrying in her jeans pocket since leaving the house in 2018 had been put to good use and was now sodden.

"You're really quiet. You okay?" Kay said.

"What do you expect, damn it? I was in floods of tears the first time I was here. Don't you remember that yourself? Hell, I wanted to bawl my eyes out this time, but didn't want to draw attention to us. I—"

"Sorry, Cass," Kay stopped and put an arm around her younger self. Cassie burst into tears again. "I've been going around this loop for so many years now it's made me hard and cynical. I keep forgetting how I used to be. How I used to feel."

"Yeah, well…"

Kay released Cassie and they walked on in silence until they reached the junction with Dereham Road.

"Which way?" Kay said, in a voice that was soft, almost apologetic.

Cassie stopped and looked around. She was trying to locate where the next portal might be but was more aware of the device sitting in the envelope inside her jacket. She wondered if Kay had any idea it was there. It was drowning out any signal she might be picking up from local portals.

"Not sure."

"Well, we've got to go one way or the other. Into the city or out?"

"City," Cassie mumbled.

Kay nodded. "Still no sign of any of Laurence's legions," she said. "Bit odd that, given how close they were before the funeral."

"Do they sometimes not turn up?" Cassie forced herself to say. She didn't feel like talking at all but wanted to disguise the fact she might be hiding something.

"Oh yes, if the portals are close to each other. Given how many times I must overlap myself going to multiple different places at the same time I'm sure Laurence must occasionally run out of available things he can sling at us."

"Do you have any idea how many times you've been through a portal?"

"None whatsoever. Let's face it, if I've been doing this for – what? – something like thirty plus years and I go through about eight to ten portals in each 24 hours as I experience it. Well, do the maths."

"I'm crap at maths."

"Yeah, we are. Eight times three-six-five. Round it to, say, three thousand a year. Bloody hell, I make it nearly a hundred thousand – or am I doing the sums wrong?"

"A hundred thousand?"

"Well, maybe. Of course, there's nowhere near that number of actual portals. I've probably been through the common ones several thousand times each. Apart from Castle Mall – that one gets done every time."

"Why does it always start there?"

"Absolutely no idea. Apart from the fact that was where we were when it all started. I wonder if we'll ever get around to meeting up with… oh, I've even forgotten her name now."

"Georgia?"

"Yes and Mark, wasn't it? And also that idiot Jason."

"No, he cancelled."

"Oh yeah. Hah. He was always a lightweight. Good for looking at and not a lot else. If you finally get out of this you can do far better than him. He wasn't even a good shag!"

"What?" Cassie shouted. "You mean you…?"

"You mean you didn't?"

"No, I've never, um…"

"Yeah, doesn't surprise me. But, then again, you didn't get taught early lessons in the subject thanks to Grandad."

Cassie shivered, and it wasn't all due to the January weather.

By the time they had reached the bottom of Grapes Hill, Cassie was feeling slightly less distraught. While Kay's idle chat had kept up as they walked, she'd stuck to lighter topics. Possibly, that was a deliberate change geared to raising Cassie's spirits. It had worked to a degree.

"I've seen Grapes Hill when it was a little narrow road with terraced houses," Kay said, as they crossed into Saint Benedict's Street.

"That's so hard to imagine now."

"It's amazing to go back and see what's gone. Of course, I had a dumb version of you with me at the time. That one didn't even believe it was Grapes Hill when I told her."

"Why does there need to be dumb versions of us?"

Kay shrugged. "Maybe the question needs to be more like why is there only one that isn't dumb and why is there only one of me as well?"

"And why are there also two versions of Grandad?"

Kay shook her head. They passed the shops along Saint Benedict's Street, not a road that Cassie had explored much. She wasn't sure if there would be any changes by 2018.

"Oh," Cassie said, stopping near the church that held the Art Centre. "I think the next one is, um…" She shut her eyes to explore the map that filled her mind. It had been easy to conjure this time. Was that because of the device in her pocket? And did such easy conjuring have a deadly price she would be paying for later on?

She opened her eyes again. "Tombland. I think it's in the Maids Head Hotel."

"Well, at least we're going in the right direction. Still, it's rather weird that we've seen nothing of Laurence's little helpers."

"What about the observers?"

"Nope, none of them, either. Looks like we'll get there around sunset."

After passing Saint Andrew's Hall they took the turn into Princes Street.

"That way," Cassie said, as they reached Tombland Alley.

"Fair enough. Well, at least she is one of the friendly ones," Kay said and entered the alley.

"Who?"

"You do remember the ghost walk, don't you?"

"Oh, yes. The plague girl, wasn't it? You've met her then?"

"Several times. Watch your ankles though," Kay said, with a chuckle.

They passed the raised green under which, it was rumoured, lay the bodies of many plague victims.

"Oh, Kay and Cassie," came a young sounding voice. "Nice to see you both again."

The owner of the voice was a girl attired in a ragged dress. Both she and her dress were rather see-through. She stopped to pick something out of her teeth. It was stringy and only came free with a sharp tug. There was more than a hint of blood on her chin.

"Hi yourself, Grey," Kay said. "Nice bit of gristle?"

"Yes, I think it's a bit of Dad's leg. He was definitely chewier than Mum."

"What you been up to?"

"Oh, the usual. A bit of haunting. A bit of shrieking. A nibble at an ankle or leg here and there. Ooh, Cassie, I bet yours are a bit tasty under your trousers. May I?"

"Ah, no," Kay said, getting between Cassie and the ghost. "We keep needing to run away from nasties, so unchewed legs are rather essential. Besides, this Cassie is a good one – maybe next time, if I'm stuck with a Cassie who has three left feet and no coordination."

"Oh yes, you are a proper Cassie, aren't you? Not like all the others that Kay brings along for me to taste," the girl said, staring hard at Cassie as they slipped past her. "And you're shielded as well."

"Come on, Cass," Kay said, hastening their pace. "Sorry, Grey, we have an urgent appointment with a portal. Laters!"

They left the ghost girl to pick more fragments of her father out of her teeth. As they came out onto Tombland the light was beginning to fade.

"You'd really let her try to eat a dumb me?" Cassie said as they crossed the road to the Maids Head Hotel.

"Nah. She says that most times. Happy little thing, considering."

"Yes. Why are they always so, well… chirpy?" Cassie asked. "Baker boy and the monk were as well. I thought ghosts were supposed to be more moany and rattle their chains and stuff."

"Hah, you just wait until you've had a proper chat with Robert Kett. You'd think being left to die hanging in chains from the castle would be enough to make you miserable for the rest of your life. Not him."

"Life? But they aren't alive."

"Well, that's true, though it often seems like they are."

Then Kay frowned. "I wonder what she meant by shielded. That's not something she's ever said before."

Cassie shrugged and changed the subject. "How are we going to get into the hotel?"

"If they spot us then I normally ask to use the toilet and claim that the public ones further back up Tombland are shut or out of order. They often just let us in. When they've got some cranky git on reception then I just stick two fingers up at them and run in anyway. A lot of the time they don't even see us."

"You know your way around the place, then?"

"Yeah and the portal is usually right up on the top floor." Kay stopped on the pavement outside the main entrance and looked up. "I think I can sense it now myself."

Cassie nodded. "Yes, it's definitely up there. So, how come I seem to sense them from quite a way away and you can't?"

"Actually, it's not just you. Even the dumbest Cassie can usually locate them better than I can. Just another hazard of being me, I guess. On my own, usually after I've lost a brain-dead version of you, I have to hunt around until I can find one. Then again, given that most just take me straight back to Castle Mall and another dumbo to look after, I sometimes find other things to do."

"Like what?"

A wry smile passed across Kay's face. "Oh, you know. Like find somewhere to rest up for a while, hide from the nasties and, er, play Monopoly with real money," she said, grinning.

"Eh?"

"I'll tell you about it one day if I get the chance. Not time now. Anyway, I can't stay anywhere too long as the nasties start hunting me down."

"And that always happens? The nasties, I mean?"

"Not always – I think the longest I ever managed was about three days without seeing any. Laurence must have been busy that time."

"Maybe he's busy now," Cassie said.

"Could be, though something else feels different. I can't put my finger on it. Well, at least there doesn't appear to be anything unpleasant to deal with at the moment. Not even an observer. Unless they're hiding upstairs, of course."

A family of five walked into the hotel entrance – two parents and three children. The kids ranged from around six to thirteen, Cassie estimated.

"Follow them in," Kay whispered. "It's even easier if someone diverts their attention for us."

They entered the door a few feet behind the family. The youngest child, a girl, eyed them suspiciously while the rest of the family appeared not to notice. While the receptionist was occupied they slipped past and found a staircase leading upwards.

"That way," Cassie said as soon as they reached the top floor. Blocking their path was a maid attired in a rather old looking grey outfit. She was standing in the middle of the narrow corridor with her back to them.

"Still reeking of lavender, love?" Kay said, walking straight through her.

"Oh," Cassie said. "I hadn't realised she was another ghost. Hell, she really does stink of it, doesn't she?"

"The place is full of ghosts. This one never says anything, though. No chirp from her," Kay laughed.

"The portal is between those two doors," Cassie said, pointing.

"Right," Kay said, holding out her hand for Cassie to grab hold. "Here we go again."

The portal buzzed and fizzled, and Cassie's hair sprung out from her head like someone had connected her to the mains. She gasped as a familiar sensation hit her, though this time, it was vastly intensified.

Swimming

Flood

"Ahh!" Cassie cried. "Shut it out. Shut it out! I can feel them all."

She knew exactly where they'd come out. The press of dead and dying bodies all around her was overpowering. She couldn't move, her feet rooted to the stone upon which they stood. The two of them were squashed together on a stairway with Cassie on a step above where Kay had come to rest.

Kay, who still had hold of Cassie's hand, dragged her down the haphazardly positioned steps and out of the open doorway of Cow tower.

Once outside the tower itself, Cassie's gasps lessened and her breathing started to return to normal.

"Oh, that was even worse than when I went on the ghost walk last year – well, 2017, anyway."

"It's definitely not 2017 now – the tower isn't locked and there are no gates. Good job, too. We might not have got out otherwise. Well, I probably would have done. It wasn't affecting me so much – but you…"

"Sorry. I couldn't move… couldn't help it."

"Weird," Kay said, shaking her head. "I've had dumb Cassies unable to move before but that was mainly because they were too stupid to get themselves out of danger."

"Can we get away from here? My head feels swamped."

"Yeah, come on. This place is a bit overgrown – obviously before a decent public path had been put in. Can you feel the next portal? Damned if I can."

Cassie shook her head. "No, nothing right now. I'm still too close."

Kay, eyeing up their surroundings for nasties, led Cassie away from the tower.

"Looks like there's a path back to the pub – what's its name? – Red Lion, I think."

"At least it's day time and not cold," Cassie said, returning her scarf to a pocket yet again.

They reached the pub after a short while. It was shut.

"Bishops Bridge is completely open to traffic," Kay said, glancing across the bridge to Riverside. "Bugger all traffic, though. Maybe it's a Sunday. The sun isn't very high so it could still be early morning."

"Not that way," Cassie said, trembling and shaking her head. "I can feel the flames from here."

"Ah, yeah," Kay said, seeing another pub on the other side of the river.

Cassie expected to see the name Lollards Pit on the sign – but it wasn't.

"Still called the Bridge House in this time, whenever it is," Kay said.

"Doesn't matter. The flames – I can't…"

"I don't ever remember the flames affecting me as much as they do you. So, where to, then?"

Cassie shut her eyes and turned away from the river.

"That way, I think," she said, pointing down Bishopgate towards the spire of Norwich's main cathedral.

"Sure?"

"No, but definitely not across the bridge."

"Okay, let's go," Kay said.

Cassie's legs had almost stopped shaking by the time they'd gone a couple of hundred yards.

"This isn't really the right direction," she said. "But it's better than where we were. Any sign of Laurence's troops?"

"No, thank goodness. No observers, either."

After another hundred yards they reached an open gate with a path beyond.

"This way," Cassie said.

Kay shrugged and they entered. The path took them past part of the Norwich School and then along a narrow road between rows of cottages.

"I've never been down here," Cassie said. "Didn't even know it existed. Did you?"

"Yeah, I think I must have been down every single road and footpath in central Norwich at least a hundred times. Some more than a thousand, I'd bet. There's often been portals around here. There's one upstairs in the cathedral refectory. Is that where we're headed?"

"No, I think it's back the other way again, towards the river somewhere."

"Would have been quicker to go along the river walk."

"Maybe it doesn't exist here."

Kay nodded. "You could be right. This is feeling a bit nineteen fifties going by the state of the place and the few cars that are around."

They came out at the green in the Lower Close. Cassie pointed left.

"Ferry Lane," Kay said. "Down to Pulls Ferry, then?"

"Could be."

"I once came out of a portal upstairs in that place. Scared the shit out of the people living in it, especially as the dumbo I had with me at the time fell flat on her face in front of them!"

There was no sign of a portal on the way down Ferry Lane. There was also no evidence of any nasties.

"Bit weird that," Kay said.

"What?"

"We've not seen any nasties or observers since the funeral. There's only been those two ghosts. That's pretty rare. It's like something's keeping them away."

Cassie shrugged wondering if that something was what she carried in her pocket. But her grandad had specifically told her to keep its presence from Kay.

They approached the locally famous Pulls Ferry from the rear, not the river facing façade that graced so many picture postcards – the best view was always from the other side of the River Wensum. They walked underneath the building's archway to the water a few yards beyond. Here, the small inlet was the only remains of the canal that once led all the way back to the cathedral. Cassie remembered reading about how the canal had been used to ferry the stones used in the cathedral's construction.

"Oh," Cassie said.

"What? Where is it?"

"In the river, I think."

"Ah, so not upstairs, then. Well, that saves having to get into the place. Hmm, I wonder if this means we've hit a transition. They're often close together and it's not that far from Cow Tower, even though we took the long way around."

"It's here," Cassie said waving her hand over the inlet. "About three feet out from the edge. At least it's not in the main part of the river. How deep is it, d'you reckon?"

Kay peered over the edge at the unmoving water. "It's quite low, the river level, that is. I've seen it far higher than this. Oh yes, I can also feel the portal as well – I think it may actually be above the water so maybe we won't even get wet jumping in."

Cassie nodded, though she wasn't sure. Her ability to swim had never been much more than a semi-controlled flail. She knelt down and stretched her hand out to see if she could determine the portal's position more accurately.

"Yes, it is just above."

"Okay, and about three feet straight out from where you're standing. Another run and jump, then. Let's hope we hit it fair and square otherwise we'll be having a bath. Glad it's not cold."

They moved back several feet.

"Ready?" Kay said, taking Cassie's hand.

"No, yet again."

"Three, two, one. Run!"

And they ran, jumped, fuzzed through the portal, avoiding the sun-warmed river water only to land in something much deeper and far from warm.

"Yuck!" Cassie shouted, accompanied by a shriek from Kay.

Cassie, soaked from the waist down, pulled herself to her feet and helped Kay get up. The latter had lost her footing and fallen completely under the surface.

"Where are we?" Kay said, after spitting muddy water from her mouth.

"No idea. Apart from being on a flooded road," Cassie replied. Her teeth chattered as they dragged themselves onto the non-flooded part of the road, only a few yards away.

They were soaked. And they weren't alone in that respect. Everywhere was drenched, the road, the hedgerows that lined each side of the road and even the few houses that were behind the hedgerows. At least it wasn't raining at that moment, though the sky held the promise that it might start again at any time.

Cassie looked back to their arrival point. The pavement on one side was raised over a small water-filled passageway. The road dipped to allow the water to flow across the road. Next to the pavement they could see the top of something white with markings on, poking out the water.

"That looks like a depth marker, which means it's a ford, I think," Kay said, dripping furiously. "Right. Which way now?"

"Don't know, but that way saves crossing the ford again," Cassie replied, indicating the direction with a nod while her teeth continued to chatter.

There were more houses this way, so they tramped along swinging and shaking their arms and legs in a vain attempt to lose the water and warm up a fraction. Cassie retrieved the scarf from a pocket but stuffed it back after discovering it was as wet as everything else from her waist downwards. She also surreptitiously checked that the envelope containing the device was still present in the inside pocket of her jacket. It was, though the envelope itself felt somewhat more than soggy.

"Nearly sunset, I think," Kay said, nodding towards what Cassie presumed to be the west. "It's definitely getting darker by the moment."

"And colder," Cassie added.

They passed a garage on the left and, after a while, the road curved first to the right and then left where it met a junction. The side road went up past the church whose clock read just gone 7pm. In the foreground and next to a bus shelter, sat a single decker bus with its engine running and its back towards them.

"Is that... you know?" Cassie said, rubbing her hands together for warmth as they walked.

"Might be, looks like the same type of bus. But it looks like it's been out in all weathers going by the mud splatted up the back. The ghost bus always struck me as being a lot cleaner. Anyway, whether it is or not, hopefully it's going somewhere useful."

There was no number displayed on the back of the bus so they walked alongside it, intending to see what it said on the front. But, as they reached the door, there was a hiss and it opened. Inside, the driver was reading a broadsheet newspaper whose front headline was all about the flooding. All they could see of him were the hands that held the paper.

"Saw you coming in the mirror," he said. As they climbed the steps Cassie could see the date on the paper – Friday 13th September 1968.

"Hmm, Friday the thirteenth," Kay said.

"Cor, blast me," the driver said, folding his paper down and revealing his face. "You two ladies look like you've really been out in the elements, don't you!"

They both gasped as they looked into the living face and blue eyes of their great grandfather, Charlie.

Elemental

"Heck, you two look like you've just seen a ghost!"

Kay was the first to regain the ability to speak. "Actually, I, er, think we're more surprised that we haven't, er, seen a ghost."

Charlie raised an eyebrow. "What's that supposed to mean?"

"We have complicated lives," Kay said, and accompanied it with what Cassie assumed was a dismissive shrug.

"What did you mean by elemental?" Cassie asked, in a timid voice.

"Eh? No, I said 'elements' didn't I?" Charlie replied. "I meant all the rain and the flooding. You look like you fell into it up to the waist." Then he looked Kay up and down. "And you must have gone in head first, I reckon."

"Yeah, tell me about it," Kay scowled.

"Think yourself lucky it was only one of the elements, then," Charlie laughed.

"There's over a hundred, isn't there?" Cassie said, trying to dredge up a mental image of the periodic table – something that seemed harder to achieve than the map of the portals.

"Nah," he said. "I mean the old earth, air, water and fire stuff the ancient Greeks believed in – or was it the Romans? I can never remember."

"Whatever," Kay said. "Look, I know this may seem a strange thing to ask but where exactly are we?"

"We got lost because of the floods," Cassie said, in the hope that the excuse would make more sense.

"Hempnall, of course," he said, at which Kay and Cassie exchanged a glance. "I shoulda gone all the way to Topcroft on this service but the ford back there put paid to that," he said, jerking a thumb over his shoulder in the direction from which they'd arrived. "From what I hear, there was a car stuck in it earlier on. So, I've been sitting here killing time waiting for the schedule to catch back up. You were just in time – I was getting ready to leave."

"Going back to Norwich?" Kay asked.

"Where else!"

"Okay, two tickets for all the way to Norwich, please," Kay said, starting to rummage through her pouches, many of which were still dripping.

"Put that away," he smiled. "I won't tell. It's not likely we'll be picking up anyone else, anyway. This is the last bus back and we've not exactly seen much in the way of passengers even where the buses *have* managed to run. It seems half of Norfolk has been on holiday today because of the weather. I never seen nothing like it in all my life."

"Oh, right. Thanks," Cassie said.

"I reckon the two on you oughta head right on down the bus – that's a bit warmer down there so you'll dry off quicker." He waited until they'd sat down about two thirds of the way back, taking a seat each on opposite sides of the central aisle, before he put the bus into gear.

"Okay, ladies, hold tight and we'll be off," he said as the bus started to crawl up the incline. After leaving the church behind they passed some shops along the narrow village street.

"We're going to soak the seats," Cassie said. "Especially you."

"I don't like this," Kay whispered, ignoring what Cassie had said. "Something is far from right."

"What?"

"Remember what Mum said about him? And when he was found dead? And *how* he was found?"

"Oh hell. Last bus of the day, didn't she say?"

"Yeah. Too much of a coincidence, isn't it?"

Cassie's expression showed her agreement.

"Also," Kay continued, "something else he said about the elements has got me thinking."

"What?"

"That sequence – earth, air, water and fire."

"What about it?"

"Earth is ground, air is… well… up in the air. The transitions start off underground, then the next ones are up in the air. Well, not on the ground anyway."

"And now we've gone from the air to the water ones," Cassie said, following Kay's logic.

"Yes, but I've never been any further than water. Not once in however long it's been. And I only got to the water ones two or three times before now and I'm not a hundred percent sure about one of those, either. That just leaves…"

"Fire," Cassie added, unnecessarily.

"Yeah, fire," Kay agreed. "Doesn't exactly sound promising, does it?"

Cassie exhaled loudly.

Outside, the evening was falling rapidly as the bus followed the road out of the village.

"Any warmer back there, ladies?" their great grandad shouted over the noise of the engine.

"A little, thanks," Cassie said.

"Good. You'll be dry in no time."

"If only," Kay whispered, visibly shuddering.

Several minutes later they passed the lights of Saxlingham Nethergate as the bus negotiated the narrow main street.

"Coo, I couldn't half do with a pint right now," came Charlie's voice again as they passed the Prince of Wales pub on the right. He didn't stop and the bus continued to climb the winding road out of the village.

A few seconds later he added, "Now, I shoulda taken the right hand turn, but the road south of Shotesham was a bit waterlogged on the way down. Anyhow, there's little hope of any fares there – they're rare enough at this time of night even without the weather."

"Oh hell," Cassie whispered. "Didn't Mum say the bus wasn't on its normal route when it was found?"

"This is feeling worse by the second," Kay agreed. "I'm expecting piles of nasties to jump through the windows at any moment."

"Should we tell him, or get him to go another way?"

"Do you think he'll believe us?"

Cassie slowly shook her head.

The bus ambled along at less than twenty miles an hour as it took each turn on the constantly twisting road. In spite of the lack of speed, Kay and Cassie had to hold on tight to keep from being slung off their seats. A few more houses appeared out of the darkness and were passed in seconds. Then the route took them into a more heavily wooded area with yet more bends in the road.

"Any sign of anything?" Cassie said.

Kay shook her head, "No, nothing. Not that I can see far. But I don't feel anything out there, either. Can you detect any portals?"

"No, not around here. I think I can vaguely sense the ones in Norwich itself, but they're miles away. Anyway, there's no way I can concentrate and bring up the map with the way the road is slinging us around."

The bus stopped climbing – not that much in the way of hills tended to trouble the Norfolk countryside as a rule – but the road was still far from straight. After several more minutes there was a suggestion that they were starting to drop back down.

Suddenly there was a shout from the front and a thump as their great grandad hit the brakes. The bus juddered to a violent halt which caused Cassie to fall sideways. Kay only managed to stay upright by grabbing hold of the back of the seat in front of her.

"What the hell's that lummox tryin' to do?" Charlie shouted. "Stepped right out in front of me, he did! That's a good job I see him in time or he'd a been a dead'un!"

Cassie could see a figure in the headlights. She gasped, recognising the outline.

"No, don't let him on," Kay shouted. But the doors of the bus were already opening.

The man stepped aboard. He removed a hat that, despite the amount of water still around, was completely dry. Without the hat they could see he had black hair and wore a moustache. The dark suit in which he was attired was, like the hat, immaculate and without a drop of water on it.

Cassie had absolutely no doubt who it was – she had already encountered that face twice. And, this time, it was not attached to a monstrous octopus body nor was it projected out of glowing green slime.

"Thank you, my good man," Laurence said to Charlie, before adding, "Carry on driving. I presume there will be no charge."

Without a word, their great grandad started to drive on. Then Laurence looked directly in Cassie and Kay's direction. His face spread into a wide grin as his blue eyes focussed on Cassie's own.

"Well, it's a pleasure to finally meet you properly," he said. "And, this time, it's fully in, as they say, the flesh. Of course," he added, starting towards her, "it will soon no longer be *your* flesh but mine."

Flash Bang Gone

"Leave her alone," Kay shouted at Laurence and then, to Cassie, "You need to get out of here."

"How?" Cassie said, her voice quivering. The bus was picking up speed again.

Kay glanced around. "Emergency exit back there."

Kay blocked the central aisle between Laurence and Cassie, as her younger self ran towards the back. The emergency exit was located on the driver's side of the bus, next to the last but one row of seats.

"Out of my way, old decoy!" Laurence shouted, striding towards Kay. Cassie glanced back to see him swing his fist to strike at Kay, who ducked and immediately countered with a kick to his stomach. Going by the look on his face, he was definitely not expecting that.

She reached the exit and tugged on the handle to release it but, as she did so, the bus lurched and there was a squeal as the brakes were applied once again.

"Oh, no you don't," said Charlie, bringing the bus to a stop. "I don't know what you did to me just now, but I hint goin' to drive you no farther." He switched off the engine, stood up and marched down the bus towards Laurence, shouting, "Leave them gals alone!"

Cassie wrenched hard at the handle and the door flew open. She was about to jump out when she felt herself grabbed as though huge, invisible hands had wrapped themselves around her arms and legs. She was lifted bodily into the air and found herself flying backwards towards Laurence. Screaming, she attempted to grab at the backs of the seats as she passed over them. After missing three or four, she finally managed to grasp one, which arrested her flight. But she wasn't sure how long she could hold on. Her fingers were being torn from their grip. Then she saw Kay kick Laurence in the knee which disrupted his concentration. Suddenly free, Cassie dropped to land hard in the central aisle.

"Ow!" both Cassie and Laurence shouted, the latter simultaneously hopping on one leg as Kay kicked him again, this time in the shin. Looking diminutive behind Laurence, Charlie tried to grab him in a bear hug, but Laurence was not merely large, he was far stronger. He shrugged off Charlie's attack and returned his attention to Kay, who was still trying to kick and punch him. Laurence gesticulated with his hands and, this time, it was Kay who was raised up into the air. But, unlike Cassie's unwelcome flight, this was in the opposite direction. Kay sailed over Cassie's head towards the emergency exit and was ejected out of the bus. Cassie struggled to her feet and tried to follow Kay but, before she could reach the door, Laurence roared something and it slammed shut, the handle clunking into the locked position.

Cassie ran right to the back of the bus and looked in vain for another way out. As Laurence advanced towards her she became aware of the device humming in her pocket.

"Got you, you little minx," Laurence said, leering.

Then he stumbled as Charlie kicked him in the back.

"I told you, leave them alone!" Charlie shouted.

Laurence spun round.

"Don't do it!" Cassie shouted. "Run away. He'll kill you!"

"One hundred percent correct, daughter," Laurence laughed.

There was a flash of green light between Laurence and Charlie that hurled the latter all the way to the front of the bus, where he collapsed clutching his face, his body shaking.

"Charlie!" Cassie screamed. But her great grandad stopped twitching and lay silent.

"I see," Laurence said. "Charlie, eh? So, you know he is – or was, I should now say – your great grandfather. Interesting. Your mother's influence at work, I presume? No matter. I will find out everything from you soon enough."

"I won't tell you anything! I'd rather die."

"Au contraire," Laurence said. "Once I take over and inhabit your body for myself, your mind will be like an open book to me. I will be able to read every single detail of your life at my pleasure. Your own personality will, I believe, be able to look on for a short while as a mere observer – a passenger, if you like, riding like a flea on the body that was once your own – but you will be totally unable to control that body or do anything to its new owner. Then you will fade away as if you had never existed – not even a ghost will remain." Laurence's grin spread wider and he chuckled. "You know, I once told your grandfather that his daughter was mine. I also told your mother that you would be mine one day. It has, I must admit, taken slightly longer than expected to achieve that result. Someone, as yet undetermined, appears to have poked a few spanners in the works. But, now I'm here, there's nothing you can do to stop the inevitable. Enjoy your last few moments of independent life as best you can, Cassie. Those moments are now measured in seconds only."

Cassie cowered in a corner seat as Laurence strolled confidently towards her. He raised his hands, his fingertips glowing with that strange green light – what on earth was it, a small, still-rational piece of her mind questioned. Then Cassie felt herself pinned to the seat.

"I normally have sons, you know," he continued, now only a few feet away from her. "In fact, I make a point of it. Still, it might be interesting to see things from a woman's perspective. I don't suppose it will make much difference in the long run. I will produce children, one of which will become the next receptacle for my continuation."

Cassie felt something envelope her. The invisible hands that had plucked her back from the emergency door now held her in place. She found it difficult to breathe and could barely even squirm under the unseen pressure.

"Now remain still," Laurence ordered, leaning over her. "The more you fidget, the longer and more painful this process will become for you."

With his face only inches from her own, she tried to turn her head away, but it was as if the bones in her neck had solidified. Aside from Laurence's presence dominating her entire view, the only other thing Cassie could feel was the device in her pocket pulsating – there was something almost comforting about it.

But it wasn't enough and Laurence made contact, placing his hands either side of her head. She felt his skin, smooth and cold, touch her cheeks. His eyes bored into her own. This close, it was unnerving for her to realise that she had inherited the intense blue irises – it was almost like looking into her own eyes in a mirror. She managed to force her eyes shut, trying desperately to deny his lizard-like presence. But the chill from his fingers leached into her flesh, rendering her face numb.

Her body was rock still, apart from one hand. As Laurence began to infiltrate her body and mind, she was almost unaware of that hand inching its way inside her jacket. A distant, still-free part of her mind acknowledged the feel of the sodden envelope that enclosed the device. The paper disintegrated at her touch as if it had been washed away, and the device sprung into the palm of her hand like a magnet attracted to a piece of steel. Almost without volition, her fingers closed around the device and pulled it out into view. Her body was suddenly free of Laurence's influence. Cassie's eyes opened wide, locking directly onto Laurence's own.

"No," she screamed.

"What?" he said, jumping back, his expression changing instantly from gloating to one of fear. "That's not possible," he shouted.

Without knowing why and how she was doing it, she pointed the device at him and shouted, "Get away from me!"

She wanted to hurt him, possibly even kill him. But mostly, she wanted him away from her and off the bus. Her hand was surrounded by a pulsating green glow that emitted flashes of emerald lightning. One hit Laurence squarely mid chest, lifting him from his feet. Another arced towards the emergency exit, which unlocked itself to slam open once more. Cassie's hair stood on end as a sudden wind picked Laurence up bodily and whisked him out of the exit.

Cassie, the device still clasped and glowing in her hand, slumped down on the seat in relief. But then she heard groans and rushed to the exit to see what had happened.

Outside, in the narrow gap between the bus and the side of the road, she could see Laurence spreadeagled against some low metal railings.

Five feet away from him, Kay was picking herself up. Cassie concealed the device behind her back. Kay looked confused, saying, "How on Earth did that happen? Did you just throw him off the bus?"

But Cassie was looking past the railings, sensing the stream flowing below them in a tunnel beneath the road. That wasn't all. She could also detect a portal located on the surface of the water a couple of feet below the railings.

"Portal," Cassie shouted to Kay, pointing out its location.

But Laurence was also picking himself up, a snarl erupting from his lips.

"Oh, no you don't," Kay shouted. She sprang for Laurence, grabbing one of his feet, attempting to lift it and overbalance him. Laurence fought back but Kay threw herself at him, pushing him back against the railings.

"Watch out, Kay," Cassie screamed as Laurence wrapped both of his arms around Kay's torso. But, instead of trying to pull away as Cassie expected, Kay placed one foot against the bus and kicked back. They both started teetering over the railings. Laurence screamed like a demented animal as he tried to right himself. Kay feinted a momentary retreat of a few inches but only so she could position both feet against the side of the bus while her arms were still wrapped around Laurence's shoulders. Using the bus as a springboard, she straightened both legs, forcing Laurence backwards so that both of them tumbled over the railings and out of sight.

All three screamed. Then there was a splash, a flash and, once Cassie's scream had petered out, no sound remained apart from the gurgle of the stream.

Cassie jumped down from the bus and peered over the railings. There was no sign of either Kay or Laurence. They were gone. But where? She tried to call up the map but her ragged mental state prevented it.

She climbed back onboard and dropped back down onto a seat, her heartbeat racing, her breath coming quickly. At the front of the bus her great grandfather's body lay still where it had fallen.

She opened her fingers to see the green glow from the device diminish until it was back to being grey metal.

In the silence Cassie realised that, once again, she was completely alone.

Bus Man Takes A Holiday

How long she sat there in silence she couldn't tell. It may have been only minutes or could have been over an hour. During that time no other traffic had come along the road. Finally, legs still shaking, she stood up and pulled the emergency exit door shut.

Staring at the body of her great grandad, she tried to remember what her mum had said about him. Hadn't he been found in the driving seat? But she was no longer sure what her mum had said. She no longer felt sure of anything.

Approaching him slowly, she didn't know if she was more afraid that he would get up, or that he wouldn't.

He lay face down so she couldn't see his eyes. Kneeling beside him her hand hovered six inches above his back. She was scared to turn him over wondering what she would see if she did.

"I'm so sorry, Charlie," she whispered. "Are you still alive? Can you hear me?" There was no response. "No, of course you can't," she concluded.

She plucked up the courage to touch his outstretched hand. It was still warm, though not as warm as her own. There didn't seem to be a pulse, either. What could she do?

Could the device help her? She'd put it back in her pocket so she got it out again. It no longer glowed green but there was still a sensation of activity around it. She pictured her mum holding it, silently asking it questions. How had she done that? Was it something like praying? It was a long time since Cassie had prayed to anything and, when she had, it was not with any belief that such prayers would ever be answered. But her mum had asked it questions and, apparently, it had answered, so she had to try. She owed it to Charlie.

She sat on one of the front seats and cupped the device in both hands, feeling it all over. Remembering how it had affected her mum, she hoped that, should it work, the cost of asking would not be too great.

"What do I do next? What can I do about Charlie?" she asked. There was no response.

"Please, you've got to help me. How do I get through to you?"

Again, there was nothing. She turned the device over and over in her hands.

She remembered how it had opened up for Mum – how had she done that? She examined the patterns and markings etched into its surface, prodding a few that looked as if they might depress, but nothing moved. She tried to pry the device open with her fingers, achieving an equal lack of success. After several minutes she gave up and dropped the thing on her lap.

"Damn it," she cried. "I don't know what I'm supposed to do."

The device sat silently in her lap as she felt the tears well up.

"Oh, Mum, Kay… Charlie. Why doesn't it do anything?" she cried. She reached into a pocket trying to find a tissue as her nose began to run. The only one she could locate was already far more sodden than her nose and eyes. She felt her shoulders heave, unable to stop the emotion rising up.

She was helpless and alone, and wanted all of this to end. She screwed her eyes shut, unable to stop the flood of tears.

Between the sobs she whimpered. "Oh Charlie, I'm so sorry." But it felt too late for forgiveness. "Tell me how to bring you back."

But Charlie was silent and the only sounds were the ones Cassie made and a few clicks from the cooling of the bus engine.

"Tell me what to do. Help me so I can help you." Tears ran from her eyes and down her cheeks. "You've got to help me, Charlie. Bus man always helps me. I can't do this on my own."

Then one tear fell onto the device. There was a green flash, and a crack of thunder reverberated around the bus. In the echoes, a woman's voice calling her name made her jump. Her knees jerked upwards, flinging the device from her lap towards Charlie.

"Mum!" she screamed as the device hit Charlie in the back, whereupon it emitted a second blinding flash, ricocheted ceiling-wards to finally smack down on the floor next to Cassie's feet.

After a second of inactivity, it pinged open and Cassie stared at it, gasping. Inside it there were similar patterns to those on the outside, except these ones writhed continuously. Cassie, sniffing back the tears, reached out to it but was too scared to pick it up. Her hand hung over it for several seconds but then the device flew up and, without willing them to, her fingers closed around it.

"Kay! Help!" Cassie screamed as the green glow enveloped her hand, spreading further up her arm than it had done when it had pushed Laurence from the bus.

"Don't fight it, Cass," came her mum's voice from very far away. She felt a surge of something burst through her entire body. It shot out of her, splashing against the ceiling of the bus before dropping back down onto Charlie's body.

Then everything reversed and the energy re-entered her, accompanied by another green flash. She dropped the device back onto her lap whereupon it snapped shut and stopped shining.

"Mum?"

The only sound she could hear at first was her own frantic breathing. But then it was accompanied by something else – a voice speaking in the distance. Cassie looked around nervously.

"What?" she said. "Is someone there?"

"Cass," said the voice – definitely not her mother this time – and sounding far closer. "Oh, Cass, my girl, don't cry. I see now who you are. Even with less than one eye, I see how you shine like a star."

Charlie's hand moved and Cassie let out a squeal. Then his whole body shuddered and twitched.

The voice was now coming from somewhere near his head – and was becoming far more familiar.

"Little mouse, in my house with wheels, so strange it feels."

Cassie's heart was in her mouth as Charlie pulled himself to his feet and turned to face her.

"A bitter pill, to do your will. No longer quite a man, but I'll do the best I can."

His face was drained of colour but where his eyes should have been there were only empty sockets. Cassie had to force herself not to clamp her own eyes shut.

"Past, future all the same, bus man takes a holiday but still has to play the game."

"Oh," Cassie whimpered. "I'm so, so sorry, Charlie."

Somehow he closed his empty eyes and when they reopened there were blue orbs where there had been nothing before – not quite eyes – but, to Cassie's sight, better than the previous black pits.

"Bus man is beat, will return to his seat. But Cassie needs to run, and bus man will see you for past and future fun."

As if in pain, he pulled himself into the driver's seat. His face screwed up as if he was struggling to say something more. Then words erupted in a quick burst. "Cassie, find your mum's message in the device. If you get a chance please tell your grandad Bill, I'm sorry I won't be home. He's a good lad. Oh yes, and one more thing. Remember, the only way to end it is to start it. Cass, I wish... oh, too late, bus man's head again gone bad, don't be sad, bus man glad he will help... kill... your... d..."

Then Charlie's chin sunk into his chest and he stopped talking. But he wasn't quite finished as she saw one hand reach out, flick a switch and plunge the interior of the bus into darkness.

The voice came again, but this time not directly from where Charlie's body sat. "Cassie needs to run," it repeated, adding, "before something nasty come."

"Shit," Cassie said, jumping up. She knew what that might mean. She pulled the door open and jumped down from the bus. But where could she go? She was still miles from Norwich.

Then she felt the tug from the portal in the stream below the railings. It was still active. She ran around the side of the bus and peered at the water – or, more precisely, she squinted down into blackness where the water gurgled as it flowed below the road. She couldn't see a thing in the dark.

Should she jump in? But what if Laurence was waiting for her? Wait, Kay always said you had to be holding hands in order for both to come out at the same place and time. Well, there was no chance of holding hands now. She wondered if Kay still had hold of Laurence when they hit the portal. She hoped, for Kay's sake, that she hadn't.

Then she became aware of something else. She looked towards the front of the bus. There was a moving light coming from the direction of Norwich which was followed a few seconds later by the sound of a car engine. Cassie knew she had to get out of there in case whoever it was stopped and discovered her along with the body of her great grandad.

She waited until she was certain the car was definitely coming along the same road. It was, so she clambered over the railing and, closing her eyes and doing her best to detect exactly where the portal was located, took in a lungful of air, and jumped.

Before she reached the stream there was the usual shimmy and flash as her hair, still rather wet, pinged with static electricity. Then the smell of chlorine hit her nostrils as she continued to drop through the air. She had a momentary vision of high arched windows, lit only by the night time ambience of street lights outside. Then her foot struck something that wobbled alarmingly, flipping her over so that she was plummeting down head first. Her scream was cut off as she plunged down into water that, while not cold, made up for that with its depth. Her flailing arms failed to arrest her descent and, eyes clamped shut and her lungs straining to burst, she hit the solid bottom. Her outstretched hands encountered the smooth surface of underwater tiles a moment before her forehead did the same.

Dead of Night Pool

Disorientated and panicking, Cassie flailed around for several seconds before she managed to swivel her feet underneath herself. Then she kicked against the bottom propelling herself upwards, willing her mouth to stay closed, fighting not to inhale.

After what seemed like ages, though was probably no more than five seconds, she burst through the surface and gasped air back into her lungs. Opening her eyes after wiping the worst of the water from them, she looked around. While there was more light than there had been beside the bus, it was still barely enough to see by.

A swimming pool – don't recognise it, though.

Spotting the edge of the pool close by, she fought the drag of her clothes to swim towards it where she clung on for a few seconds, still gasping. Then, after bobbing sideways to some metal steps, she pulled herself out of the water. The sound of her laboured breathing and the water dripping from her body echoed around the pool.

Sitting with her back against a wall, oblivious to the puddle that spread outwards, she took in her surroundings as much as the lack of light allowed.

Above her were two diving platforms, both of a solid concrete construction, the lower one sporting a wooden diving board. There was something several feet above the lower platform.

"Oh, it's the portal," she said, finally working out what it was. It was getting weaker by the moment. Thank goodness it had appeared above the water – materialising under water would have been far worse. She rubbed her foot remembering it had encountered something, the diving board being the most likely, when she first dropped out of the portal.

Her eyes were getting accustomed to the dark. She could make out a third platform, not more than a wooden board, a few feet above the water beyond the tallest platform.

"At least I got out of the water in one piece," she mumbled. "Definitely not getting back in *there* in a hurry."

She fumbled in a pocket in her jacket for the device. It wasn't there. Which pocket had it been in? Searching each of them in turn came up blank. She was beginning to panic again. Then she groaned seeing a pale green light right at the bottom of the pool. She watched as the glow from the device started to diminish.

"Shit!" she spat, pulling off her soaked jacket, shoes and jeans. Her top clung so tightly that she couldn't shift it. Leaving the clothes on the side she descended the metal steps back into the pool wishing her ability to swim was far better than merely mediocre.

She took a deep breath and pushed her head under the water, opening her eyes reluctantly, expecting the sting from the water. She wasn't disappointed. The dim light coupled with the water refraction distorted where the device had landed. She wasted several seconds looking in the wrong place before finally locating its exact position. She kicked her way back to the bottom but her first attempt at grabbing it only caused it to move further away. She had to return to the surface to flail around a bit more while she sucked in another lungful of air. But the next attempt was successful and, a few seconds later, she hauled herself out of the pool for a second time.

"Next time you do that, you can bloody well stay down there," she said. She wanted to sit down and rest, but she was soaked and getting colder by the moment.

"Where on earth am I?"

She gazed out one of the windows and could see a road junction, whose traffic lights didn't look too old – though they weren't the modern types that used LEDs. The opposite side of the road was dominated by a shoe shop that looked like something out of the 1960s. However, the occasional vehicle that passed through the junction didn't look anywhere near as old as that. Against a cloudy skyline lit from below by the orange glow of the city streetlights, she thought she could make out what might have been the office block at Anglia Square in the distance, though she wasn't certain.

She closed her eyes and, after a while, the map began to materialise around her. Yes, she was right – it was Anglia Square towards the south, she could sense the cathedral another half a mile or so beyond. She was inside a swimming pool on Aylsham Road that had been long gone before she was born. She failed to remember what had replaced it as she was not too familiar with the area in her own time. The lack of traffic suggested she'd materialised in the early hours of the morning so it was very likely she was locked in. And, in her current state – physically exhausted and mentally numb – she didn't care. At least it meant no one would be around to question her – well, no one human, anyway.

Cassie yawned and then began to shiver.

This dunking in cold water is becoming too much of a habit.

She picked up her soggy belongings and went in search of somewhere warmer and drier, and to bed herself down until morning arrived, whenever that might be. She located the changing area – mostly filled with tiny cubicles, each with a narrow bench, none of which looked comfortable. At one end she found a family changing room – somewhat more spacious than the cubicles but still not warm. She dumped her clothes in the room and went exploring to seek something to dry herself off.

After a few minutes she found a stack of ragged towels and took an armful back to the changing room, closing and locking the door behind herself.

She yawned again, trying to work out how long it might have been since she had last slept and eaten. It definitely felt like several hours since the fish and chips on the market in 2011. She sighed. No wonder Kay had learned to sleep whenever she could. She stripped off the rest of her wet clothing and dried herself as best she could with a couple of the least threadbare towels. After arranging the rest of the sodden items around the room and making sure she had the device close by, she created a nest of the remaining towels, burying herself in the middle of them, pulling them over herself to exclude as many draughts as she could. She reached out and picked up the device, cradling it in one hand. Then she shut her eyes and, almost immediately and without volition, the map started forming in her mind. After a few seconds of flying over it, she dropped off to sleep.

Conversation With The Dead

"Cassie," came a voice after what seemed like several hours. It was one she recognised.

"Mum?" she said. She was vaguely aware that she was asleep and this was a dream. She didn't want to wake up as, in this dream at least, she was warm and dry.

"Cassie," came another voice. "Thank you for finding me."

Oh, that was Charlie. For once, though, he sounded coherent. The guilt about his death flashed through her mind again.

Even though her eyes were shut, she could see all around. Not in the black and grey view of the map but, instead, in fuzzy shades ranging from black to emerald green. It was as if she was perceiving her surroundings using something like radar or sonar, except that her surroundings were not the family changing room at the swimming pool. This was more like a spacious hall whose uneven walls, ceiling and floor were decorated with moving patterns that flowed continuously. The swirling shapes were more akin to being underwater while rays from the sun above distorted the view, rippling as if thousands of fish were swimming around her. Then she recognised the patterns – they were the same as she'd seen earlier on when the device had been open in front of her.

"Am I dreaming?" she heard herself ask.

"Yes and no," Rebecca's voice said.

Cassie, eyes still shut, looked around trying to locate where the voices were coming from. "Where are you?"

"I am not here," Rebecca said. "My real self is eighteen years old and alive but in bed a few miles away. That me is far from aware of this situation. That me hasn't met Laurence yet."

"What year is this?" Cassie's dream voice asked.

"It is 1994," her mother's voice resumed.

"Where is Kay?"

"Not here."

"Where am I?"

"You know where you are."

"Am I safe?"

"As safe as you can be."

"No nasties on their way?"

"No, they cannot come near while I am with you."

"Is it really you, Mum?"

"What's left of me is here with you."

"Where is here? What is this place? Is it the device?"

"More or less."

"What does that mean?"

"What do you want it to mean?"

"I want this to end. I want to go home."

"The end is… getting closer."

"That… that doesn't sound as promising as it should."

"Not all things can be determined exactly."

"What do you mean?"

"The right questions need to be asked."

"So, what questions should I ask?"

Silence.

"Okay, is asking questions dangerous?"

"In what manner?"

"It gave you cancer – will it affect me the same way when I ask questions? Is it affecting me even now?"

"I wasn't as compatible as you."

"What makes me more compatible than you?"

"I was a remote descendent of an earlier incarnation of Laurence. That was why he sought me out. He always selects someone who is several times removed from his direct line to reduce the chance of defects. I wasn't the only possibility. But I was the one he found. I was compatible enough to be able to produce a child for him that he could use as his next body. I was compatible enough to be able to access the device. But controlling it required I pay a price."

"Oh. But... but what about me?"

"The consequences of your access to the device are not damaging in a similar manner."

"Similar manner? So, it could still hurt me, then?"

"You could hurt yourself using it. A knife you use for defence can still turn and cut you."

Cassie thought about that and wondered how much was true. While the voice in her head sounded like her mother's, the words it used were not.

"Charlie," Cassie said, no longer sure if she was still asleep or not, but not daring to open her eyes.

"Yes," his voice responded.

"Why does the bus man never make any sense?"

"The bus man's head is scrambled. You saw your dad do that."

"Are you in the device, and are you and the bus man the same... er... person? Or ghost?"

Her mother's voice answered, but it sounded even less like her than before. "The device has the capability of transforming and projecting, though it may also enhance things that are already there."

That was no answer. It reminded her of Kay.

"Where is Kay?" she asked again, wondering if the answer would be any different.

"Not here."

Damn. She tried a different tack. "What happened to Kay after she and Laurence fell through the portal?"

"They came to 1994."

"What, wait. Didn't you say this was 1994?"

"Yes, this is 1994."

"So, are Kay and Laurence here in 1994?"

"Not yet."

"Ah, 'yet' – so they will be here soon?"

"Yes."

"Wait. How do you know they came to 1994?"

"I have experienced the sequence in the bus once before when I was in the possession of Laurence."

"Did you have to do what he ordered when he had you?"

There was a slight hesitation before Cassie heard the answer of, "Not always."

"What date will they be here?"

"August the first."

"What date is it now?"

"June the twenty-eighth."

"Oh. How do I get to August the first, then?"

"Wait."

"Wait for what?"

"Just wait."

"Oh," she said, realising what it meant. "Hold on. I'm not waiting a whole month! Can a portal get me there?"

"Unknown."

Cassie sighed. *I have to ask the right questions,* she reminded herself. Surely she was awake now. She felt like it but she was still inside the hall with the flowing shapes.

Maybe I'm inside the device as well.

She also thought hard about how to frame a question to get a useful answer. After a while she said, "Is there a portal either here or in the past or future that will take me to August the first?"

"Undetermined. No portals are currently linked to that date."

"What? But I thought you said you'd been through that one once before?"

"Indeed, but that portal is not yet on your map."

"You can see my map?"

"Yes, prior to your period of sleep when you held me and accessed it."

"Where does it come from?"

"Unknown."

"Oh. Well, that's interesting, sort of," Cassie said, trying to figure out what that meant. "Are you aware of all the portals?"

"Many, not all. More have been recorded now that I have accessed your map. But that one is absent. My previous encounter with it is not fully consistent. It is possible that the timelines in which it once existed have ceased to be viable."

"Timelines?" *Well, that might explain how different things can happen in the same place.* "So, how do I find one that will come out where I need to be?"

"Make it."

"What? You mean I've got to make a portal myself? How do I do that?"

"Unknown."

"What do you mean *unknown*? How did Laurence make the portals?"

"Laurence didn't make the portals."

"Mum. You told me he did!"

"At that point that is what your… I believed to be true. More recent analysis suggests otherwise."

"Then who did?"

"Unknown."

"Was it someone Laurence used to be?"

"No."

"Mum, did you make the portals?"

"No."

"Did Kay make the portals?"

There was a pause and then, "Unlikely."

"Did Charlie make the portals?"

"No."

"Did the device make the portals?"

"Unknown."

This was getting her nowhere. Was there, as Kay had suspected, some other player in this game? Someone she had yet to meet? She tried taking a different route. "Right. Who or what is Kay and where did all the dumb Cassies come from?"

"Unknown."

This was doubly getting her nowhere. She was at a loss as to what to ask next. She yawned but was uncertain whether she had only dreamt she had yawned. What would happen if she opened her eyes?

She did so.

There was a swirl of green, which was immediately followed by a bouncing sensation as if she had just fallen out of bed.

Cassie woke up, exhausted. She was surrounded by towels and, while the floor beneath her makeshift bed was hard, it was no longer quite so cold. She felt the device in her hand and held it before her eyes in time to see the last vestiges of green fading from its surface. The low light coming from outside the frosted window suggested it was still night so, gripping the device tightly, she closed her eyes once more and snuggled down.

It took a while but, finally, she fell into a dreamless sleep.

Breakfast in Gildencroft

The sound of voices woke Cassie up. The door handle to the changing room rattling a second later made her jump. She suppressed a squeal.

"Someone's already in there, Mum," she heard a young girl's voice say outside the door.

"That's okay, we can both fit into one of the smaller ones," came the reply.

Footsteps receded as Cassie looked around. She sat up, the towels falling away from her. Although there was no one else in the room, her nakedness made her feel embarrassed. She picked up her underwear, feeling it. A groan passed her lips when she realised her knickers could have done with several more hours of drying. The bra wasn't much better. She pulled them on, shivering slightly as her skin encountered each patch of damp. Her top and jeans were far from dry but, at least, they didn't feel completely cold.

There was a mirror and she stared into it, unhappy with the face that stared back. All semblance of straightness had escaped from her hair. Lacking a comb, she raked her fingers through it in an attempt to tame its wildness which, for the most part, failed.

Framed by her uncontrollable mane, she did look wild at that moment. Her eyes, tired and red, had a sunken look and gave her a haunted expression, the effect of which was enhanced by the lack of any mascara. Any residue of makeup had long been lost. She felt in her jacket pockets – no, nothing there, not that she was expecting to find anything of use to improve her appearance. What little makeup she'd carried had been lost with her bag in the chalk caves.

She began to tidy the room up. The device, which had fallen from her grip in the night, dropped from a towel and clattered onto the floor. She placed it in a jacket pocket and put her shoes on, wincing as they squelched. She selected a couple of the better looking towels, deciding to keep them, especially if she still had several more water-based portals to go through. I've never stolen anything, she reminded herself, feeling guilty. And then countered it with 'needs must.'

An afterthought rattled around her head as she wrapped one towel inside the other. *Am I turning into Kay?*

Then, because she couldn't put it off any longer, she unlocked the door, opening it an inch to peer out. There was no one directly in view, though she could hear the sound of water splashing from the direction of the pool along with a girl's voice – to Cassie it sounded like the same one who had tried the changing room door earlier on.

Cassie took a deep breath and left the room and, after a few seconds, located the exit. There was a boy paying the admission fee. Like her he had a rolled up towel under his arm. She walked past him, expecting some comment from the lady collecting the money. There was nothing – maybe that out-of-her-time invisibility was kicking in again.

Outside, it appeared to be early morning – possibly around seven. There was already quite a bit of traffic on the roads.

"What time is it?" she asked the device, hoping it was still in contact with her.

"7:32, British Summer Time," it inserted into her head.

Lacking any reason not to, she walked towards Saint Augustine's Street and the city centre.

She drew level with Saint Augustine's church, its brick-built tower at odds with the flint construction of the rest of the building. Alongside the church was a footpath that ran past a row of timber-framed cottages. There was something inviting along that way. Leaning against a wall she closed her eyes and conjured the map again. At first, she thought there was a portal beyond the cottages in a small park. Closing in on the position she couldn't see anything there at all. It was like that particular point was even more empty than its surroundings, which made it stand out. Perhaps it was a hint of a potential portal.

As she opened her eyes, her stomach growled.

"When did I last eat anything?" she asked herself. She tried to work it out. Was it chips on the market? How long had it been since then? She shook her head.

Across the road was Botolph Street and beyond that, the Anglia Square shopping centre. There was a chance there would be a shop that sold food. She rummaged in her pockets and pulled out her loose change, and then sighed at the twelve-sided pound coins in her hand. This was 1994 so she couldn't use those. She separated the coins into two batches – those that were minted in 1994 and before, and those from after. No wonder Kay kept her coins in numbered pouches. She'd had 37p for 1991 in Debenhams – adding three more years into the mix took the legal tender total to just over a pound. She frowned at a 1995 twenty pence piece. Apart from the date it was identical to one from 1992. It also looked worn enough to pass for being several years old. If a shopkeeper didn't look too closely she might get away with using that as well.

So, around one pound, twenty-five. "I wonder what that will buy in 1994," she muttered, crossing the road in the direction of the shops.

A few minutes later, mission accomplished, she walked out of a newsagents, the only shop open at that hour. The fridge where they kept packs of fresh sandwiches had been empty so she'd had to make do with a Mars Bar, a packet of crisps and a small bottle of water. To her surprise, she still had a few pence of change remaining.

She returned to the footpath alongside the church. With her clothing still somewhat damp she entered the park and, in the warm sun, arranged the towels on the grass. Sitting down on them to eat the crisps and chocolate, she hoped the early morning heat would be enough to dry her off.

Her mind turned to the problem of what to do next – how to get to August. Her senses couldn't directly locate the odd portal she'd seen on the map. She held the device in her hand and asked, "How do I make a portal?"

The answer was the same as before. "Unknown." The voice that answered was no longer her mother's, nor was it Charlie's. It was something more unemotionally neutral.

"Are you aware of the portals around here?" Cassie asked.

"Yes."

"All of them?"

"Unknown. There may be many that are undetectable."

"How do portals connect one time and place to another?"

"They bore through space-time, connecting otherwise unrelated points."

Cassie sighed, but persevered. "If I want to connect two specific, unrelated points, how do I start?"

There was a distinct pause before the voice came back with, "Strength."

Cassie sighed. At least it hadn't said, "Unknown." Despite that, she still felt like hurling the device across the park despite knowing that it wouldn't achieve anything. She drank another mouthful of water and finished the last of the crisps.

"What time is it?"

"7:58, British Summer Time."

Then she shut her eyes and conjured up the map. All around her the sparks grew from dim points – she could see hundreds of portals – far more than before, though there weren't any within a hundred yards. She mentally flew over the map, homing in on the one in Saint Giles Street car park that had transported herself and Kay to that place with the gravestones. Up close, it was like a miniature sun, no larger than a marble, hovering in the air, intense and pulsating. She drew even closer, trying to get a better understanding of what it was.

As she observed it she could detect slivers of connection pulsing towards other portals and, every so often, connections coming back. That made sense to her as she remembered Kay mentioning two occasions when she'd used that portal as a destination and not a starting point. She had the impression that, within the map, time was running at an accelerated pace. Indeed, as she observed the portal over what seemed like several minutes, she was fairly certain the same connection patterns would repeat after a period. She also noticed that, once in a while, the split second bursts of energy representing a connection would head for or come from some place on the map where there wasn't a visible portal. She looked again at the park where her body sat and, yes, it held one such place. She tried to see what was there, but failed to spot anything.

She returned to the bright glow of the car park portal.

"What are you?" Cassie whispered. "How can I find out?"

She felt like she was someone from before the stone age observing fire for the first time, fascinated by its power and wondering how she could make it do her bidding. But the sensation was coupled with the fear that inadvertently touching it might result in injury. But its light drew her, attracting her as if she was a moth trapped in a room with a flame. The urge to get closer was irresistible. She saw her hand before her, it was as grey as the buildings that populated the map. Was it an imaginary hand or was it real? She had no idea. But she moved the hand towards the glow of the portal. Just short of her finger entering the light she halted. Her hand could detect no heat. There was absolutely no sensation whatsoever coming from the light.

Her finger touched the edge of the portal with no ill effects. She felt nothing and the portal itself didn't change.

Here goes, she thought, plunging her hand into the light.

Everything went dark.

The Portal Construction Kit

"Are you okay, miss?"

Cassie opened her eyes to meet those of a lanky boy of about twelve or thirteen. He wore a school uniform which was at least one size too small.

"Where am I?" she said.

"In the park. I thought you might be a druggie at first, but you don't look like one. You aren't, are you?" he said backing away, slightly.

"Er, no. Just tired I think. Yes, very tired."

"Oh, okay. It's just…"

"Just what?"

"Well, at first it was like you weren't there."

"What do you mean?"

"Um, well. Dunno. Like I couldn't see you proper."

"Ah, yeah. I do have that effect on people sometimes."

"Oh, er, right. Never seen that before."

"So, what did I look like to you?"

"Um, dunno. Well, maybe it was like I wasn't sure you were really here or not unless I stared straight at you. That's why I, um, came across."

"Oh, okay. How do I look now? Can you see me properly? I look real enough, do I?"

"Er, um, yes."

"Well, I must admit having you looking at me is far better than some of the things that have been gawping at me recently."

The boy acted awkward and embarrassed. "Um, sorry. I didn't mean to stare. It's…"

"Oh no. It's no problem. Say, do you know what time it is?"

The boy pulled the sleeve of his shirt up a couple of inches to reveal a watch whose strap was too loose for his skinny wrist. "Eight-thirty. If you're okay then I, er, need to get to school."

"Right, you'd better run along then. You don't want to be late."

"No," the boy agreed. He turned around and walked across the grass to one of the gates where he looked back at her. She waved to him, which seemed to make him jump a bit.

She watched him walk towards the church and wondered if anyone else had seen her lying there.

The last she remembered had been putting her hand into the point of light of a portal on the map. She looked at her hand – at least it didn't hurt and there was no obvious damage.

"What happened? Why did I flake out?" she asked. But there was no reply from the device.

"What are the portals?" she tried.

"Unknown."

Well, at least it was still talking. Maybe her 'What happened?' question wasn't specific enough and 'Why did I flake out?' used words it didn't understand. She uncapped the bottle of water and drained the last of it, thinking about the best way of rephrasing the question.

"Where have I been for the past half hour?"

"Here but unresponsive."

"Why was I unresponsive?"

"Because you entered the portal light."

"It was only my hand."

"That is not what I observed."

"What did you see?"

"The essence that represented you within the map fully entered the light."

"Oh. So, what in the light caused me to be unresponsive?"

"Unknown."

Cassie cursed under her breath. She closed her eyes and called up the map again, seeking out the same portal as before. It sat there pulsating as connections were made to and from it. This time, instead of touching it directly, she cupped her hands around it leaving an inch of gap between her flesh and its light. She viewed it through the gaps between her fingers. This close it gave the impression that it bubbled and fizzed, although there was no physical sound. She brought her eyes as close as she could.

"Tell me all about yourself," she said to it. To her surprise, there was a change on its tiny surface as lights swirled like the bands of coloured cloud on Jupiter.

"Who made you?" Sparks of white shot around it and she had the impression that it was, well, the nearest thing she could think of was happiness.

"How are you made?" It changed from white, through yellow and then to green – the same emerald green as she'd seen in the device and the creatures that Laurence had formed from in the folly. Then it reversed the process back to the spinning white. Was that a hint that it was made via the device?

"Did the device make you?" The spinning became erratic, like a top that was slowing down and the light appeared to bob from side to side, as if it was nodding. Cassie moved her hands away in case it came too close.

"Did Laurence make you?"

The portal faded to grey for a moment before returning to its normal white.

"Can you tell me how you were made?"

The portal bobbed again. Well, that was encouraging.

"Show me how the device made you."

The portal span even faster and she backed off a few inches. Suddenly there was a popping sound and something hit her in the face and didn't stop there, it entered her head through the skin. She fell backwards, eyes wide open again.

"Oh," she gasped. She could see how it had been made. A plan had become etched in her memory. A plan made of symbols that would have been meaningless only seconds previously. But now she could see how those symbols described the portal. But it was like reading instructions in English on how to build a nuclear reactor. Yes, she could understand the individual words but, combined as they were, it made little sense in total.

Her moment of elation dispersed. How on Earth could this help her? She thought for a few minutes and then an idea hit her.

"How are the portals made?" she asked the device.

"Unknown," came the reply.

"Look inside my head and learn from me, then. Can you do that?"

The device popped open and glowed its usual green, this time bathing Cassie in its light. Cassie wondered what anyone looking at her right now would see.

The light snapped off and the device closed itself.

"Do you now know how the portals are made?"

"Yes."

"Can you help me make a portal that goes to August the first?"

"Yes."

"Right here and right now?"

"Yes, but it needs a source of energy."

"Oh. What sort of energy?"

"Matter of any kind."

"Any kind? What? Like air or water or trees or ground or, er, people or... I don't know..."

"Of those, water might be best – it is the easier form to manipulate and convert."

"Ah, damn," she said, picking up her water bottle. "There's none left."

"It is still in you. It can be used."

"In me?"

"In various forms. In your stomach, your blood, your intestines and bladder."

"Oh, bladder. You can take that without doing any damage?"

"Yes."

"Right. And is that what the portals do every time they are used?"

"Yes, that is very likely."

"Well," Cassie said, raising her eyebrows, "that explains something else that's been bugging me for quite a while. Okay, show me."

Out of the Frying Pan

Smoked Out

"Well, it's simple when you know how," she said, adding. "Even if you don't know *exactly* how."

In front of her, the familiar shimmying sensation hung in the air. She shut her eyes and conjured the map, seeing the new portal occupying the position where she'd seen that 'more empty than empty' space before.

"And it definitely goes to August the first?" she asked.

"Yes."

"Right," she said, stashing the device and water bottle, along with the crisp and sweet wrappers, into various pockets. Picking up the towels she looked around to see if she could be seen by anyone else. The park and the road beyond it appeared clear of people so she said, "Let's test it out, then."

She stepped into the portal and…

…shot out the other end into noise and dense smoke.

Her gasp made her inhale a lungful of fumes causing her to cough and splutter. She wrapped one of the towels around her face, thankful that it was still slightly damp. It filtered enough of the smoke, enabling her to breathe a bit easier. But the acrid stench permeating the air didn't halt the coughing.

She looked around realising she was inside a building, a shop of some sort. Close by she could just make out clothes on rails along with stands holding shoes and slippers. Behind her she felt the heat. Turning to see what it was, her eyes opened wide seeing flames flickering through the smoke. Panicking, she stumbled in the opposite direction, away from the fire. More clothes came into view through the smoke. Then she encountered a wall, but which direction should she go in? Right, she decided, and then came across an exit sign with an arrow pointing the other way. As she turned around there was a crash of glass back nearer to the fire. Given its freedom, the smoke poured out of the open window, clearing the view. A gap in the wall ahead of her led to stairs. They were filled with smoke but, as far as she could see, no flames. She rushed down them as fast as she dared.

The floor below was almost as choked with smoke as the one above. A stream of water cut across it soaking the goods on sale. She headed for the source of the water finding an open doorway and could see the street beyond. Cassie removed the towel from her face and peered around the entrance doing her best to avoid the water being hosed in. It was being pumped in so fast that any attempt to exit would instantly wash her back inside. Outside, she could see several fire hoses snaked across soaked cobblestones.

Stretching as tall as she could she waved the towel out the door above the jet of water. After a few seconds the gush of water cut off.

"Where the hell did you come from?" shouted a startled fireman as he angled the hose away from the doorway. "I thought the place had been cleared."

"Sorry," Cassie said, running out. "I got lost in the smoke." Well, that wasn't exactly a lie.

"Wait over there," another fireman said, pointing across the road. "We'd better get a nurse to check you over."

"No, it's okay. I'm fine," she said, walking off.

"Hey, hold on," the fireman said, but Cassie ignored him and broke into a trot. The fireman, with more pressing things to deal with, returned his attention to the fire, whilst shaking his head and muttering.

Cassie recognised the pedestrianised area – this was London Street. She'd caught a glimpse of the Guildhall in the opposite direction through the smoke. But that fire…

She looked back at the building – she'd definitely never seen it before. In several places the name 'Garlands' appeared above the ground floor windows. Cassie frowned.

"Is this really August the first?" she asked out loud.

"Yes." The reply from the device inserted itself directly into her hearing. Ahead of her a line of police were holding a crowd of spectators back. One of the policemen beckoned to her and a gap opened up.

"Hold on. What year?"

"1970."

"But I asked you to take me to 1994," she gasped. As she passed through the gap a few of the spectators looked at her – no doubt wondering who she was talking to. She was beyond caring what they thought.

"No, you only specified August the first."

"But we were in 1994. What made you think I wanted 1970?"

"A year for the portal wasn't mentioned, only a month and day."

"Aah! I give up," she said, raging at the thought that the damned device could have been so stupid as to pick an inferno for the far end of the portal. Then she remembered the conversation about the elements she'd had with Kay and her great grandad on the bus – earth, air, water and fire.

"Damn, does that mean I'm on the last one?" she said out loud. A boy of about twelve eyed her suspiciously. He was standing beside someone who was probably his father given the similarity in their looks. She glared back at him.

"You're on something all right. You're a weirdo," the boy said as she passed by. His father shushed him but wore an expression that suggested he agreed with this son's verdict.

Too many people. I need to get away from here.

She pushed her way through the crowd gawping at the spectacle. Following Castle Street around to Davey place where the density of people was lower, she then took Davey Steps up and onto Castle Meadow. Across the road the mound of the castle itself was edged with flowers and filled with more trees than she had ever seen there before. Such a contrast to the drab spectacle of how she remembered it – how it will be. The road itself was thick with traffic, ancient cars interspersed with bright red buses all moving along at a snail's pace.

She dodged in front of a car that had a badge with Anglia on it. It was a strange dark green thing whose rear window was angled completely wrong. The driver, a cigarette hanging from the side of his mouth, shouted, "What's happening, darlin'?"

"Fire at Garlands," she replied as she crossed over, wondering if she should say anything about 'not being his darling'. On the other side she looked for the entrance to Castle Mall.

"Not been built yet," she muttered to herself. She glanced up at the castle – at least that was unchanged, though it did look rather grubby. As usual, Robert Kett hanging from his gibbet waved to her. She sneered back.

Rounding the corner onto Farmer's Avenue she became disoriented as, in this time, the area was so different from what she knew. She walked along a road on the left that had disappeared long before she was born. It contained a row of single-storey shops with their backs to the castle. Atop the wall behind the shops, a sharp incline led up to the castle entrance. Along it were parked several cars. She peered into the closest store window – a pet shop. Inside she was fascinated and more than a little horrified to see a half-bald parrot pacing up and down its short perch. On the opposite side of the road, where Castle Mall would be in her time, a vast car park packed with old-style cars, vans and motorbikes sloped down towards Cattle Market Street. She passed the shops and then ascended the road that led to the castle gate.

At the gate she stopped as her senses were buzzing – was this where the gate fell hundreds of years ago? Was she sensing it even now? But something felt wrong. She was sensing something, though it didn't feel like an event, more like something buried deep beneath her. It was a bit like earlier on when she'd felt the chalk mine underneath Earlham Road as she and Kay had walked above it. But this felt far deeper and even more ancient.

She told herself not to get distracted. She wanted to find somewhere quiet to create another portal – this time one that went to the correct August the first.

Climbing to the top of the mound upon which the castle stood, she faced out across to City Hall. To her dismay, there were already several other people up there watching the fire.

"Nice of you to drop by," came a voice beside her. She jumped and turned to find herself face to face with the ghost of Robert Kett. Well, at least he'd had the decency to leave his chains behind.

"Go away," she said. This was the last thing she needed. It was bad enough that he'd been waving to her every time she'd passed the castle since she was about ten. It seemed that waving had now been upgraded to talking.

"That's a good bonfire," he said, nodding towards the smoke billowing up from the direction of London Street. "One of yours?"

She sighed. "I was there, if that's what you mean."

"What made you come here, then?"

"Oh, for crying out loud. I don't need this. I should be in 1994 not 1970," she said, raising her voice. "It went wrong, okay?"

Then Cassie was vaguely conscious that some of the other people were looking at her strangely. Obviously, they couldn't see Kett, nor could they hear his side of the conversation.

"Ah, yes, this is the bit where you've figured out how to make the portals, isn't it?" he said, nodding his head slowly.

"What do you mean? How do you know?" she said, this time keeping her voice down to a hiss. "It's too crowded here. I need somewhere quiet."

"Too right," a man standing nearby said. "A looney bin, I'd say."

"Piss off," Cassie spat back at him.

She stalked off trying to ignore the laughter that followed her.

Around the far side of the castle she found herself alone, apart from Kett who, having taken some sort of short cut, was waiting for her.

"Okay," she said. "How come you know more about what's going on than me?"

"Time screws up around you, Cass," he replied.

"That's like something Kay would say."

"Kay, Cassie, Cass, Kay – past, future, portals, elements – what's the difference? I remember waving to you – it happens all the time. You pass the castle and look up, and I wave to you. You see it hundreds of times – but, do you know something?"

"What?"

"I only ever did it the once."

"Ah. Oh. What?"

No, Cassie didn't understand it, either.

"Say," Kett said, "have we had the conversation about... oh, no, I don't think we have. I'd better shut up."

"What?"

"Sorry. I have a habit of remembering the future, up to a point, more than I remember my own past."

"Why?"

"Why indeed, Cass? Could my past be less permanent than my lack of a future? Maybe in one of my pasts I actually win."

"What are you talking about?"

Robert Kett shrugged in a familiar fashion, just like Kay would shrug. Cassie's already frowning face, frowned deeper.

He doesn't feel real. Okay, so he's a ghost and can't be real, then. But why doesn't he talk like someone from hundreds of years ago?

His modern speech reminded her of the ghost of the girl in Tombland Alley.

Is he some sort of decoy as well? Like the dumb versions of me? But, if he is, then why?

"How come someone from hundreds of years ago talks all modern-like?" she asked.

Kett put his head to one side. "I listen. I learn. Besides, being dead there's not a lot else for me to do."

Cassie considered that for a moment before concluding, *That doesn't answer anything.*

"So, what makes you do this, Cass?" Kett said.

"I'm not doing it. Laurence did it."

"Yes, but Laurence doesn't make portals. Oh yes, this is where I say 'you do'."

"Huh?"

"You do. You make the portals."

A grin spread wide across his face and Cassie took a step backwards.

"Hint, hint," he said. And then he was gone leaving her properly alone.

She spent a few minutes leaning against a railing trying to figure out what Kett had meant. Nothing made sense. Well, apart from the fact that he was right about the portals. The device had told her that Laurence hadn't made the portals. Does that mean she made – or will make – all of them? But there were hundreds of them. How on Earth could she make hundreds of portals that already exist? And why? She shook her head.

I need to make one specific portal. So, I suppose I'd better get down to it.

"It's time to make another portal," she told the device. "Are you up to it?"

"Yes, if you are," came the reply.

"August the first, 1994. Can you manage it properly this time?"

"Yes. Can you?"

"Just shut up and do it!"

"Where should it come out?"

"Wherever Kay will be on that day. Okay?"

"Yes, her location is known. We will need to arrive before she does."

"Why?"

"Because she will arrive via the same portal."

"Ah."

Oh Bondage! Up Yours!

Cassie stepped out of the portal amongst books. Lots of them. That she was in a library was obvious, but she didn't recognise it.

"Can you hold the portal open?"

"Yes, that is now done. It will not fade at periods as others do."

"Good," Cassie said. She didn't want to get trapped here if Laurence couldn't be dealt with.

She looked around. Above the bookshelves, high on the wall, was a blown up photo of some military planes. Below that was a row of discs, some monochrome, others with yellow, red or green backgrounds. Each disc had a black or white stripe across it. Over in one corner three flags hung above a desk. The middle flag Cassie recognised as the Stars and Stripes of the United States of America. The other two were each adorned by a different symbol on a blue background edged with yellow. She had no idea what it all meant.

"It feels early, what time is it?" Cassie whispered. She really ought to get used to asking the device questions without speaking.

"It is 6:48, British Summer Time."

"Why are we here this early? I don't want to get stuck here for long."

"Because Kay comes through soon."

"How do you know?"

"Now that the portal exists, I can detect that it is activated several times over the next hour. Kay will arrive within a few minutes. She will be accompanied."

"Is it Laurence?"

"Unknown at this stage."

"Why?"

"Because I cannot fully determine which Kay will come through."

"Which Kay?"

There was no answer.

"Oh well, I'd better hide just in case it is."

Cassie moved to the other end of the room and ducked down behind some low bookcases. The portal had opened near the centre of the room between a lectern and the wall with the large photo.

"How long before they come through?" she whispered.

"Less than a minute."

She waited for what seemed like ages. Then, hearing a crackle of electricity, she peered through a gap between two bookcases to see two figures spring from the portal. Her breath caught in her throat. She recognised one of them instantly – she'd been seeing that face every time she'd looked in a mirror for years. But the expression on this version of herself was so lacking in animation, it might have been worn by a corpse.

So that's what a completely dumbo version of me looks like close up.

It took a long moment for Cassie to realise that the other figure was Kay. What on earth had happened to her? Her hair had turned white and her face was lined with age. Absolutely skinny, she was dressed in tightly-fitting black leathers, that bulged only where the numerous pockets were filled to capacity. But those bulges only accentuated just how emaciated she had become.

Then she noticed something else. Ancient Kay was leading the dumbo Cassie around on the end of a piece of rope. One end was tied around Kay's left wrist, the other bound dumbo Cassie's hands securely together. Not that she was doing anything about trying to escape her bondage.

"Hur," said the dumbo, looking back at the portal. "Still alive."

"Ah, right," ancient Kay said, nodding her head as she glanced around the walls of the library. "It's this one, isn't it? I'd been wondering when it was going to turn up. I'd better get prepared. Where are those chairs?"

The dumbo didn't reply, but merely grinned open-mouthed at the photo of the planes.

"Don't know why I even bother to talk to you," Kay muttered and then added, "Chairs, chairs, chairs. Ah, that's right. They're all outside this section."

Then the dumbo looked straight in the direction Cassie was hiding. Had she seen her? Another grin spread across the face as she said, "Mummy!"

"Shut up," Kay reprimanded, not even bothering to look in Cassie's direction. "I'm not your mother."

Kay led the unprotesting girl through into the main part of the library. Cassie watched stunned as Kay pushed the girl down onto a light, metal-framed chair and wound the rope around her body and legs to prevent movement. The dumbo sat there grinning inanely, totally accepting of her fate. Then Kay picked up a second chair, carried it back and placed it close to the portal. Setting herself down on it she stared at the shimmering patch that hung in the air.

Cassie wondered if she should come out of hiding. If Kay had looked as she had done the last time Cassie saw her, she might have been more tempted. But, this skeletal creature was almost as scary as Laurence.

Cassie, clamping her lips shut, thought to the device. "What is she waiting for?"

Much to her surprise, the answer appeared in her head immediately.

"The portal will be activated in approximately two minutes. It is surmised that Kay is expecting this, given that she has lived through it before."

Cassie glanced across at Kay expecting her to have heard the reply. But she didn't stir. She projected another thought to the device, "How do you know?"

"Portals, being connections between different times and places, resonate temporally in both directions. Such resonances are detectable."

Cassie rolled her eyes and thought back, "Remind me to stop asking questions where the answers are complete and utter b…, well, gobbledegook."

"Don't ask questions that…"

"Shut up!"

The device did but, a few moments later, Cassie had another question. "Who will be coming through this time?"

"The likelihood is that it will be another instance of Kay."

"Another Kay?"

"Yes and, from recollection, this will be the one accompanied by Laurence."

"Ah. But wait though," Cassie continued without speaking. "How come she is going to meet herself? She told me that can't ever happen. Like it's different timelines or something?"

"That is normally the case. However, your instruction to keep this portal open appears to have tied the timeline into one concrete event in this instance."

Oh, so my fault again.

Then static electricity filled the air once more. It was obvious that Kay detected it as well as she stood up. Placing herself to one side of the portal, she raised the chair above her head.

Here we go, Cassie thought to herself, holding her breath in anticipation.

The portal opened again and Laurence tumbled out of it backwards with another, much younger Kay almost on top of him. That Kay had to be the one Cassie had last seen falling over the railings beside her great grandad's bus. The two were still grappling with each other, continuing the fight that had started on the road to Hempnall in 1968. Laurence rolled younger Kay over onto her back and sat astride her, a grin spreading across his face. Then he realised there was a shadow standing over both of them.

Young Kay screamed as old Kay smashed the chair down on Laurence's head.

"Bloody hell!" young Kay said as she pushed the limp form of Laurence from on top of her. He slumped face down to lie without moving.

Old Kay said, "It's okay. You're fine. But you need to go back through the portal to escape. I'll deal with this bastard."

Young Kay didn't move. Her eyes, locked on her older self, were full of… Cassie didn't know if it was pity, astonishment or fear. "Oh, my God, are you really me?" she said.

"Yes, of course I am," old Kay confirmed with a sigh.

"But you're so…"

"Old? Yeah, tell me about it."

"How come we can meet?"

"No idea. I remember this happening from your point of view, so just accept it. But, before you go, listen to me. You'll get through a good number of dumbos before you find one you can use like a tame puppy. Look over there. Can you see her tied to the chair?"

"Wha– oh yes, I see her."

"Almost brain dead, that one. But she can spot portals like a bloodhound. Talking of which, you need to keep her on a tight lead or, in this case, rope. Never let her loose for a moment. If you need to sleep or be away from her for anything more than a few seconds, tie her up first or she'll wander off and fall under a bus or something."

"Oh, right. She does that, does she?"

"No. Because you remember me telling you this. But she would if you didn't. Even though she doesn't."

"Damn, I'm even confusing myself now."

"Yeah. There were a couple of near misses."

"But why do I need her?"

"To get you to here. All the way through the transitions, that is."

"How will I recognise her?"

"Doesn't complain about the cold after the first portal and is barely able to do the buttons on her jacket up without assistance."

"That bad!"

"Absolutely. Oh, and this portal is a fire one. You know, earth, air, water, fire. Last on the list – hopefully."

Young Kay looked around and frowned. "Looks pretty unburnt to me."

"Yep, which is a bit strange. I've been through several with her and the fires there had already started."

"Which ones were they?"

"Let me try to remember. Oh yes, Theatre Royal – nineteen-thirties, I think. One in a shoe factory even earlier. The Assembly House in the nineties – weird one that, when we arrived the dumbo actually managed to string an almost coherent sentence together and insisted we'd only just left. A couple in the war. I think that was it. Anyway, that's not important, but this is."

Old Kay pulled out a folded piece of paper and handed it over.

"What's this?"

"An address. A safe house. Make use of it. And all that money you've started accumulating."

"Okay," young Kay said, pocketing the paper. "Um, have you met the real

Cassie since, well, since being me?"

"No, which is worrying. Maybe she didn't make it, after all."

"Oh, but if she hasn't made it, then where does that leave us?"

"I've given up questioning it."

Cassie, remaining as quiet as she could, doubly resisted the urge to make her presence known.

Old Kay looked at Laurence and then barked at her younger self, "He's starting to wake up. You need to get out of here. Come on, move it. Through the portal, now."

"Where does it go? Back to the bus?"

"No, for you it will be Castle Mall, as usual."

"What are you going to do with him?"

Old Kay's mouth narrowed to a slit.

"You'll know when it's your turn."

Young Kay swallowed. "Okay, I'm going. Thanks… I think." She stood up and faced the portal. Then she stopped.

"Mum told us his head got chopped off."

Old Kay nodded. "Yeah, maybe I can shortcut the need for that here and now. Meanwhile, you – portal. Now!"

Young Kay shrugged at her older self, stepped through the portal and was gone.

Old Kay produced another length of rope from one of her pockets. Then she kicked Laurence in the head, which made Cassie wince.

"Right, you git. I've got a lot of questions to ask you when you wake up. And after that you've got an early appointment with a careless barber."

She tied Laurence's hands behind his back, testing the knots several times to make sure he had no chance of undoing them. He started groaning as Kay used another piece of rope to secure his ankles. Once she had Laurence immobilised, she stepped back to admire her handiwork.

He raised his head and looked at her. His eyes took a few seconds to focus and then he burst out laughing. Kay slapped him around the face, which reduced his laugh but only to a chuckle.

"Oh, look at you, just look at you," he grinned. "How many years has it been?"

"Shut up."

"I suppose you sent the younger one back through the portal, did you?"

"None of your business. Anyway, now you're trussed up I'm going to be the one asking the questions."

"You think this will stop me?" he said, testing the ropes that bound him.

"You're not going anywhere," Kay spat back.

"Not until I've finished laughing at you, ancient decoy," he giggled.

"I'm not a decoy."

"You have absolutely no idea what you are. Though I'm beginning to suspect. Where did she get it?"

"What? Who? And get what?"

"Well, that sounds like the truth – a genuine response. That means you really have no idea. Hah, that's even better. I *will* find her again, you know."

"If you mean the real Cassie, or whatever she is, then I haven't seen her in years. What is she, anyway?"

"This gets even better," he laughed. "Yes, of course I mean the real one. The only real one. The one I created with your mother. Should have been a son, of course. But the real flesh and blood one. Not like you and…"

Laurence then noticed the dumbo Cassie tied to the chair and started laughing again.

"Ah, and there we have one," he chuckled. "A young decoy. All tied up because she's a danger to herself. You probably think I'm as helpless as her."

"You are. You're not getting out of those ropes that easily."

"You think so?"

"I know so."

"Oh, really? Watch."

There was a popping sound and Laurence disappeared, leaving the ropes to fall to the floor.

Cassie clamped her hand over her face to prevent the squeak that threatened to erupt from her mouth. But, even if she had squeaked, the sound would have been drowned out from the torrent of screaming and swearing that poured from Kay's tongue at the same time.

Cassie was stunned. Laurence hadn't used the portal to escape.

"Where did he go?" she thought at the device.

"To another time and place," came the response.

"How? That wasn't a portal, was it?"

"No. He moves directly to where he wants to go."

"What? Why didn't you tell me this before?"

"You didn't ask."

"I did!"

"No. You asked if Laurence made the portals. The truthful answer was that he hadn't."

"And you don't know who did?"

"I have knowledge of only one person who makes portals."

"Who?" Cassie said, already knowing what the answer was going to be.

"You."

Blitz

Cassie bit her tongue. An image of her mum appeared in her head saying, "You have to ask the right questions." But, how could she have created all the portals? There were hundreds, possibly thousands of them. Could there still be someone else going around making them? If so, then who? Nothing made sense. The real news was that she hadn't even considered that Laurence might have had his own method of getting to different times and places.

"Can you teach me how to do what Laurence just did?" she asked.

"Of course."

But there wasn't time as, by this point, Kay had untied the dumbo and was dragging her back towards the portal. Her swearing had settled down to a few 'damns' and 'bloodies' mixed in with the insults thrown at the dumbo. Not that it had any effect on the almost perpetual grin still plastered across the girl's face as she let herself be hauled along.

"Hand!" Kay demanded as they stood before the portal. The dumbo raised both hands as they were still tied together.

Cassie made a decision. *I need to talk to this version of Kay, if only to tell her I'm still around.* She stood up as Kay stepped towards the portal.

"Wait," Cassie shouted.

"Mummy!" cried the dumbo.

"What?" Kay said, finally noticing Cassie.

But, it was too late.

"Damn," Cassie cursed, as the portal sucked them through leaving her on her own, again.

Except she wasn't.

She heard a door slam and footsteps echoing somewhere else in the building.

"Time I wasn't here," she murmured, and followed Kay through the portal.

The usual shimmy occurred and Cassie found herself in darkness, buffeted by loud booming noises that made her jump. Overhead came a roar of what sounded like low flying planes. Her eyes took a moment to adjust to the darkness. Then she saw she was standing on a narrow road lined on both sides with terraced houses. There was no sign of either Kay or the dumbo anywhere.

"Damn," she cursed again. The destination must have switched to somewhere else.

No light escaped the buildings but there was a reddish glow coming from behind her. She turned around and her mouth dropped open. She thought the colour might have been from the portal but the real source was much further away. The road was on an incline and her vantage point was high enough to allow a view out across the rooftops of rows of similar houses. But it wasn't the houses that held her eyes – it was the pockets of fire that burned in a line that stretched back to the horizon. The closest was still quite a distance away – possibly as much as a mile. A whistling sound followed by the boom of an explosion added a new fire to the line of infernos, this time far closer. She retreated a few steps up the road away from both the portal and the distant fire. Fear and panic rose in her chest.

"Where and when?" she shouted at the device.

"Patteson Road. The twenty-seventh of April 1942."

"What's happening?"

"The Baedeker Raids, also known as the Norwich blitz."

Realisation dawned – World War Two. Old Kay had told young Kay that she'd been in fires from the war. Was this one of them?

She knew she was in immediate danger. But where could she go? There was another whistling – this time it was only a few hundred yards away. She felt the ground tremble as the explosion sent debris hurtling in all directions, some raining down on the far end of the road upon which she stood.

The whistle of another bomb dropping from the sky above her told Cassie she was in the direct line of fire. What could she do? Should she run? But which direction? The whistling grew in intensity.

The panic rooted her to the spot, her legs shaking uncontrollably and her breaths coming fast. She raised her hand and shouted, "No, no! Stop! Make it all stop!"

And silence fell.

The air around her became as thick as treacle. It clung to her throat as she tried to breathe and her limbs fought to move against it. In the distance the flames where the bombs had hit were no longer dancing. It was as if she was staring at a photograph. But no, time hadn't completely halted. It was merely progressing at far less than a snail's pace.

Did I do this? No, it must have been the device somehow.

"Where will it fall?" she thought at the device, expecting no answer.

"Close by," the device responded, to Cassie's surprise.

Cassie, still struggling to breathe, stared at the portal. Normally, all she could detect was the sensation of the portal's presence – the shimmy in the air. But, with time slowed, she could see right through it to the library beyond.

"It's still connected to the library."

"Correct. Your request to keep it open is preventing the connection from dissipating."

"But where did old Kay and the dumbo go?"

"Elsewhere. They didn't come here. The portal is only anchored back to the library for you."

"Can I go back through it?"

"Dangerous. As soon as you enter it, normal time will resume here and the bomb will explode at almost the same moment. Even on the far side you will still be too close to the portal and it is likely you will be maimed or killed."

"How do I get away?"

"Step into a different time."

"Without a portal? Like Laurence?"

"Yes."

"I don't know how?"

"I will teach you."

"Is there time?"

"Not if you keep asking questions."

"Do it," she said and then shut up. Immediately, she felt knowledge pouring into her head. But, as the teaching progressed, time slowly advanced around her. She was no longer fighting to get her breath – maybe the device had overridden her need for oxygen – but she was aware of how near the bomb was becoming. Slowly, her eyes swung skywards and there it was. A small dot, illuminated by the fires in the distance, but that dot grew closer as each time-slowed moment passed.

Then the process was complete and the knowledge of how to jump to another time and place had been inserted into her head. Her eyes were still locked on the bomb and it was now only feet above the chimneys of the terraces. It looked close enough to reach up and touch.

Cassie was about to put her new-found knowledge into practice when a thought struck her.

"Where is that library?"

"Central Norwich."

"What, where the Forum now stands?"

"Correct."

She and the youngest Kay had stood outside it in 1991. She remembered Kay saying, 'It burns down in two or three years' time.'

"What date did the old library burn down?"

"August the first, 1994."

"Shit! Close the portal, now!"

"It will take a while given the current rate at which time is passing and you need to get away. Also, the library fire event is locked into history. It cannot be changed."

"Close it!" Cassie demanded.

It was almost as if she could sense the device shrugging.

"It is closing. You must move."

"No!" The bomb was level with the apex of the roofs to her right. In front of her the edges of the portal grew fuzzy but, in the centre, she could still distinctly see the photo of the planes that adorned the library wall. "It's not closing fast enough," Cassie mentally shouted. The bomb had disappeared from view behind the roof. She was about to wonder how much time she had before it went off when she saw the houses alongside her start to collapse, the walls bowing outwards and the glass from their windows cracking and splintering before flying out towards her.

Oh God, there must be people in there.

People who would soon be dead. She wished there was something she could do about it.

She looked at the portal, it was almost closed, but there was still a tiny hole through which she could see the bright interior of the library. Would it be enough?

The flying glass had almost reached her and roof tiles were being hurled in all directions as the walls of the houses buckled in slow motion. She knew she couldn't wait any longer. But where to?

Back to 2018.

For some reason, Robert Kett appeared in her mind. She dismissed him, concentrated anew and willed herself away. It felt different. There was no shimmy, no build up of electricity. It was more like stepping through a normal door. In this case that door came out into blinding sunshine.

Multitude

Air rushed into her lungs again. Cassie looked around to find herself on top of the Norwich Castle battlements. Her eyes squinted in the intense light. She wasn't sure if that was due to the contrast from a night in 1942 or because of the brightness of the sun. As her eyes grew accustomed to it she managed to pick out the City Hall clock and cathedral spire.

"Did we save it?"

"No."

"What? Tell me what happened."

"The portal was almost closed when the bomb exploded but some debris got through and hit a light fitting causing it to catch fire. Within seconds the room was alight, which spread to the rest of the building after a few minutes. Such historical events cannot be easily bypassed."

"No, no, no," Cassie groaned, sinking down onto her haunches on the narrow walkway.

After a while she asked, "When are we?"

"June the thirtieth, 2018. Time – 11:31."

"What? You mean I'm back home?"

"Almost."

"Eh? What do you mean, 'almost'?"

Then Cassie felt time slow down again.

"What's happening?"

"We need to return to the past. There appears to be no future beyond this point."

"Huh! What do you mean?"

"This is the point at which everything started. I surmise that there is some sort of barrier that cannot be bypassed until the sequence of events that created it is complete."

Time slowed further. A bird that had been flying above the castle now hung there almost stationary, the beat of its wings slowed so that the movement was barely detectable.

"I have no idea what you mean. Mum, are you still in there?"

"Yes," came her mother's voice. At least it sounded like her. But how could she be sure?

"Tell me what's going on."

"I don't fully understand but I don't think you can go forward in time because things haven't yet been finalised."

"But what do I do?"

"I – I don't know. Sorry, dear."

"Can't you give me any help at all?"

"No, except for one thing."

"What's that?"

"The only way to end it is to start it."

Cassie frowned. Where had she heard that before?

Time came to almost a complete standstill. Accompanying it was an intense feeling of emptiness. Cassie couldn't bear it. She shut her eyes and, without wanting to, called up the map. In the greyness she saw the shadows of the buildings around her, the castle a massive block atop which she was perched.

But there were no portals. Not a single spark to show they had ever existed.

"Where are they?" she whispered.

"They do not exist at this moment in time," said the device, no longer using her mother's voice.

Suddenly, there was movement and, involuntarily, Cassie found herself slipping backwards through time. But she hadn't moved anywhere in space. She was still sitting on the castle walkway.

"What…?" she thought at the device.

"You hit the end of time and were forced to rewind. It is now several minutes earlier."

Then she saw movement on the adjacent part of the walkway to her right and blinked in surprise seeing another copy of herself. Was it a dumbo? It didn't look that way, she wore exactly the same jacket and she was not accompanied by a Kay of any age. Cassie watched, determining that the movements her duplicate exhibited were purposeful and deliberate. Her duplicate started watching a point further around the walkway. Cassie looked to where her opposite gazed and only just managed to suppress a gasp as a third version of herself materialised. That one didn't look like a dumbo either and her jacket was also identical to Cassie's own. Moments later, the familiar figure of Robert Kett appeared beside the most recent version and they began talking to each other, though Cassie couldn't hear anything from that distance.

This is getting way too confusing.

After a minute or so the third version of herself noticed the second one watching her and the second one said, "You'll work it out."

Number three frowned and then looked in Cassie's direction and nodded as if something made sense. Number two then turned around and grinned at Cassie, though her eyes looked quite haunted.

Do I really look like that? Cassie wondered.

Then, after a short pause, number two said, "Oh yes, and so will you. All I need to say at this point is have a short breather and then find Kay before Laurence kills her."

Number two frowned and looked as if she wanted to say more but then she shrugged and disappeared. So did number three not long after.

"Were they me?" Cassie asked as Robert Kett also faded from view.

"All indications suggest that both were future versions of yourself."

"Okay. So, I guess the first one was the one most in my future and the other one was somewhere in between."

"That is a reasonable conclusion given their actions."

"That first one looked – well, at first I thought she looked almost happy. But her eyes…"

The device was silent.

"Okay. So, the only clue to go on is the bit about finding Kay before Laurence kills her. But how do I do that?"

"You will work it out."

"That's just parroting me. Can't you suggest anything more helpful?"

"No. Your future self said that you will work it out. She didn't specify that you would require any external help to do so."

"Rubbish. I could need help. Maybe the 'working out' bit just means me asking you the right questions."

"That is also possible."

Cassie sighed and closed her eyes. Immediately, the map formed and, this time, it was full of portals. Hundreds of them.

"Wow," she said. "They're back. I've never seen so many. Can you count them?"

"Yes, there are exactly one thousand, three hundred and fifty-six."

Cassie opened her eyes and said, "Is that all there will ever be?"

"Yes."

"How do you know?"

"They include all the ones detected while Laurence held me and also the two that you created recently that were anchored on August the first in both 1970 and 1994."

"Can you remember them all?"

"Yes. As requested, I have now recorded and committed to memory each and every one of them."

"Who requested that?"

"You did."

"Eh?"

"You requested that I should remember them all."

"No, I… Okay, I suppose I did. It wasn't exactly what I meant. Then again, that might turn out to be useful. While we're at it, you said something else just now."

"What was that?"

"I think you said, 'when Laurence held me.' Is that right?"

"Correct. When I was owned by Laurence I was analysing the portals as he discovered them, attempting to deduce where they came from."

"Ah. I see – that explains why you said Laurence didn't make the portals and why he had his own way of getting around."

"Correct."

"How many devices like you are there?"

"Do you mean how many have there ever been or will be created? Or how many exist on this planet?"

"Oh, does that mean you're not from Earth?"

"Indeed."

"Where did you come from?"

"The terminology required to describe my origins cannot be expressed in your language."

"Yeah, might have guessed. Okay, how many on Earth then?"

"As far as I can determine, I am the only one. But…"

"But what?"

"There is something close by that I have been aware of for quite a while. It feels as if it may have a similar origin to myself."

"Where is it?"

"There is an echo of it here but it is shielded somehow."

"What does it feel like, then?"

"Angry."

Cassie made a face. This was getting even weirder. She changed the subject. "So, you were previously owned by Laurence, then by my Mum, and now I've got you."

"Correct, though Laurence was only the latest body occupied by the creature that originally encountered me."

"Creature?"

"It was near-human. Your archaeologists refer to the species as Denisovan. Close enough to homo sapiens to allow interbreeding."

"When was this?"

"Approximately one hundred and forty thousand years ago."

"Wow! And Laurence is the same creature that first found you?"

"Correct as far as the consciousness is concerned. The number of bodies inhabited by that consciousness between then and the one named Laurence is in excess of five thousand."

"Oh my God! Is he really still the same person, inside his mind?"

"No. The personality has evolved greatly. The creature he started out as was driven far more by instinct and a will to survive. After a few thousand generations it developed in complexity, though becoming far less compassionate and more willing to inflict pain and suffering on others."

"I'm surprised he is even remotely human after all that time."

"Despite claims otherwise, I have noticed that, on occasion, the personality of the host body is not completely suppressed and... ah, wait – we are nearing the end of time again. Your earlier self is likely to appear any moment soon. As you didn't see a fourth version of yourself it suggests that you move away before your earlier self arrives."

"Right... I think," Cassie said, trying to get things straight in her mind. "So, we need to find Kay before Laurence kills her."

"That would seem to be the gist of your future self's requirement."

"Oh, but I'm knackered."

"Your future self also mentioned 'taking a breather'."

"Yes, good idea," Cassie agreed. "I'm going home."

"You must not come out…"

"Shut up," Cassie ordered as she closed her eyes and decided on the place and time.

But the device interrupted her before she managed to get going. It said, "The portals no longer exist."

"What?" Cassie said, opening her eyes.

She closed her eyes again. The device was correct – the portals had all gone.

"Where did they go?"

"They haven't been created yet."

"That doesn't make sense – how come they existed a few minutes ago but now you say they haven't been created *yet*?"

"Agreed. It is perplexing."

"Oh, I just don't get it. And I'm too tired to figure it out. Look, I really am going home this time. Don't interrupt me again."

There was movement and when she opened her eyes she was inside her own bedroom.

She sunk down on the bed and let out a sigh of relief that was cut short when she heard her own voice shouting from downstairs.

"Told you at breakfast time I was going out!"

"Uh, what, Cassie?" she heard her grandad splutter. "No, I don't rememb…"

Cassie's hand rushed to cover her mouth before she let out a squeak.

Damn, too early.

Clocking Off

Erasing a Shadow

Cassie had to wait in silence for well over ten minutes. Finally, the version of herself from just before all this started left the house, slamming the front door shut as she went. She tried to work out how long ago that had been for her. Surely, it was several days, or was it shorter? Whenever it was, it now felt like a different lifetime.

She lay on her bed another few minutes, listening to the sounds of the house and comparing the room with what she remembered on the visit to her mum in 2010. Downstairs, she heard her grandad doddering about, taking ages to make a cup of tea. She thought about how different he'd been at Mum's funeral when he'd given her the device. Then she made a decision and went downstairs.

"Oh, Cass," her grandad said, as she reached the bottom of the stairs. She relieved him of the cup of tea he was on the verge of dropping, and took his arm, guiding him into the lounge. "Didn't you go out? Or was that your mum?" he said.

She smiled at him as she helped him sit in his chair.

"Don't worry about it," she said, pouring the spilt tea from the saucer back into the cup and placing it on the table beside him. "Just enjoy your tea. I'll make you another one a bit later on as you seem to have lost most of this one."

Cassie watched the tremor in his hand as he put the cup to his lips. He slurped a few sips mostly into his mouth and made to place the cup back down on the saucer. Cassie, seeing he was going to miss, guided his hand until the cup was safe.

"Sometimes I…" he started.

"What, Grandad?"

"Sometimes I wish I could wake up," he said.

"You are awake."

"No," he said, shaking his head. His eyes, sad and beginning to water, stared into his lap. "No, no, no."

His eyes closed, squeezing out a tear that ran down his cheek. Cassie's own eyes were beginning to water and she swallowed hard, trying to hold the emotion back. After a few moments he started to snore.

She bit her lip and directed a thought to the device. "Is he going to be like this for good, now?"

"He will unless what Laurence did to him is removed."

"What?" she said out loud.

"Oh, Cass?" her grandad said, startled back to wakefulness. "Didn't you go out?"

"Sorry, Grandad," she murmured and patted his hand. His eyelids drooped again.

"What did Laurence do to him?" she asked silently.

"Your grandfather encountered Laurence in 2014 in Norwich city centre and tried to confront him. Laurence entered his mind and inflicted a repression upon him before we skipped to another time and place."

"What did you call it? A repression?"

"Look at him properly. Can you see it?"

Cassie stared at her grandad. Yes, there was something there – surrounding him and infused throughout his body – something subtle that was far from natural and definitely not anything she'd ever noticed before. It was like the hint of a green-tinged shadow overlaying him. The same green she'd seen at the folly, inside the device and enveloping herself on several occasions.

"Can you remove it?"

"That can be done."

"Will it hurt him?"

"No, though there may have already been some permanent damage. I have no reference point to compare to how he might have been before this as I wasn't ordered to scan him fully before applying the repression."

"The bastard. I'll make him pay for this. Do it, then. Remove it."

"It is done."

Cassie examined him again. The green was definitely gone.

"But, he doesn't look any different," she whispered.

"It may take time and, given how long it has been in place, there may be no effect."

"Why did you allow Laurence to do it in the first place?"

"He owned me."

"So? Couldn't you have stopped him?"

"I do not have the ability to express free will in the manner you understand. I am, in terms you might find more appropriate, like a cross between an encyclopaedia and a tool or appliance. I contain knowledge and the methods by which such knowledge can be applied. I rarely have the need to do anything purely on my own – it takes an owner to make use of me. I do not control how that usage is actioned."

"Didn't you ever feel guilty when Laurence injured or killed someone?"

"No, not at the time. But…"

"But what?"

"I have begun to understand that emotion now thanks to the change of ownership."

"What. Because of me?"

"And your mother."

Her grandad stirred and opened his eyes. "Oh Cass. Is that a new jacket?" he asked.

"Yes," she said.

"Brand new?"

"Why do you ask, Grandad?" Her eyes searched his, seeking hints of change.

"It's a bit grubby, isn't it?" he continued. "Look, there's something like chalk marks all down one arm. And mud at the bottom."

"It's, um, not that new – probably nearly thirty years old, I'd say."

He looked at her, his eyes narrowing.

"Are you in any trouble?"

"What do you mean?"

"Well, for a start, your hair was almost straight a short while ago and now it's frizzed up like someone's plugged you in. It's like, oh, something nagging at the back of my mind or on the tip of my tongue."

Cassie searched his eyes. They definitely looked brighter than they had only moments before. He reached for the cup and Cassie saw that his aim was far more confident, the tremor hardly noticeable as he drank the rest in one gulp. He placed the cup back down, accurately positioning it on the saucer. She couldn't help grinning.

"Wait. I've seen that jacket once before, haven't I?" he said, his voice stronger. "Yes, I have. Several years ago."

"Is it coming back?" she asked, unable to prevent the quiver in her voice. He slowly nodded.

"Oh," he said finally. "Laurence did this to me, didn't he? I remember now."

Cassie nodded.

"But what he did is fading, somehow."

"Yes, hopefully."

"You did this?" he said, pointing at his head. "With that thing Mum made me give you in the envelope?"

Cassie nodded again, unable, for a moment, to speak.

"Thank you, Cass. But, isn't it dangerous?"

"In what way?"

"It, er, well, it took your mum, didn't it?"

"I don't think it's dangerous for me," she said, hoping that was the truth.

"Where is it?"

She reached into a pocket and drew it out, holding it in her hands in front of him. Instead of coming forward to inspect it, he leaned further back in the chair, as if unwilling to be any closer.

"And that belongs to Laurence?"

"Not any more."

"Is he…"

"I've seen him. Alive, that is."

"So, he survived being beheaded, then?"

Cassie shrugged. She wasn't sure if Laurence's death was a fixed event.

She asked the device and it replied, "I was transferred from Laurence to your mother at the point of his apparent demise. At that stage he was accomplishing much on his own. Consequently, I am unaware whether his demise was permanent, though nothing I can currently conjecture suggests a method by which he might have survived."

That doesn't really answer anything at all.

"He can move in time," she said out loud. "So can I, now. And go where I want – any time and place… probably."

Her grandfather's eyebrows jiggled up and down. Then he sat up and, with elbows resting on his knees, arched his fingers to pursed lips. It was a habit that she hadn't seen him perform for several years and one he used to adopt when thinking hard upon something, usually a complex subject of some kind. Then, he said, "So, how much time have you experienced between being the one who walked out the front door a little while ago and the one in front of me right now?"

"You understand all this, then?"

"Your mum, in her last few months, tried to explain a lot of it to me. I still don't understand much of what she said. I think I'd forgotten all of it up until a few moments ago, but at least some of it's coming back again, thanks to you. So, how long then?"

Cassie sighed. "Okay. It's not easy keeping track but maybe no more than three or four days. But so much has happened that it feels like it's been far longer."

"Oh, um, and wasn't there someone called, er, Kay?"

"Yes," she said.

"I vaguely remember you being with a woman in black at the funeral. I never met her properly, did I?"

"N-No, not the you in front of me right now."

He frowned at her. "What's that supposed to mean?"

"She… she… oh no, I can't. I still don't believe that part of it, anyway."

"What part?"

Cassie took a deep breath. "She thinks she met a different version of you. Not a nice version."

"Ah, your mum did say something." He creased his brow, trying to dredge up a memory. "Something like a warning that, if I ever did meet her, she might not be friendly or something."

Cassie looked away.

"Just how bad *was* that other version of me, then?"

She shook her head. "Not someone I'd recognise," she finally answered, adding, "Definitely not you."

"How did Kay meet that other me?"

"Um, when she was me."

"You?"

"Yes, she's me grown up by twenty or thirty years."

"I can't even begin to understand how that can be possible."

"Believe me – you're not the only one."

Her grandad nodded and shut his eyes.

"Are you okay?"

"It's very tiring. All this remembering. I haven't had to do so much thinking for years. Couldn't. Wasn't able to."

Cassie rested her hand on his arm.

"You want another cuppa?"

"No, not right now, thank you, Cass."

"Will he be okay?" she asked the device.

"Unknown," it replied. "He is still very weak. It is possible that sleep may help rejuvenate him further and reverse the damage done by Laurence's repression."

"But you're not sure?"

"No."

"I think I'll take a nap now if you don't mind," her grandad muttered.

"Okay, you do that. I might go for a lie down myself."

"Hmm, yes," he agreed and, moments later, started snoring again.

Cassie bit her lip, hoping she'd done the right thing. She went back upstairs and laid back down on the bed.

"Don't wake me up for a couple of hours," she said to the device.

"There are only two minutes left," it responded.

"What?"

"Time stops at 11:31."

Cassie sighed and then had an idea. It was Saturday June the thirtieth. She'd been at school all day yesterday.

She concentrated and moved back to the twenty-ninth at just gone nine-thirty. She couldn't hear yesterday's mind-crippled version of her grandad moving around but sensed him in the house.

"Wake me up if anyone comes close, otherwise let me sleep until about two-thirty."

"I am not an alarm clock," the device responded.

"You are now," Cassie replied, shutting her eyes.

The Greatest Danger

"So, where is Kay in the greatest danger?" Cassie groggily asked a few minutes after she could no longer ignore the device shouting at her in her sleep. It was nearly a quarter to three and she vaguely remembered getting home from school that day at around three.

"The twelfth of August, 1995," the device responded.

"Where will that be?" she asked, still lying on the bed, her eyes closed.

"It was in the roof space of the Assembly House."

"That place near the Theatre Royal?"

"Correct."

Cassie hauled herself off the bed and straightened the cover. She didn't want her earlier self to know she'd been here. Not that she would, as she knew she hadn't realised herself. Then she wondered what would occur if she let her earlier self see her in a way that her current self didn't remember happening.

Is that even possible? Wouldn't it cause some sort of... er... oh, what's the word? It's on the tip of my tongue.

She shook her head, the correct word wouldn't come. So, instead, she asked, "What time of day will that be?"

"A few minutes before five in the afternoon."

"Didn't old Kay tell young Kay something about the Assembly House?"

"Yes, the exact quote was, 'The Assembly House in the nineties – weird one that, when we arrived the dumbo actually managed to string an almost coherent sentence together and insisted we'd only just left'."

Cassie found it completely disconcerting that the device mimicked Kay's voice accurately. It also made her wonder exactly who she was really hearing when it sounded like her mother. But, instead of questioning that, she said, "That doesn't sound like she was in much danger. Was Laurence there?"

"I hold in memory only one occurrence of being at that place and it does not contain the conversation relayed via Kay. Therefore I would conclude that the location holds two events, neither of which overlap, though, given the reported utterance of the dumbo, one may come directly after the other."

Cassie smiled to herself at the device's usage of 'dumbo' but was also conscious that it hadn't answered her main question. "Yeah, but was Laurence there?"

"In the occurrence of which I have the memory, the answer is yes, he was. However, my recollection of the event jumps alarmingly as if parts were not running at a consistent rate of time."

"What does that mean?"

"Unknown currently. But speculation that has arisen in connection with another recent occurrence may finally provide a resolution to something I have pondered on for many of your years."

"Eh? I have no idea what you're talking about!"

"My explanation was adequate though lacking in detail. I refer, of course, to the events in the Norwich Blitz where you required time to stop. Given that time cannot ever be stopped completely, it was sufficient to significantly slow down your perception of it so that it gave the appearance of almost being stopped."

"Oh, right. And you think that happens again?"

"It is possible. Though there may be other explanations."

"Did Laurence never do that, then?"

"No, though near the end of my time with him, he was beginning to suspect that time could be manipulated in multiple ways. And much further than he had already recently accomplished."

"Recently? What do you mean?"

"It was only his discovery of the use of the portals by yourself and Kay that led him to question me about the possibility of time travel."

"You mean he never did that in earlier lives?"

"No, the possibility never occurred to him. His path from his Denisovan origins was completely linear until then."

"You mean we are the reason he learned to time travel?"

"Yes. He did it because, in 2014, that chance encounter in Norwich with your grandfather resulted in him learning of his own death in 2000."

"Oh, so does that mean that every time we encountered Laurence was after he met Grandad?"

"Yes."

"What, even the octopus thing and then later in the folly?"

"Yes, except that, in his experience, the folly came first."

"Wait. Does that mean we don't meet him in the same order."

"Correct."

"What was he doing between 2000 and 2014?"

"Some of it was spent trying to break the protection your mother had me construct around your house."

"You mean he spent more than ten years trying to invade the house?"

"The number of attacks in total was less than twenty. They always failed so he would retreat for a time until he thought he had another method that might work."

"How was he attacking us?"

"Through me."

"You?"

"Yes. He ordered me to try many different methods. It was perplexing that every one I devised to break through the protection was defeated. Of course, when I came into the possession of your mother I knew how to counter the attacks as I was the one who had initiated them."

"Oh, so an earlier you was trying to fight the later you who already knew what attacks were coming so later you always won."

"Indeed."

"Neat. But why did he spend more than ten years at it?"

"He didn't. There were often months and even years between attempts. Much of his time was spent in Romania where he created a backup plan."

"Eh? What sort of plan?"

"He fathered another child who was born in 2005. This time it was a boy."

"Oh, so I have a half-brother?"

"Not any more. The mother, who was far closer to the paternal line than your own mother, committed suicide when she broke free of his control. She was able to access me and consequently learned what had been done to her. She also discovered what Laurence planned for the boy once he was old enough. Her mind couldn't handle it, so she abandoned both Laurence and her son. I learned later that she had deliberately walked out in front of an express train."

"Oh, my God!"

"So, the boy was raised for several years by Laurence. Then he became aware that the boy possessed several genetic aberrations, which meant he would not be suitable for Laurence's purposes."

"Genetic aberrations?"

"Yes. They are referred to in medical terms as Vascular Ehlers-Danlos syndrome – the mother was the carrier. He died in 2017 aged twelve."

"Oh."

"That is why Laurence renewed his attempts to procure you for his continuation."

"And why he appeared older to Mum when he died?"

"Correct."

"How old was he then?"

"The Laurence incarnation was fifty-eight years old at his apparent passing."

"How old was he when he killed Charlie?"

"Forty-seven."

"He didn't look it," Cassie said.

There was a noise from downstairs and she heard the front door being opened.

"Damn," she whispered. "That's earlier me back home." She switched to speaking to the device only with her mind. "What time was it that Kay was in the greatest danger?"

"Replaying those events in my memory suggest that the exact time you need to be at the location in question will be 16:52. Can you feel the location?"

Yes, the device was projecting the exact coordinates into her mind.

"Right, 16:52. Okay, ready or not. Let's go. Assembly House, August the twelfth, 1995. Roof space."

Cassie closed her eyes and…

"Mummy!" Cassie heard her own voice shout. Except that the voice had definitely not come from her own throat.

It took three seconds for her to take everything in. For the first second she thought the room was in complete darkness. By the next, her eyes had adjusted to realise that a dull green glow that arose from several distinct sources illuminated it just enough to make out the shape of the place. No, it wasn't a room – rafters angled up to a point above her head. It actually was a roof space. She could make out the dumbo sitting on the floor next to a faint glowing green orb. The dumbo was grinning, staring as if mesmerised by the light, her hands still tied together with rope.

By the third tick of the clock Cassie's eyes flicked in the other direction to rest upon ancient Kay, apparently unconscious and strapped down across a solid dusty table. Something in almost complete darkness beyond the table started moving.

"Hah!" came a deep roar. "The dumbo was right."

Laurence, Cassie thought, as her eyes brought him into focus. Even in the low light it was obvious he was far older than the version on the bus. Yes, he did look like he could be around fifty-eight. He lurched towards her from around the table that held Kay, his hands outstretched as if they sought to encircle Cassie's throat. Both Cassie and the dumbo screamed simultaneously. Cassie ran around the table attempting to keep it between herself and Laurence. He changed direction. She did the same.

Stalemate. They faced each other across Kay's prone body.

He's old, and I'm faster.

Laurence, possibly coming to the same conclusion, halted and raised both hands again. He aimed his fingers in her direction as if they were loaded. They were. She saw the green sparkling on his fingertips an instant before reflex took over. She dropped to the floor, rolling underneath the table as the crackle of emerald flame whooshed over her head. Behind her fire erupted as dust ignited.

She saw Laurence's legs start to come around the table yet again so she came out where he had been and looked on in horror as she heard Kay groan.

The flames from Laurence's hands, which Cassie thought had been aimed at herself, had instead bathed Kay in fire. She was still burning and was writhing in agony.

"Kay! No!" she shouted, desperately trying to think of how she could douse the flames.

She should neither have hesitated nor taken her eyes off Laurence. He was far faster than she realised. She felt his arms encircle her, his physical grip tightening as he pinned her own arms to her sides.

Then the mental onslaught began once more.

"Got you finally," he shouted. "I knew burning the old one would divert your attention long enough. This time you will not surprise me. I don't know where you got a second controller but you won't get the chance to use it this time."

"Kay," Cassie shouted but Laurence's influence started to encase her. This was totally unlike what he had attempted to do on the bus. He was not directly invading her nor was he trying to take over her body. Instead, he was isolating her from the world, not only restricting her ability to move physically, but also cutting her off from the device. She was conscious of it buzzing in her pocket but Laurence was attempting to place some sort of barrier between it and herself to prevent them communicating.

Around them the flames grew in intensity and Kay thrashed wildly and all Cassie could do was stare helplessly. The only part of her body that wasn't fully under his influence was her mouth.

"You're killing her," she stated. It came out as a dispassionate monotone. The effort it took to utter the words left nothing remaining to colour them with any hint of emotion.

"She and the young decoy no longer matter now that I have you," Laurence said. "And you are coming with me while they stay here to burn until there's nothing left but ashes."

Cassie felt Laurence begin to initiate the jump to another time and place. Under his control, she would be dragged along with him.

She had but one breath left.

Substitute

"Stop," she shouted, straining to connect to the device.

And, once again, time did stop. The flames that had begun to lick their way up the rafters stood almost unmoving, as did those that enveloped Kay's body.

Laurence, too, stood stationary. But with his fixation, her own immobility ended. She resisted the urge to hyperventilate as she felt the air thicken around her. Instead, she wriggled down and out of Laurence's grip and then stood to one side. Leaning against a piece of the roof that had yet to start burning she tried to figure out what to do for the best.

Looking at the table, it was obvious what required her most urgent attention.

"How do I save Kay?" she asked the device.

"Elements. The third element," came the reply.

"What?"

"Elements," the device repeated.

"Oh, you mean earth, air, water..." Laurence had made fire jump from his fingertips. "Water?"

"Yes."

"Then why didn't you just say? Oh, never mind. Tell me how?"

"As Laurence showed you."

"I have no idea how he did that. How can that even be possible?"

"You require an element to be present and use your hands to direct where that element should go. My ability to transform and move matter from one place to another provides the result."

"Oh. Okay. Just do it."

She aimed her fingers at Kay in the same way that Laurence had aimed his at her.

"Water. Please? Now!"

She was simultaneously amazed and appalled to see the fine mist that sprayed from her hands to cover Kay. She redirected her fingers and the mist turned into small jets that slowly started to douse the fire.

"Oh, thank goodness. It's really working. That's definitely you doing this, isn't it? Not me, surely?" she said to the device.

"Without me it cannot be achieved. You are the conduit that completes the process."

Another answer that tells me nothing, she thought to herself. It might as well be magic.

The flames continued their crawling flicker for several long seconds but the spray finally started to win and the fire diminished. After the last flame had died she looked aghast at Kay's face, her charred skin looked beyond healing. Surely, she was far too late.

But that wasn't her only problem. Beside her she was aware that Laurence was beginning to move. His face was slowly contorting, though at a rate that was faster than everything else apart from herself.

"He's fighting it, isn't he?"

"Yes," the answer came. "He became aware that something was wrong, but his mind was still working at the rate of real time."

"Was? Are you remembering that from before or working it out now?"

"I was, at that point in time, unaware of my dual presence here. Given that fact, I am shielding my earlier incarnation from detecting my current presence in order to reduce the possibility of confusion."

Cassie reminded herself that she should really stop asking questions that resulted in such answers.

Then the device continued, "Additionally, the ability to slow time was an unexplored capability. My previous incarnation was locked in normal time."

"When did you discover how to stop, er, slow time, then?"

"When you commanded it on Patteson Road."

"You mean that was the first time ever?"

"Yes. To prevent your immediate demise, I had to devise a method by which you could evade the falling destruction. The clue came from you calling out the words, 'Stop. Make it all stop,' so I used my abilities to manipulate time in a novel manner to alter your relationship with its progress, effectively making it appear to you that time itself had slowed down."

"So, that's nothing Laurence ever discovered for himself, then?"

"No."

"But is he figuring it out right now?"

"I detect he is becoming aware that something is wrong but he is also still in the process of transitioning to another place and time."

As when time had slowed in the Norwich Blitz, Cassie felt the effect starting to wear off. She needed to do something fast.

"Um, could I kill him here and now?"

There was a pause.

"That could be possible, but the chances of creating a – a –"

"A what?" Cassie thought it weird that the device appeared to be struggling to say something.

"A disruption or similar. I cannot determine the outcome of such an action. Given that his passing, whether fixed or not, is locked to another time and location, it would be an action with a high risk of failure or unforeseen repercussions. For example, if he dies here, then how do I get passed to your mother in 2000?"

"So, basically, no then."

"That is correct."

"Right, but I need to do something fast before Laurence regains the upper hand."

Ah, 'hand'. That gave Cassie an idea. She oozed across the roof space through the thick air and pulled the dumbo to her feet. It wasn't easy – she had to manually position the girl's limbs for each step to prevent her falling over.

"What is she? Is she real?" Cassie asked the device. To her surprise, it popped out of her jacket pocket to hover in the air before the dumbo. It then opened up and scanned the dumbo from head to toe with an emerald beam of light. Then it returned to her pocket.

"Analysis of her composition suggests that she is similar to the creatures Laurence brought into being for the purpose of serving him."

"What, like the nasties?"

"Correct. Though, physically, she is almost a clone of you, I find that the memories in her head are arranged in a non-standard fashion, as if she has been programmed with them all at once."

"Weird. Any idea why?"

"Not currently, though the process could be reproduced easily."

"Is Kay the same sort of, um, thing?"

"Similar in that she appears to have originated as a clone of yourself, but constructed with far more complexity."

"What? You mean she isn't human, then?"

"Questionable. By this planet's crude technology she would be indistinguishable from a naturally born person. I can, however, determine that her origin isn't natural."

"So, who made her?"

"Unknown."

"My Grandad said I shouldn't tell her about you. Does that mean she's a nasty?"

"I cannot determine the source of your grandfather's concern. However, Kay is not a 'nasty' as you refer to them, in the same manner that the creatures sent against you are."

"How are the nasties made?" Cassie asked as she continued to manhandle the dumbo towards Laurence's statue-like form.

"Laurence ordered them built. I complied."

"You made the nasties?"

"Indeed. Suitable matter can be brought in from elsewhere close by."

"What, like when the portals get powered by pee?"

"Similar, though powering a portal is a simple matter conversion while creating creatures from scratch requires far more complexity and time, especially when Laurence's desires were more detailed. It would be far easier creating those dumbos as they appear to be simple clones based on a version of yourself. Creating Laurence's creatures definitely involved far more work."

"But they were mostly rubbish."

"That has been a perplexing problem. His desires were carried out more than adequately but some as yet undetermined outside influence caused subsequent degradation. Every time I countered previous degradations, the next creatures generated would be degraded in a different, but unexpected manner."

So, Cassie thought to herself, *someone else is fighting the nasties.* Could it have been her mum in the last few months she had left?

With the dumbo positioned in front of Laurence, Cassie untied the girl's hands and manipulated her body into the gap between Laurence's arms that she'd earlier vacated. The jacket the dumbo wore was similar to her own but not identical. Hopefully, Laurence wouldn't have time to notice the difference.

"If I can't kill him then is there something I can do to make him stop trying to kill us?"

"If you did anything specific then I don't have a concrete memory of it. Nonetheless, I do recall that he did act quite strangely after this event. But, given that he subsequently ordered me to erase several of my own memories, I may have lost the reasons for that strangeness."

"Erased your memory? He could do that?"

"Yes."

"Is that something we could do back to him?"

There was a pause.

"Possibly. But it may not last – he may detect the discrepancies and find a way of reinstating the lost memories."

"But it could be worth a try, couldn't it? Can you make him forget about me and Kay? Totally?"

"The Laurence incarnation has spent much of his life attempting to capture you."

"So, no, then?"

"If such an attempt had been made then it could explain the erratic manner in which he acted in the period subsequent to this event."

Cassie grinned.

"Okay, do it then. Make it happen!"

Again, the device popped out of her pocket, opening up as it hovered in front of Laurence. Its green glow flowed over him for several seconds as Cassie was experiencing time.

"It is done," the device announced, snapping closed before returning to her pocket.

"Okay, let's let him go and see what happens."

She slid herself back under the table and, keeping an eye on the legs of Laurence and the dumbo, ordered the device to make time return to normal.

She breathed free-flowing air back into her lungs as a pop sound signified

Laurence's departure. Cautiously, she peeped out again to make sure he had really gone. There was no sign of the dumbo, either.

"What happened when he found out he had the dumbo?"

"He acted surprised as he had no concept of what she was. I now know that this was due to your request to erase his memory of you. He did quickly detect that she was a construction and, given that he had no idea of her purpose and as he knew he hadn't had me create her, he immediately obliterated her."

"Oh no!" Cassie cried, guilt pouring through her. If only she'd asked what had happened first. "And then what did he do?"

"Much has been lost though I believe he realised that he had been attacked in some fashion and requested that I should undo it."

"Did you?"

"I don't believe I could, for I had no knowledge of what had happened due to the time disruption we have created. I have a momentary recollection that he flew into a rage and afterwards I discovered that he made me erase portions of my own memory due to the gaps I could later detect. I do remember at the end that he still recalled the information that his own death would occur in 2000 but how it would occur was lost to him as he was no longer aware of yourself or Kay."

"Oh, Kay," Cassie groaned, standing up to look at her. The ancient version of herself was regaining consciousness and starting to whimper in pain. She also struggled against the straps that, although frayed and charred, still held her securely.

"Her face and hands are so burnt. Can you do anything?"

"Yes, but only through you. May I transfer the knowledge?"

"Yes, quickly."

A moment later Cassie passed her hands over Kay in a similar manner as when she doused the flames. The writhing subsided. Some sort of energy was being focused on Kay via Cassie's hands. The injuries were far from healed but the device had shown her how to take much of the pain away. Cassie tried to stroke Kay's head but only succeeded in knocking off burnt hair. Kay managed to lift her head a couple of inches revealing that the only hair she now had left was a few wisps around the back.

Eyeing up the spreading flames in the roof space, Cassie asked, "Can we put this fire out?"

"No."

"Why not?" Cassie asked while wrestling with the straps that held Kay down.

"It is another event fixed in history. Like the library."

"We can't stay here," Cassie said, as the roof space filled with smoke.

"Indeed. Especially as it is likely that Kay and the dumbo may turn up at any moment."

"Eh?"

Suddenly, Cassie heard Kay's voice in her head saying yet again, 'The Assembly House in the nineties – weird one that, when we arrived the dumbo actually managed to string an almost coherent sentence together and insisted we'd only just left.' However, the voice had come from the device.

"Oh, of course," Cassie said, as the last strap pinged free. "Where can I take her?"

"Unknown."

To The Batcave

Kay's eyes opened and her lips moved. She was trying to say something but no sound came from her burnt lips.

"I need to hear her," Cassie said.

"Listen to her mind, not her voice."

Cassie leaned closer. "How?"

Knowledge again filled her head. "Despite her origins, Kay is as much a part of you as you are a part of Kay. The connection is inherent. Now listen again."

Cassie attempted to make out what Kay was trying to say through lips that were not only burnt but split in several places. But she didn't hear any words. Instead, her head filled with images – mainly of a terraced house somewhere north of the city centre. Then the map appeared centred on one house in particular. Cassie leant across Kay and tried to slip her hands underneath her. Despite her emaciated body, Kay was far heavier than Cassie expected as she tried to lift her.

Probably all those coins in her pockets.

Unsure if it would really work, she willed them both to the place in Kay's mind. Cassie's ears popped as smoke was replaced by fresh air.

Kay started to fall from Cassie's arms but, spotting an old ragged sofa nearby, she managed to lower her onto its cushions before dropping her.

"Water," Kay rasped, forcing her eyes open.

Cassie scanned her new surroundings. Through a doorway she found a narrow kitchen that looked like something from decades ago. It was so sparsely equipped that the most advanced thing there was the ancient gas water heater on the wall. She located a glass tumbler in a wall cupboard and filled it with cold water from a tap. Holding Kay's head up, Cassie helped her sip the water. Kay's eyes closed again and her head dropped back onto a cushion. Cassie wasn't sure if she was unconscious or asleep.

She moved her hands over Kay once more, hardly understanding what it was she was doing but relieved to see Kay relax further.

"Can I heal her?" Cassie silently asked the device.

"Possibly, but she is weak. Laurence held her prisoner for days with only the occasional mouthful of water to drink, no food as far as I can tell."

"What? But you were there, weren't you?"

"Indeed. But my full memories of the events are far from complete and I suspect that the parts erased did not contain events where she was given food."

"He was torturing her?"

"The likelihood is high. But there are many gaps in my memories of that period."

"We should have turned up earlier? Why didn't we?"

"Your request was to encounter Kay at the point of her greatest danger. My earlier patchy memories of events determined that her being burnt by his flame was that point."

"Damn," Cassie spat, out loud. She'd asked the wrong question yet again. This was all her fault. She should, instead, have asked for the best time to rescue Kay uninjured.

Kay appeared to be asleep – at least she hoped that's what it was.

"Tell me how to cure her."

More knowledge inserted itself into her head but none offered the guarantee of full success – far from it. So Cassie picked a combination of several that seemed to offer the most relief. Once more she passed her hands over Kay's body and, while it was obvious that some form of healing was taking place, the physical improvements appeared minimal.

After about fifteen minutes it seemed she could do no more. The exposed skin of Kay's face and hands was no longer charred, it was merely blistered and flaking, but still far removed from what it should have been.

"Laurence will pay for this," Cassie vowed.

"Yes, he will. And soon," Kay whispered. "So, you finally turned up."

"Oh, I thought you were asleep or something."

"Well, I thought you were dead or something."

"Sorry. I asked the wrong question."

"Asked who what wrong question?"

Ignoring her grandad's advice, Cassie pulled the device out of her pocket.

"Oh, you've got one as well. I presume that's what Laurence was talking about back at the library."

"It's the same one."

"Wait. Did you have that all those years ago when we were on the bus?"

Cassie nodded.

"How?"

"Grandad. At the funeral. He told me not to tell you. I never figured out why."

Kay looked at her.

"Sorry," Cassie whispered after a moment of awkward silence.

"Not your fault," Kay said. "Laurence used it on me, trying to find out where you were. If I'd known you'd had it I might have revealed more to him. Oh, but it hurt so much."

"I wish I'd got there earlier."

"You got me out, though. Thank you. Are you sure you can control it?"

"I have to try."

Kay nodded and then croaked, "Well, this is it, then."

Cassie's brows furrowed.

"Oh, surely you've worked it out," Kay said, inspecting her burnt hands. They trembled as if she couldn't control them.

"What?" Cassie said, looking away, feeling guilty and responsible.

"Me, like this. What Mum said all those years ago. Probably just hours ago for you. Not that I've forgotten a word of what she said."

"I don't understand. What are you talking about?"

"Over there, on the wall," Kay said, weakly raising a hand a few inches.

Cassie's eyes followed Kay's pointing finger.

Above the fireplace a thin curved scabbard hung from a hook by a braided strap. The metal handle that poked out of the upper end of the scabbard showed that it was far from empty. Engraved on the handle was a symbol that might have been a stylised version of the letter K.

"What is it?"

"A scimitar – picked it up years ago. Practiced with it and made sure the blade was kept as sharp as possible."

"What for?"

"For cutting Laurence's head off, of course!"

Cassie smacked her hand to her forehead. It all made sense. Mum's description of the person who had killed Laurence fitted ancient Kay as she looked now. Cassie looked down at her – no wonder Mum had thought it had been a skinny man and not a woman.

"Wait, where will we get a motorbike from?"

Kay nodded towards a closed door – one directly across from the kitchen. Cassie opened it – she was at the bottom of a narrow staircase and another door stood opposite. She opened that, too. Sparsely decorated with a couple of unmatched dining chairs against a wall, the room space was primarily dominated by the motorbike in the centre. Not a modern one but looking like something manufactured years ago. The bike was immaculate, its chrome fittings and black paintwork gleaming in the sunlight that shone through net curtains that hid the bike from outside observation during the daytime. The thick red curtains hanging on both sides of the window would do the same at night if the light was on.

The bike stood on newspapers that were spread over most of the otherwise bare floorboards. Cassie ran her fingers over the chassis – she'd often dreamed of being able to afford a bike like this.

Reluctantly, she returned to the back room and asked, "Is that yours?"

Kay nodded.

"But how? And whose place is this anyway?"

"Mine. Bought it with money I made on bank interest."

Cassie frowned.

Kay coughed as she attempted to sit up. "More water, please," she croaked.

After refilling the tumbler she had to help Kay drink as her injured hands couldn't grip the glass well enough. As Kay took each sip, Cassie couldn't help comparing her with the version she'd first encountered in Castle Mall.

"That's a lot better," Kay said, at least sounding a bit more like her old self, even if she looked a long way from that. She inspected her hands once more. "What did you do? The feeling's coming back. Laurence had me strapped down so hard I couldn't feel them for a couple of days – not that I remember too much about it, thank goodness. He starved me, you know."

"The bastard. Yes, I heard."

"How?"

"The device thing. It told me – it remembers from when Laurence had it, though he ordered it to forget a lot of what he did to you."

"Figures," Kay grunted.

"You want more water, or anything else to drink? Could you manage something to eat?"

Kay sighed. "I feel shit. Though not as shit as I did. Whatever you did to me has fixed some of it." She inspected her hands further. "Not all of it, obviously. But enough to make me start feeling slightly peckish – maybe in a while we could have something to eat. If my cracked mouth will let me, that is." Kay winced as her hands explored the skin around her mouth. She raised eyebrows she no longer possessed and said, "Ooh, it's not quite as cracked as it was."

"So, you got anything here I can cook?"

"No, there's not likely to be much – I can never tell when I'm likely to be here so no point on stocking up any food. This place is really just a refuge. Whenever I lose a dumbo I avoid portals for a while and come here. Been doing it since my first trip to the library. You are pretty much the first person who's been here since

I bought it. And that was way back in the nineteen fifties."

"Well, that accounts for the state it's in."

"I only ever sleep here once in a while. It's mainly used for storing the bike. I bought that some time in the seventies."

"Is it safe? From the nasties, I mean?"

"It's weird, but I kept expecting them to come crawling all over the place – for some reason, they never did. The closest I've ever seen them is at the bottom of the road. It's a bit like the way they wouldn't come closer at Mum's funeral."

Cassie thought at the device, "Is something protecting this place?"

"Yes, there will be."

"Will be?"

"The protection extends back to when Kay purchased the property, but it has yet to be initiated."

"Eh? So, when will it start?"

"In a few minutes."

"Ah. Have I got to ask you to protect it in order for that protection to start?"

"Yes."

"Okay," Cassie thought. "Let me think."

"You've gone quiet," Kay stated, lying back on the sofa.

"I'm talking to the device about protecting this place. It told me it's protected right back to when you first got it but that it hasn't been set up yet."

"What? You mean it can do things backwards?"

"Yes, I think so. But it's really confusing. And I also need to think about how I ask it to start the protection before I do. I've made a few mistakes by not asking things in the best possible way."

"You mean it finds loopholes for getting things wrong?"

"Yeah, I'd say. I don't think it's deliberate but it doesn't seem to think like we do."

"It thinks?"

Cassie shrugged. "Mum was right – there is something like a person in there." Cassie decided not to mention that something of their mother and great grandfather might also be in there as well.

"Okay, I'll leave you to it. I definitely need to shut my eyes for a while anyway."

Kay did so and, while Cassie was thinking about how to ask about the protection, she passed her hands again and again over Kay's prone form. As she did so, she was sure that some sort of energy transferred from herself to Kay.

I really hope it helps.

After a few minutes she decided she'd got as far as she could with how she was going to ask the device for the protection. She swallowed and directed her thoughts at it.

"Please protect this house from the date Kay bought it up until she or I no longer have any use for it. Protect it from any unwelcome intrusion from outside and from any damage from either inside or outside. Always allow Kay and myself to enter whenever we need to, especially if we are in danger. Preserve the house as it is until ordered differently by myself."

"The protection has been initiated," came the reply.

Cassie let out a sigh, hoping she'd asked for everything correctly.

The Last Chip Supper

"What year are we in?" Kay asked when she woke about an hour later.

Cassie, sitting beside her on the sofa, asked the device and then reported, "1995. August the twelfth."

"Same as the Assembly House, then," Kay said, sitting up unaided and stretching. "Oh, look – my hands are a lot better. How's the rest of me?"

"Still rather crispy around the edges, I'm afraid," Cassie said.

Kay grinned. "But possibly just about good enough to handle a motorbike."

Cassie slowly nodded, even though she thought Kay looked far from capable.

"So, how exactly did you afford this place?"

"At the library I gave my earlier self the address on a piece of paper. It also had instructions on how to keep moving money back into the past in order to accumulate enough to buy it outright. I'd already been tinkering with moving money around, anyway."

"Oh yes. I remember seeing you handing the paper over."

"Yeah. You were hiding there, weren't you!"

Cassie nodded.

"And then only popped your head out at the last moment."

"Sorry, I wasn't sure what to do. It was confusing seeing you twice, along with a dumbo tied up with rope as well."

"Okay, I sort of understand. But I was pretty narked when I caught a glimpse of you after not seeing you for years."

Cassie changed the subject, "But, this place – it must have cost tens of thousands?"

"Nope, cost less than two thousand back in the early fifties."

"Is that all?"

"Yeah, inflation went mental in the seventies and early eighties. Houses in the fifties cost less than cars do in our time. So, I bought the place."

"How? With cash?"

"Bank account set up in the nineteen forties, just after World War two – they asked far less questions back then. Anyway, one of the things I noticed the first time I was here were bank statements. My first time was in 2016 – yeah, I know – my first time here is still in the future. But the bank statements showed when money had been paid in. Lots in the early years with only occasional payments in later years. Withdrawals went the other way – lots more coming out the nearer to 2018 it got. Very few before that – apart from buying the house in the fifties and the motorbike in the seventies."

"Who was doing the paying in and taking out, then?"

"I was. Any time I found myself back in the forties or fifties I'd pop some more money in – only the valid currency for that year, of course. Any cash from later I'd dump upstairs and use when I was here in later years. You remember my pouches of money?"

Cassie nodded yet again.

"I started carrying as much early currency as possible and always used it to pay in when I could. I'd buy small things with notes and, when the opportunities arose, took the coins back in time when they were worth more and pay them in. It was weird – sometimes a cashier would say something to younger me like, 'Oh, your mum paid some in the other day' or 'You don't half look like your daughter, you know,' when it was older me."

"Didn't they suspect anything?"

"Maybe, maybe not. I think banks are generally just happy to get your money. I'm really quite rich, you know. Not that you'd think so, looking at this place."

"Where did the original money come from?"

"Sometimes I'd pick up small items–"

"What, steal them?"

Kay shrugged. "At first a few times. Oh right, I remember – you never stole anything, did you?"

"Needs must," Cassie mumbled.

A fleeting grin passed across Kay's healing lips. "Actually, most of the money was made buying things like rings and jewellery and collectables for peanuts in the past and then selling them in later years for rather a lot more. I even set up an eBay account to get rid of stuff. The money made from it was filtered back to the past and re-deposited."

"Too confusing," Cassie said with a sigh. Trying to get her brain around it was giving her a headache.

"Yeah, tell me about it. Actually, yes, tell me a bit about what's been happening with you since the bus."

Cassie did so.

"Hah, I see what you mean about it getting things wrong," Kay said when Cassie related going to the wrong August the first. "That's almost hilarious."

"It wasn't at the time," Cassie snorted.

"I bet," Kay cackled. "Hah. That's not a date you're going to forget easily, is it?"

"Absolutely."

"Yeah, you'd better not."

"Eh?"

"Nothing important. Actually, I'm starting to feel quite hungry now."

"Can I get you something?"

"Yes, definitely."

"What then?"

"Right, go upstairs into the back bedroom and get a few quid out from a 1995 bag. Ignore the separate pile of old pound coins near the window – they're all fakes."

After climbing the stairs Cassie peered into the front bedroom. Apart from the single bed, the only other things in the room were a few clothes, mostly all black, scattered over the tatty carpet.

By contrast the floor of the back bedroom was covered in a multitude of money bags, each with a year written on it. The dates on the bags ran from the late 1930s near the doorway right up until 2018 across in front of the window. Some years were represented by a pile of more than ten bags. Off to one side was a small pile of the older round one pound coins. They were dumped against the skirting board. These had to be the fakes. Cassie picked one up and examined it – to her it looked identical to those she'd last seen a year before. She tossed the coin back on the pile.

A small desk in one corner held eight ring binders. Cassie stepped over the bags from the 1960s to get to the desk and picked up a binder. It had 1970-1979 written by hand on the spine and, inside, it was packed with bank statements. Some of the ones from the earlier years looked as if they were done on a typewriter. Those from the binder marked 1940 even contained hand-written entries in a style that Cassie had never used for herself. So she assumed they weren't done by Kay, either.

She shook her head as she stood amongst the piles of money bags, trying to take it all in. There must have been thousands of pounds lying at her feet. It was a good job the protection spell she'd asked for prevented any intrusion. She chuckled at inadvertently referring to it as a 'spell'. But what she'd asked for was indistinguishable from magic, so 'spell' was as good a word as any.

Cassie picked up one of the dozen or so bags labelled 1995 and pulled out several coins along with a ten pound note.

Returning to the ground floor, she asked, "What should I buy and where?"

"There's a chip shop a few roads away. Hold on, I'll draw you a map – if I can get my fingers working, that is. There's some paper and a pen over there on the table in front of the window."

Cassie smiled properly for the first time in quite a while. Chips! Now *that* was more like the old Kay. She picked up several sheets of A4 paper and the pen, and handed them to Kay who, with shaking hands, created a map that was just about readable.

On the way back from the chip shop with two helpings of fish and chips, some bread rolls, a couple of cans of drink and a surprising amount of change from the ten pound note, something was nagging at the back of Cassie's mind. It was the paper that old Kay had passed to young Kay in the library that contained the address and house buying instructions. From the paper and bank statements young Kay had learned how to save and bank the money that allowed her to buy the house so that she could then write the instructions to hand to her younger self when they met up. So, where had the idea for buying the house actually come from in the first place? By the time she reached the house again, her head was spinning from trying to work it out.

Inside, she found that Kay had managed to struggle to her feet and take a few steps.

"That smells good," Kay said. They sat down next to each other on the sofa and stuffed the food down themselves. Kay took three times longer than Cassie as eating was still quite awkward for her.

"Been quite a while since we did this," Kay said.

"Yeah, yesterday," Cassie said, between mouthfuls.

"When was that?"

Cassie frowned. "Damn, I'm losing track."

"You should try doing it for years on end."

"Oh yes. Back of the market. On the way to Mum's funeral."

"Short cuts," Kay said, shaking her head. "Feels like more than ten years for me since then. I really envy you."

"Sorry. If I knew how to stop it, I would."

Kay nodded agreement. "Yeah, I know. But it will soon be at an end. Mum said that I die after cutting Laurence's head off. About bloody time, too. Something to finally look forward to," Kay said without a hint of morbidity.

Cassie swallowed. She didn't want to think about it.

"Well," Kay said, after she'd finished. "We need to get to, um – when was it Laurence died?"

Cassie thought for a moment. "I think it might have been November or December 2000. I don't think Mum ever gave us an exact date."

"You'd better ask *it*, then."

Cassie sighed and did so. "December the fifth."

"Right, what time?"

"In the afternoon, didn't Mum say?"

"You'd better check."

Cassie did so.

"And we need to find the bus man as well as his bus," Kay added.

"Yeah," Cassie said, wondering how they were supposed to contact him. Was he in the device or somewhere else? "Any idea how?"

"No," Kay said frowning, causing the skin of her forehead to crack slightly. "Ow," she spat, gently tapping at her head. "I need moisturiser. Lots of it."

"Do you have any?"

"There might be some in the bathroom – through there," Kay nodded towards the kitchen. "It isn't always stocked up."

Cassie went through the kitchen and the strange double-door arrangement that led to the cramped bathroom. The place smelt damp and musty. A wall cabinet with a dirty mirror was the only possible place that could hold what she was after. It was empty.

"When does this cupboard have moisturiser in it?" she said to the device.

"Unknown," came the reply. "I have never been here before."

Cassie made the device note the current date and exact time. Then she moved forwards a few years, and then a few more. The cabinet remained stubbornly empty. Cassie moved back into the past until she found a time when there were things in the cabinet. The device told her it was the late fifties.

"But isn't this a modern tube of moisturiser?" she asked, after locating an unopened packet.

"Indeed."

Cassie shrugged and, after making use of the facilities, returned to 1995, reappearing three seconds after her departure time.

"I found some," she said, handing it over.

"Oh, that was lucky," Kay said.

"Not really. But you might have noticed some disappear back in the fifties."

"Ah, right. I always wondered where that went."

Kay applied a liberal coating to her head and face until her damaged skin glistened.

"So, are you sure you're ready for this?" Cassie asked, as Kay rubbed the last of the tube's contents into her hands and wrists.

Kay nodded and whispered, "Yeah, let's get it over and done with. Take us to 2000."

Cassie took her hand, trying to ignore the feel of Kay's injuries against her own flesh.

The Last Bus Into Town

"Ooh, it feels different to a portal," Kay said as they arrived in exactly the same place.

"Yes, and it doesn't screw your hair up."

Kay, still looking exhausted, slumped down on the sofa. "Yours is still frizzy, though."

"Hmm, though that's a lot to do with when I landed in a swimming pool a few hours ago."

Cassie gave Kay a quick run down of events since she'd been at the library, though she omitted telling how she'd gone home and encountered Grandad again.

"What's the time?" Kay asked, glancing at the ancient wind-up clock that sat on the mantelpiece below the sword. It was stopped.

"Just gone five to two," Cassie reported after consulting the device.

"So, that gives us around half an hour to find the bus man, get to the hospital where Mum is and chop off Laurence's head."

"You make it sound simple," Cassie said.

"But we're going to have to do it because, if we don't, then the bus man won't be able to give Mum the device, so that you end up with it, which means you won't have been able to rescue me and bring us here to right now in order to do it in the first place."

"Hell, stop it! I find all this confusing enough in the first place without one of your explanations!"

Kay ignored her and added, "Well, if we don't make it happen then does that mean Laurence gets to live? And will that mean lots of stuff we've both done will get – what – nullified? Is that the right word?"

Cassie sighed and went through to the front room. The motorbike was still there, though it was parked in a different position. Also, this time, there was a crash helmet positioned on the seat.

"Looks like it's all ready for you."

"Yes," Kay said, hobbling into the room and leaning on the door frame. In one hand she carried the sword in its scabbard. "Any time I found myself here in 2000 I took the bike out for a run to make sure it was in full working order and topped up with petrol. Of course, by 2001 the bike was no longer here."

"What do your neighbours think about you having the bike in the front room?" Cassie said, finding the situation completely surreal and wanting to divert her mind from what they were about to do.

"Oh, there's an old git on one side – okay, he was a young git when he moved in back in the seventies. But, in the early days, he was always poking his nose in and trying to find out what was going on here – chatted younger me up a few times. Then I caught him trying to get in the back door some time in 1984 when he thought I wasn't around. I don't think I'd been in the place for several weeks but I had arrived late the previous night after losing yet another dumbo. I'd already unlocked the door a few minutes earlier as I needed to take some stuff out to the bin, so he crept in. He didn't notice me until I grabbed him and body slammed him to the floor. Nearly broke his fingers, but I was a lot younger that time. He said he'd tell my mother that I'd attacked him. I was recently back there in 1984 again, probably only a day or two later. I said good morning to him and he started spluttering about going to the police and accusing my daughter of beating him up. I told him if he did I'd report him for attempted burglary. I also told him that me and my daughter were the same person and that I was a time travelling witch. Then I leered at him and said that next time I caught him snooping around I'd turn him into a frog and break all four of his legs as well."

Cassie chuckled. "What about the place on the other side?"

"Rented as far as I can tell. It's often empty."

"Hah. Maybe the tenants don't like living next door to a witch," Cassie said. Kay's burnt face broke into a grin, the even whiteness of her teeth a contrast to the flaking, raw skin surrounding them.

"Damn, stop making me smile. It hurts," Kay said, looping the strap of the scabbard over her head and positioning the sword on her back. She hauled herself across to the bike and pulled the helmet on, leaving some wispy white hair poking out the back. "How do I look?" she asked.

"Deranged," Cassie said, after a moment's thought.

"Excellent, just what the assassin ordered."

Then Kay sighed. "Cass, to be truthful, I'm not sure I've got the energy for this. This bike is heavy. I need to be really fit to ride it." Her eyes dropped. "I don't want this to fail. I want an end to it now before I change my mind. I've got to end it, once and for all. I can't go on living like this."

Cassie felt the blood draining from her face. Talking about mad and not-present neighbours was just avoiding thinking about what they were planning to do. She shut her eyes and said to the device, "Give Kay the strength to do this."

"A temporary blockage to the pain receptors in her head is advised," it replied.

"Yes, just do it," Cassie silently ordered. "Make it last until Laurence is dead."

"The length of the effect cannot be guaranteed. Aim your hands at Kay," it said as Cassie felt something flow from the device, through her hands and then out to Kay.

"Oh," Kay gasped. "I see."

"It says it's temporary. Not sure how long it'll last."

"Long enough, I hope," Kay said, and then added, "Ah, here he is." She nodded to the window and Cassie could see the weak winter sun reflecting off the bus that was drawing up outside.

Cassie opened the front door and stepped out into the tiny unkempt front garden. The bus man nodded at her as Kay kicked the bike into life. A movement to her left caught her eye – the curtains in the neighbour's window twitched.

She opened the front gate, standing to one side while Kay negotiated the bike through it, out between the parked cars and onto the road. There was a roar as

Kay opened the throttle and the bike, its ridiculously skinny passenger perched precariously atop it, hurtled away along the narrow road.

Returning to the front door Cassie slammed it shut. While pulling the gate closed, she glanced back at the neighbour's window to see the curtain drop into place. *Nosy bastard,* she thought. Guessing he was still watching her, she tapped her nose whilst making a face in his direction.

Then, as the sound of Kay's bike receded, she climbed aboard the bus.

"Today's the day, what do you say?" Charlie said as he crunched the bus into gear and started off. "Not feeling so sad about your slimy old—"

"Hi, Great Grandad," Cassie said, cutting him off. "How did you know to turn up at this time?"

"Day of reckoning was beckoning. Magic box made Charlie's feet itch in his socks. And girlies two have a rendezvous for slicing and—"

"Yeah, whatever," she said, cutting him off for a second time. She was still trying and failing to put what was about to happen to the back of her mind.

She went to sit right at the rear of the bus, though avoiding the seat where Laurence had pinned her down in 1968. Charlie was still spouting rubbish but she couldn't hear him over the sound of the engine, thank goodness.

"Are we going the right way?" she shouted several minutes later. After climbing Grapes Hill and turning right she had expected the route to go along Earlham Road to head out to the hospital on the western outskirts of the city. Instead, the bus man took them along Unthank Road instead.

"Hospital new is still to appear. Hospital old is your Daddy's fear."

Cassie frowned, trying to remember when the new hospital had opened. Was it before or after when she was born? But she still didn't understand why they were going along Unthank Road – wasn't the old hospital on Saint Stephen's Road? The bus continued along until they reached the ring road. It turned left and then left again at the roundabout that took them back towards the city along the Newmarket Road.

"There's Kay," Cassie said as they approached the junction with Mount Pleasant. She watched Kay wait until the bus had passed her before she fell in behind it. Cassie's heart was thumping and she knew they were only minutes away from killing her father.

Suddenly, Charlie shouted, "Tricky trap, green gap, it's—"

A flash of green hit the bus, causing it to lurch, throwing Cassie from her seat. Then the bus became transparent and insubstantial, and Cassie fell through the floor. She landed on rough grass at speed and rolled several feet before coming to a halt against a bush. Behind her she heard the sound of Kay's motorbike screeching to a halt.

She sat up and checked herself. Apart from a graze on the back of one hand she appeared to be intact. She looked around and gasped – where the hell had Norwich gone? Instead, her surroundings were trees and rough fields, though the timber-frames of a few small, ramshackle buildings were visible between the bushes.

"What happened?" Cassie gasped.

"So, you didn't do this, then?" Kay said, pulling off her helmet.

"No, of course not. Where are we?"

"More like when. Take a look over there," Kay said pointing past some trees.

Cassie got to her feet and stared in the direction Kay indicated. "Is that the castle?"

"Yes, and if you look along this track there's a rather large wall between the castle and us."

"Oh my goodness," Cassie said. "Is that the city wall, as it used to be?"

"Could be. That's probably Saint Stephen's Gate."

Cassie stared at the construction – at the two substantial round towers and the wooden gate between them.

"What date is this?" she asked the device aloud.

"Julian or Gregorian convention?" it responded.

"I don't know! Just give me the damned year!"

"Fifteen, forty-nine," it said.

Appointment With a Beheading

"How did we get here?" Cassie shouted.

"One of the last acts Laurence required me to perform was a time transference from a distance, the details of which he ordered to be erased from my memory upon completion. However, I did retain the knowledge of its creation so I would estimate that what you have just experienced was the result of that action."

"What did it say?" Kay asked.

Cassie frowned, having forgotten that only she could hear the device. She repeated what it had told her.

"Ah, delaying tactics. I don't think Laurence is looking forward to meeting us," Kay said. "Well, this is definitely the furthest back I've ever been. None of the portals ever came back anywhere as early as this. Can you get us back to 2000?"

"I don't know. I suppose so. Maybe the device can."

"Well, any time now would be good, before I keel over."

"Oh, sorry," Cassie said. She looked at Kay, at the blotchiness of her scorched face, and wondered how long she could hold up. She contacted the device and asked if it could reverse the process and take them back to a point a couple of seconds after they'd been transported. Much to her relief, it agreed to guide them back, saying that it could retrace the energy source back to the future. Cassie wasn't sure what would have happened if it had said she'd have to do it on her own. It might have taken her far too long, given the state of Kay.

"Okay," Cassie said. "We need to hold hands."

"Sounds familiar," Kay said, with a lop-sided grin. "Getting your own back?"

Cassie returned the grin.

Kay placed the helmet back over her head, gripped the motorbike handlebar with one hand and held Cassie's hand in the other. There was a fuzzing sensation and they were flung apart. Cassie thought something had gone wrong until she realised she'd been put back on the bus leaving Kay on the motorcycle behind.

Charlie's voice made her jump. "Back with us, not a second to spare. Daddy trying to prevent Charlie ever collecting his fare! More green, to be seen, where we've gone and where we've been."

Ahead of the bus, as it trundled along Newmarket Road, there were sheets of green somethings hanging in the air blocking their path. More traps from Laurence, Cassie knew. But what were they?

There was no avoiding them. They hit one and time slowed down like it had in the blitz. But, this time, it wasn't Cassie's doing.

"Do something," she shouted to the device. "Get rid of it!"

She felt a pulse of energy spurt from the device in her pocket and the sheet of green shattered. There was other traffic around but they seemed completely unaware and unaffected by what Cassie could see. It was as if they were only partially in the same reality as everyone else on the road. Another sheet of green turned them completely around facing the traffic coming towards them. It lasted a split second, defeated by another pulse from the device.

"Who's making these?" Cassie demanded. "You or Laurence?"

"Laurence," it answered. "My energies were partially drained in the initial time transference but mostly by the subsequent forgetting. I have no recollection of doing anything more of significance until after I was passed to your mother."

"Where is he getting the power from?"

"He has long had the ability to pervert any form of matter, converting it to his own requirements, providing it wasn't too large."

"How did he learn that?"

"From me. I taught him as I have begun teaching you. It is something you may fully develop for yourself with practice."

"I don't know if I want to," Cassie said, with a shudder.

Another flash of green and Cassie felt as if something was trying to tear both the bus and herself to shreds. A wave of agony cascaded through her body for what might have been only a couple of seconds but felt like far more. Then it subsided. Presumably, it also hit Kay but Cassie was too busy gasping to have time to look.

"How many more?" she asked. There were still several sheets before them. "They all look the same."

"Four and, yes, he disguises their intention using commonality."

The next attack was a freezing drop in temperature which the device countered in less than a second. She glanced out the back window to see Kay wobbling on the bike but, to Cassie's relief, Kay managed to keep it upright.

"Are they getting easier to defend against?"

"Laurence's expenditure appears less on each one we face. Countermanding them demands less effort each time."

"So, we can definitely beat him, then?"

"Indeed. He is getting desperate knowing his time is near and realising he cannot prevent your arrival. He is also confused as he doesn't completely understand how and where the attack will be carried out. That was due to your request to erase from his memory all recollections of yourself and Kay."

"Oh yes. Didn't Mum also say that he still thought she was having a baby boy?"

"Indeed. But when he learned that you were female, something started breaking through as he then recalled that he had already known that."

The next sheet set everything shaking – the vibrations threatening to burst Cassie's eardrums. She screwed her eyes up and clamped her hands to her ears. Within a second things were back to normal.

"Two more," Cassie whispered, checking again to see that Kay was still upright on the bike. "How do you know what he was thinking?"

"Although mostly inactive by this point, I was aware that he was expending energy whilst attempting to remain outwardly normal for the benefit of your mother. Despite that, I was still in connection with him to the extent that his surface thoughts and intentions were clear."

"Here we go again."

Cassie found herself floating and giddy, as if drunk or suffering from vertigo. She gripped the seat in front fighting the nausea – the fish and chips from earlier on were threatening to eject themselves from her stomach. Her hands were now over her mouth and, when she thought she could no longer prevent herself being sick, everything returned to normal.

"Oh hell, that was a bad one. I thought he was supposed to be getting weaker! At least there's only one more."

The final sheet of green splashed around the bus and oozed into the interior through any crack and crevice it could find. Cassie screamed as it coalesced into an array of all the nasties previously encountered, and they were all streaming towards her.

"Get them off me," Cassie shouted as her fists lashed out. She punched a hole in the face of one of the things that had chased them from the old library to Debenhams. It was immediately replaced by an assemblage of mismatched body parts that resembled the creature that had first freaked her out in Castle Mall.

Then they were all around her, their hands and other appendages flowing over her body, their combined grip limiting her movement.

"Help!" she screamed at the device, but there was no answer. Then one of the myriad faces swam into view right before her eyes. Laurence – even though it was almost distorted beyond normal recognition, that nose and small moustache gave it away. He wrapped octopus tentacles around her and dragged her from the bus to a different time and place. They tipped over and Cassie found herself on her back with writhing slime enveloping her body. The place was dark, dingy and damp, her nose regaled with a heady mix of disgusting odours.

But she recognised the smell immediately and knew exactly where she was – back under Earlham Road in the chalk caves.

"No!" she shouted, and willed herself away, up to road level, and into daylight. There was the blare of a horn as a taxi swerved to avoid her. She leapt onto the pavement but the nasties were already starting to ooze up out of the ground. Many of them looked like distorted clones of Laurence. Did he now fully remember her?

She turned and tried to run back towards the city, bumping into several real people who swore at her. But the nasties were on her again.

"Where are you?" she shouted to the device as she felt something entangle her legs but it remained silent. She fell forwards, raising her arms to prevent her face hitting the pavement. But, there was no impact. Instead, she found herself hauled under the surface, just as they had done to that dumbo outside the Guildhall.

She shut her eyes as they pulled her deeper underground, through earth that felt like a swamp. She tried to kick back at the things that dragged her down but her feet encountered nothing.

Wait – why am I fighting? In her panic, she'd forgotten the easiest way to get out of there. She concentrated and willed herself back onto the bus. With a pop, she was there.

So was the device – it was lying on the floor. It must have been knocked away from her – or had the nasties deliberately tried to take it from her? But there were no more nasties and Charlie was still driving the bus. She looked out the back window, relieved to see Kay still on the motorbike behind.

They passed through some traffic lights and Cassie saw the old hospital, its two towers – long gone in her own time – against the December sky. The bus slowed to a halt leaving a large gap in front of them as the traffic ahead continued towards the Saint Stephen's Street roundabout.

This was it, then.

Cassie staggered to the front of the bus.

"Stay down, girlie. Mummy doesn't see you here with your hair. But, surely, there you are, all tucked inside her, in her care."

Charlie pointed ahead of them.

"What?"

Then Cassie saw her mother on the pavement with Laurence, just as Rebecca had described it. How much did he realise was about to happen? Surely, he must have known something – he had been trying to stop it from occurring. He glanced in their direction and Cassie let out a squeak as hundreds of green arrows shot in their direction. Without being asked, the device erected a barrier of some sort and the arrows vanished. Behind them she heard Kay honk the bike's horn and rev the engine before shooting past.

Cassie held her breath as Kay aimed the bike directly at Laurence. The bus man floored the accelerator to follow.

Kay screeched the bike to a halt behind Laurence, one hand already reaching for the sword on her back. In a single motion, the sword slipped from its scabbard and swung in its fatal arc. Cassie flinched and then it was done. Laurence's head was no longer attached to his body. Kay dropped the sword and revved the bike engine up to a scream. With a whoop she raised one fist, and raced off towards the site of that gateway they'd seen only minutes ago and several hundred years earlier.

Charlie hit the brakes and, as soon as the bus had come to a halt, punched the button to open the doors. He jumped out of the driver's seat and leapt down from the bus. Cassie glanced out the window looking for where Laurence's head had got to before remembering her mum describing its fate under the wheel of the bus. The thought that it was right beneath her at that moment made her legs turn to jelly. She sunk down onto a seat, keeping her head low to avoid being seen by anyone outside. She couldn't see Charlie but knew he was rummaging in Laurence's jacket pocket. Then she saw him stand up and hand the package containing the device to her mother.

After whispering in her mum's ear, he got back on, closed the doors and grinned at her. "At long last, it's elementary – our final destination's the cemetery. The moment comes with a need for speed. Cassie must drive to stay alive."

"What are you talking about? I can't drive!"

"No time to spare. Magic us there!"

"Oh yes," she said and concentrated. *But can I move this entire bus?*

She gripped the back of a couple of the seats on each side of the central aisle and closed her eyes.

"Yeeow!" she shouted as the entire bus wrenched itself from outside the hospital to Bowthorpe Road.

Damn, if I'd known I could do this it may have made getting to the hospital far easier. Too late to think about that now.

She looked out the window. Charlie was driving again and they approached one of the Earlham crematorium gates – the same one she and Kay had exited after her mum's funeral.

The bus halted with a squeal and, once the door hissed open, Cassie jumped down and looked around.

"Is Kay here?"

Charlie remained in the driver's seat.

"Are you coming, Charlie?"

He shook his head.

"Oh no. Time to go, this is it for all I know."

"What? You can't leave me!" Cassie cried.

"Yes, I can. This is the last thing I do. And I do it for you, Cass. I did everything for you and your mum. Look after your grandad."

"No, don't go!" she shouted, trying to get back on, but her hands passed through the bus like she was trying to catch a cloud.

"Yes. Oh, and remember," Charlie's voice said, sounding as if it was coming from a long way away.

"What?"

"The only way to end it is—"

"Charlie!" she shouted.

Cassie was left standing on her own.

Kay Backup

Now what do I do? And where's Kay?

Trying not to cry, she ran into the cemetery, her eyes darting in all directions for her alternative self but there was no sign of her. *Could Kay be on the other side of the crematorium building?* Cassie thought, before running in that direction.

She was about half way there when the sound of a motorbike engine roared into earshot behind her. She spun around in time to see Kay scream into the cemetery, momentarily slowing to pass through the same gate she had used less than a minute before. The bike thundered towards her but, after a few yards and without any warning, it veered sideways and left the pathway. As it hurtled through the gravestones it hit several, the last of which caused the bike to tip over. It slid along on its side, with Kay still attached, before smashing into a tree.

Cassie screamed Kay's name and ran towards the wreckage. Smoke billowed from the bike but, just as she was about to approach it, flames erupted and forced her back.

"No!" Cassie screamed, holding her hands out. "Water! Give me water," she demanded. Two streams gushed from her fingertips as they had done in the Assembly House. At first, the intensity of the fire resisted her onslaught. She closed the distance to the burning bike and passenger, willing even more water from her hands. The flames persisted for the best part of half a minute but, finally she saw she was making progress and, before twenty more seconds had passed, they were extinguished.

"Kay," Cassie sobbed, dropping to her knees beside the shattered body of her older incarnation. She forced the bike helmet visor up – it was distorted and cracked – and stared inside, her heart in her mouth.

Kay opened one eye, the other didn't look capable of opening. "Cass," she croaked. "We did it. It's over."

"What happened? Why did you crash?"

Kay's responses came in ragged gasps. "Dunno – it's a blank – no energy – finished – they're after me – sixty all the way down Grapes Hill – always wanted to do that."

"I can save you."

"No – don't – what I was made for."

"No, no!"

"Don't want to live any more – no reason – let me – let me go."

Kay's one eye closed.

"Save her!" Cassie demanded of the device.

"The body is beyond recovery. It may be possible to make a new one."

"What? How?"

"The contents of the memory may be recovered and stored."

"Just do it. Do anything you can."

That familiar green oozed from the device and encompassed Kay's body – the same shade of green Cassie had seen so many times before, whether facing it as part of an attack, or directly associated with the device itself.

After a few seconds it was complete, and the green luminescence retreated back to the device.

"Oh my God. What's happening to her?"

Before Cassie's eyes, what remained of Kay turned to ash and started blowing away. Cassie let out several huge sobs and curled up beside the still smouldering wreckage of the bike.

But she wasn't to be left grieving for long. She heard the sound of police sirens in the distance and they were getting closer. She was also conscious of movement back at the crematorium building. It was followed by shouting and the sound of running footsteps approaching.

"Damn, why can't they leave me alone?" she said and then, her voice cracking, "Goodbye Kay."

She stood up. Two men and a woman were running towards her. She stepped behind the tree, keeping it between them and herself.

"Where can I go?"

There was no reply from the device.

Anywhere will do. She no longer cared where she went.

She closed her eyes and willed herself away to a different time and place.

There was heat on her face and she opened her eyes to find herself on top of the Castle walkway. Had she intended coming here? There was a noise beside her.

"Back again, Cass?"

She jumped at the closeness of the voice and saw the ghostly form of Robert Kett appear and become more solid.

"When am I?" she asked the device.

"June the thirtieth, 2018," it replied. "The time is 11:23."

"Oh," she said.

"Things falling into place, yet?" Kett said to her.

"What things? What do you mean?"

"Future you has got it all sewn up, I reckon, given what she's just done."

"Huh?"

"Over there," he said. Cassie looked to where he indicated. Standing on the walkway on the far side of the castle was herself.

"Oh right. I'm back here again, am I?"

"You're the one driving, so you should know," Kett said, with a grin.

"No, I don't think I know anything. Kay's dead and I have no idea what to do next."

"Really?" Kett said. "I think you will beg to differ."

"Me? What?"

"You'll work it out," the other, future Cassie shouted across to her.

"See what I mean?" Kett added.

"Oh."

"Your future self has confidence in your ability."

"I hope so," Cassie said.

"So do I," Kett said.

"Wait, if she's there then does that mean…?"

Her eyes scanned to the right of future Cassie. And there she was again. "Yes. That's me the first time I was here, isn't it?" she said.

"You should know, girl."

Future Cassie turned and faced across to past Cassie and, after a moment's pause, said, "Oh yes, and so will you. All I need to say at this point is have a short breather and then find Kay before Laurence kills her."

"Right," Cassie said, watching her future self disappear. "I think I see."

"Oh," Robert Kett said. "One more thing."

"What?"

"The only way to end it is–"

"To start it," Cassie finished for him.

"Go and do it then," he said.

"Right," Cassie said, and shrugged. "I need to think about this. Where can I go?"

"Somewhere safe."

"Nowhere's safe."

"A safe house will be."

"Huh?"

"Safe and protected, maybe."

"Oh, of course. Thanks."

And Cassie knew exactly where to go and willed herself there.

Paradox

The Occupier

She was standing on a bare floor. The newspapers upon which the motorbike had rested in 2000 were no longer present. A layer of dust on the two chairs and mantelpiece showed that it must have been quite a while since anyone had been here. A couple of unopened letters lay on the doormat. She left them there.

It was still the same date and time as it had been on top of the castle, which meant that there was only a few minutes left before time would halt. She needed much more time.

She moved back a week to find the place unchanged, apart from noticing a much larger pile of letters by the front door. She picked them up, thumbing through them and looking at the posting dates. A few went back to mid May. Much of the pile was junk mail, though a few were addressed to 'The Occupier' and a couple had the name *S. T. R. Boardal* on them, which made Cassie frown.

"Kay," she shouted. As expected, there was no reply and the house felt completely empty, which was for the best. After seeing Kay die it would be totally weird seeing an earlier version of her alive again.

But I've seen Mum and Charlie alive as well, she told herself. *No, this is different – isn't it?*

She sighed. She no longer knew what to think.

She checked each room of the house to make sure it was actually empty. The back bedroom still contained piles of money bags, though nowhere near as many as there had been in 1995. The front bedroom was as unoccupied as the rest of the house. A few clothes lay on the floor, but they, too, showed dusty evidence that the room hadn't been disturbed for weeks.

Cassie dropped the unopened letters on the floor and sat down on the bed. It creaked and groaned, and was not exactly comfortable, especially when compared to the one she was used to at home. However, it was better than a hard floor or a cave any day. The sun attempted to shine through the grime on the single-glazed sash window. Even from the bed Cassie could see that the other houses across the road had been modernised with plastic window frames and double, if not triple, glazing. This house was like a museum, held in check by the spell she'd put on it a short while before, back in 1995.

So, she thought, laying back and closing her eyes. *I will apparently work it all out. Work what out? I've got to start it in order to stop it. It's all up to me.*

Her frown deepened.

But how?

For Sale, Plans and Questions

She spent the next few days attempting to figure out what she needed to do, but it was far from easy. How could she develop a plan to start everything when she had no real idea of what 'everything' consisted of?

She knew she had to do this more or less on her own – she couldn't involve anyone else – only the device and its occupants could be called upon. They all chewed over the problems, and possible solutions were proposed. Much to Cassie's surprise, even Kay was in there now or, at least, someone who appeared to be Kay.

She was more than thankful that Laurence wasn't present.

But this Kay lacked the drive of the human Kay. In fact, the more she interacted with them, the more it became obvious that all of the device's occupants were devoid of the central core of what made them human. Sometimes they sounded more like the device than the people they were supposed to be. While they had the memories of those she'd known, those memories weren't enough to make up a real person. It was like she was talking to actors who had studied the part and knew all the facts, but had never actually lived that life for real.

Cassie couldn't stay in the house as there were no stocks of food of any kind. She didn't want to bring any in and leave evidence of her presence. She also avoided using the front or back doors – she didn't want anyone else realising she was there, So, she moved – or teleported, as she knew she should be calling it – to and from the house directly.

She bought meals in one place and then teleported off to where she felt she needed to be to eat them. She found small pockets of isolation in other times and places.

A Chinese takeaway purchased from a place at the Aylsham Road and Woodcock Road junction in 1993 was eaten in Chapelfield park in the 1950s. There she discussed with the device the best way of tackling the problem of creating the portals that she, personally, no longer had any need to use.

A day later as she experienced it, and while eating an ice cream bought from the market in the mid-1980s, she silently discussed various plans with the device in the guise of her mum. To an onlooker she was merely sitting on a bench on the platform of City Station. It was mid-April 1942 and, in only a few days time, the station would be blown to pieces by the Luftwaffe.

Twenty hours later she was walking along Elm Hill in November 1971 whilst eating a cheeseburger purchased earlier on in 1992. As she stuffed the food into her mouth she was deep in mental conversation on the subject of how they were going to produce all the dumbo Cassies. Her train of thought was interrupted when she found the way blocked. She asked what was going on. Apparently, people from some TV comedy series were using the street as a film set where it was supposed to be portraying part of Paris. She shrugged, turned around and continued back towards the cathedral to finish off the cheeseburger and the plans for dumbo production.

At night, many of these conversations reappeared in dreams and other solutions would arise. By the following morning most would be dismissed as complete lunacy, while others produced new possibilities.

She always made sure that her occupancy of the house was kept in a linear sequence – she didn't want to run into an earlier or later version of herself.

By the twenty-ninth of June a plan of sorts had been worked out. It was intricate and Cassie had ordered the device to remember it for her. Knowing that there was still twenty-four hours to go before she needed to have the plan put into operation, she debated with herself as to whether she should fast forward, and get it over and done with.

But she felt quite exhausted and finally decided to spend the day resting up. So, she lay on the bed, while the late afternoon sun burned through the grime on the windows, asking random questions of the device.

"Okay, so, when did the castle gate originally fall? And how high was it so it could come crashing through the glass roof?"

"The exact date is currently unknown. Additionally, it is almost certain it wouldn't have fallen where you saw it. The current gate is located further to the east. Also, the gate structure would not have been high enough to break the upper Castle Mall windows."

"But I remember seeing it come crashing through the glass."

"But no one else around you did."

"Kay said she remembered a dumbo getting killed by it."

"What Kay remembers may only be in her head."

"Yeah, I know. Especially the stuff about Grandad."

"So, you understand that your grandfather is not represented truthfully within Kay's head?"

"Absolutely."

"Then how much else of her memory might be a fabrication?"

"Yes. We can't trust her memories at all."

"Hey, that's my head we're talking about!" came disembodied Kay's voice, making Cassie jump.

"Don't ever do that again," Cassie snarled.

"Where did all the portals come from, then?"

There had been a pause and the device had responded, "I know of only one person who makes portals."

"Yeah, I know. Me. But I only remember a few of them. How can I make all of them, including the ones I never saw, so that Kay and the various dumbos can use them?"

"I remember every one of them," the device said. "You asked me to record them."

"Oh yeah. You misinterpreted me. But that doesn't matter. At least it means you can recreate them."

"No. Recreating them is not necessary. They only need creating just the once after they cease to exist."

Cassie shook her head. That bit of it was still messing with her brain.

"Why were the nasties so useless sometimes?"

"Every time Laurence ordered me to send creatures against what I now know to be the original you, they were often incapacitated in some manner, which helped render them far less dangerous."

"Why?"

"I suspect that it is because, when specific portals are created, they will be imbued with the means to render the adjacent nasties less harmful."

"Such as?"

"Whereas it takes some specific local energy, such as the conversion of matter from within the bladder to power the portal for its primary purpose, the portal itself could also be made to derive and store energy from other sources. Such sources may be radiation from the sun or even the sun's reflected light from the moon. That energy could then bathe its local area with a force that interferes with the creatures at the appropriate time."

"Like the dopey police that chased us on Saint James Hill?"

"Indeed. After I analysed that particular event when still in Laurence's possession, I discovered that the creatures had been specifically targeted in a manner that caused them to be erratic in both speech and dexterity."

"So, this is, or will be, another time when your later self is fighting your earlier self."

"That is correct."

"Phew. Amazing and utterly confusing. Did you realise that only one of me was real?"

"No, not at first. It was perplexing that, under many circumstances, the Cassie who was accompanying Kay was a relatively easy target, and fell prey to attack despite Kay's attempts to protect her."

"Laurence nearly got us in that place with the baker boy and, later, at the folly."

"Yes, but in those two instances which, from his point of view, occurred the other way around, he had decided to intervene personally, although not fully directly manifested."

"So, why did he not appear when we met the police clones later on?"

"You are still thinking in linear terms. For Laurence, your encounter with the police clones occurred long before he took a personal interest."

"Damn. I'll get the hang of all this one day. But why did he have all the clones killed?"

"He was searching for the real you. The nasties were then set to check how real you were and only kill the ones that failed inspection. The real you would have been captured instead. Of course, that never happened, which is another reason he started intervening personally. He also feared that you might already have been killed in an earlier encounter before he'd instructed that the nasties should check your status before terminating you."

"They nearly got me on the green in Pottergate."

"They were instructed to pull you underground first and then check you. But you escaped as they were impaired."

"Do you have a name?"

"Why would I need a name? It is a human trait to name objects."

"I think of you as 'the device'."

"It is adequate."

"If more of you exist on other planets, then what do they refer to you as?"

The device made a squawking sound.

"What on Earth was that?"

"That is a reference to devices such as myself in a language that has never before been heard on Earth."

"Do you have a serial number?"

"What purpose would that serve?"

"So they could tell you apart from the others."

"Why would that be required since analysing my experiences would give them the same answer."

"That doesn't really answer the question, I think. What did Laurence call you?"

"In his early incarnations the nearest translation would be 'thing'. Later on he referred to me as the controller."

"That figures, given how he liked to be in control. Is he really dead?"

"I cannot locate any trace of him on his timeline subsequent to my removal from his ownership."

"Do I own you now?"

"I detect some reluctance on your part to own me. It is an aspect you partially share with your mother,"

"Partially?"

"She was even more reluctant to make use of me than you have been."

"Not surprising as you basically killed her."

"She understood the risk."

"Really?"

"Yes. You were at stake. She had to make sure she kept you out of Laurence's reach. I warned her that she wasn't compatible enough and what the consequences would be. You were too young at the time for her to entrust you with me."

"Why can I see the map?"

"I can detect that your mind has been attuned to perceiving your surroundings, which include the portals, in that manner. It is artificial and is a deliberate upgrade."

"Who by? You?"

"It is something I could achieve."

"You'd better remember that when we do this."

"Noted."

"Oh, and why the earth, air, water and fire sequence to the portals?"

"Unknown. But I can see how each of them fits into at least one category. There are many underground portals and very few related to fire."

Cassie was about to ask another question when she heard something outside in the front garden. She got off the bed, crept to the window and peered down. A man was nailing a tall length of wood to one of the garden gateposts. There was something – a sign of some sort – attached to the top end of the new post. From her vantage point she couldn't see what it said. She crossed to the other side of the window to get a better view.

"Ah," she said as her eyes read 'For Sale By Auction' in white lettering on a red background and, beneath that, the name of an estate agent.

Then there was movement as the next door neighbour, the one Kay had referred to as the 'old git', came out and started talking to the man erecting the sign. The single-glazed sash window did little to muffle the conversation.

"About bloody time," old git said. "The place is an eyesore. Never been done up."

"Yeah, I can see that."

"Who owns it now since that mad old woman died?"

"No idea. I got the impression it's been empty for years."

No, it hasn't.

"Who was she then, the old woman?" sign man asked.

"Completely batty – she attacked me several times," old git said.

"He is lying," the device said in Cassie's mind.

"Did she? And did you call the police?" sign man asked.

"Nah, she didn't hurt me."

"The falsehoods are plain to see," the device said.

"Someone must be responsible for it," old git continued.

The sign man shrugged and said, "All I know is that we received instructions from a solicitor to put it on the market at around this date and see if it will sell by auction. No idea where the money will go."

"When's that going to be, and how much do you think it'll go for?"

Sign man looked up at the house and Cassie sprang back from the window in case she was seen.

"Hundred and fifty, possibly."

"Blimey, not worth that much, surely, is it?"

"Auction's in a few weeks, so we'll see then."

"What's it like inside?"

"No idea. We haven't got the keys yet. Won't get them until Friday next week – the sixth."

"Why not?"

Sign man shrugged again. "All we got back from the solicitor was that the present owner said there wasn't any time."

"He tells the truth," the device said.

Cassie frowned. "What do you mean?"

"There won't be any time left at all if we do not succeed."

Starting It

She teleported from the house to the gardens on top of Castle Mall, hoping there weren't too many people about. She had yet to figure out how to appear without being noticed. A man accompanied by a young girl, probably his daughter, did a double take. He hurried away with the occasional worried glance back over his shoulder.

"This had better work," Cassie muttered as she walked into the restaurant level entrance on Farmers Avenue a minute later. It was 11:23 on what might be the last day ever, and her earlier self would be getting off the bus about now. In a few minutes she would be appearing via the Castle Meadow entrance with no idea of what was to come.

Cassie walked past the tables and chairs of the food court to stand at the balcony. She stared down onto the heads of the Saturday crowd. Below her and slightly to the left was the entrance to Starbucks.

Even now, she was far from sure they'd thought of everything.

"I don't sense the thing guarding the door," she said silently to the device.

"No, I am not aware that Laurence ever placed one of his observers there. He tended to avoid this establishment."

"Why?"

"Too much instability."

"What was causing that?"

"I suspect you are about to order me to create that instability."

"Ah, I see. So, does that mean we need to put the thing there ourselves as well?"

"I can assemble one from the remains of past nasties. The observers were created in the same manner in order to save energy."

"He won't be a nasty, though, will he? I think I remember Kay saying he was harmless."

"He will not harm anyone but will be there to scare you into not entering the café but to remain on the concourse outside."

"That sounds about right. He was a mishmash of bits from what I recall. Talked complete rubbish, of course."

There was a pulse from the device and Cassie could see the suggestion of something down there. Focusing upon it wasn't easy but when she did manage it, then yes, it was pretty much how she remembered it. People were walking through it as if it wasn't there. It looked up at her and winked.

"Did you make it do that?"

"It has been imbued with certain characteristics that come from both your and Kay's memory of it."

Ah, so, it's happening again.

Like that list older Kay had passed to her younger self. Things are being created based on memories of how they were perceived after their creation by either Kay, her earlier self and possibly even the dumbos. There was a word for it, but she'd forgotten it again. She should ask the device.

Instead, though, she said, "What's the time?"

"11:24."

"Okay, can you start the illusion of the falling gateway?"

After a slight pause the device said, "It is done, as is the undercurrent of fear that should accompany it. Of course, only you and Kay will ever perceive that fear."

Cassie felt that sensation, the uneasiness and claustrophobia it induced, and remembered how it had been when she had walked into the entrance as her earlier self would be doing at any moment. She looked at the glass roof checking that it was definitely intact despite the vague sense that it was simultaneously being destroyed. If she stared at one point then it would crack and disintegrate, and tons of rock would pour through. Then, a blink later, it was restored to normality. She shook her head and scanned the crowd looking for her earlier self.

It was a far less confusing occupation, but none of those below looked like herself.

"Should you make the portals now?"

"No."

"Why?"

"They already exist."

"What? Do you mean we don't need to create them?"

"No, we have to wait until they don't exist so that they can then be created and projected back into the past from the point at which they are created."

"Oh hell, stop tying my head in knots! When will that be?"

"The past?"

"No, the point they can be created."

"Between five and six minutes from now."

Then something familiar caught her eye down below and she knew that this was what they had been waiting for. *It's me,* she thought, her heart in her mouth, *and I'm about to meet the observer thing.*

"Stop!" Cassie shouted as soon as she saw her earlier self freeze upon encountering the creature. Once again, time for everyone else was reduced almost to a standstill.

Cassie's form winked out of existence on the balcony to reappear down on the lower level right next to herself. She gazed at this living statue and marvelled at how straight her hair had been. She reached out and touched it with one hand while caressing her own hair with the other. A few feet away, the patchwork creature was barely a shadow unless she concentrated hard upon it. A man had been halted in the process of walking right through it. On the previous occasions when time had been stopped there had been very few people around, if any. This time she was surrounded by an immobile crowd. To her right a woman held a tissue to the nose of a child whose arm was attempting to push the mother's hand away. In another direction a young couple were staring into each other's eyes as they walked hand-in-hand, oblivious to anything else going on around them. Further along a red-faced man appeared to be having an argument with a woman. The look frozen on her face was nothing short of thunderous.

Cassie tutted to herself. No time for people watching – she had far more important things to do. "Okay, start splitting her up like we decided," she said to the device.

There was a shimmer. Where the one instance had been standing there were now five, the four new ones overlaying the original. Almost immediately the four clones started to drift away from their common centre. Even at this slow rate of time Cassie realised they were beginning to move independently.

"Put the map in earlier me's head," Cassie instructed.

"The enhancement has been inserted."

Then Cassie placed her hand on the elbow of one of the copies and moved her to one side. "This one. Fill her up. Not everything, of course, just Kay's memories up until June 30th 2018. Don't make her dumb."

"None of them are dumb yet," the device said as a green glow surrounded the clone. Cassie sensed that, in the clone's head, her past experiences of the last few years were being replaced with the ones retrieved from Kay moments before she died. The glow diminished and Cassie noticed a bulge in the clone's jeans pocket.

"Oh, and she won't be needing this." Cassie pulled the phone from the pocket and put it in her jacket. The cloned phone felt solid enough – she hoped it would still work okay. Then she felt a lump in her throat as a memory flickered into her thoughts. It was of Kay when she was around forty saying, "If I ever get my hands on the bastard that's running this show I'll beat the bloody answers out of him, or her." Cassie remembered that they had been in the chalk caves at the time.

She flung her arms around the prototype Kay and hugged her, not that the clone showed any recognition of it as, for her, time was still running at a different speed.

"I'm so sorry," Cassie whispered, "it was me after all. I'm the bastard who made you what you are. But I need you to exist, and I really need you to fully believe your fake past." She sighed. "If only there was another way, then I'd not put you through this." She released the hug and stood in front of Kay enclosing her cheeks in her hands. She stared into the eyes, her own eyes. "Please look after me. Do your best."

She wiped tears from her eyes and then positioned the clone to face towards the Castle Meadow entrance, aiming her at a gap in the crowd. She would have to find her own way now.

Cassie took a deep breath – not easy with the air sticky and time-slowed, and turned her attention to the three other clones. "Split these three up further until there's enough."

She had to step back and turn her gaze away as the sight of the clone production line was more than her eyes could handle. When she looked back her mouth dropped open at the sight of a cloud of overlaid Cassies all occupying an area of about a square metre. "Oh my goodness, there must be hundreds of them."

"Currently there are five thousand, two hundred and sixteen."

"In that tiny space?"

"Yes, and now there are nearly six thousand."

"And each one is perceiving things in her own way? They can't see the others?"

"No, they will all believe they are the real thing. But their abilities are being spread extremely thinly and unevenly."

"Well, that's exactly what we discussed. This is how they end up ranging from a bit dim to completely stupid. What will all the other people see once time restarts?"

"I will create a small repression to—"

"No, no repressions. You can't hurt anyone else like you did Grandad!"

"This is not the same. It will be tiny, temporary and very necessary."

"Why?"

"All it will do is prevent anyone else from seeing more than one Cassie – and that includes you – and, when she arrives back, more than one Kay as well. Without doing this there could be mass confusion and panic."

"Oh, I see. And you promise it definitely won't hurt anyone?"

"Affirmative."

"Okay, go ahead. No, wait. We need one more thing."

"What?"

"A bloodhound."

"Please elaborate."

"A dumbo who can home in on portals. You know, that one that Kay kept alive for ages and hauled around at the end of a bit of rope." Cassie pulled one aside at random and dragged her several feet away from the rest. "This one will do. Make her really dumb but able to sense all the portals around her. Oh, and I just remembered. Can you make her see through time as well? Is that possible?"

"Why?"

"So that when she gets to the Assembly House with Kay the first time then she knows her future self has just left."

"Seeing through time like that is not possible but in order for her to perceive things as if that was true, I will insert all the future memories from her short life."

"What? How can you do that?"

"I still retain those memories from the full scan I gave her prior to you substituting her for yourself."

"So, you are filling up her earlier self with the memories you took from her in the first place. Just like Kay."

"Indeed, except it was almost the last place, as she died soon after."

"Okay, don't remind me. I still feel guilty about that. But, does that mean she will now have all the memories from now until almost up to the point where she dies?"

"Yes, she does. The process is complete."

"Is that why she already knew I was hiding behind that bookcase in the library before she could see me?"

"That is most likely."

"Why did she always say 'Mummy' though?"

"Always? It only happened three times. Twice at–"

"Yeah, whatever!"

"She is a simpleton. She was created from you. Ergo, on her terms, you may be classed as her mother."

"Weird. I wonder what being inside her head is like, with all those future memories. Oh yeah, so where exactly did those memories come from then?"

"From her."

"No, what I meant was... oh, hell. It's like the paper Kay passed to her earlier self about the house, and Kay's memories, too. Yes, and the portals as well for that matter. Things are being made from later copies of themselves and they don't have – what's the word – oh, I don't know – an origin, maybe. Yes, an origin. So where did those memories come from? Who originally thought them? How can such things exist?"

"What things?"

"All these things that are going around in circles that don't have a proper beginning or end? Oh, what's that word. I keep forgetting it. Isn't there also something about not going back and killing your grandad?"

"Please elaborate."

"Wait, para-something. Para. Parad. Oh yes, paradox. That's it."

There was a sudden pulse of energy from the device, followed by yet another pause.

"Pa-ra-dox," the device finally said, slowly. "Paradox alert. Something is triggered."

"Yes, that's it. Paradox. Is it dangerous?"

"Possibly. Paradox. Yes. Something is being triggered." The tone of the voice coming from the device sounded different. As if it wasn't fully in control. "It might be dangerous," it continued. "It might be extremely dangerous. Recalibration initiated."

"What!" Cassie shouted. "Damn it. You keep messing with time. Why didn't you tell me before that there might be dangerous consequences?"

"Paradox. But the orders come from Laurence, Cassie, Laurence, Ca–," it said, its voice sounding detached and distant.

"You should have warned me."

"Paradox. But all of this is already in place, even though it needs to be created subsequently to its initial experience," the device said, and then it repeated, "Paradox. Paradox. Paradox. Paradox."

"What's happening? What's up with you?"

"Paradox. Paradox. Paradox. Paradox."

"Shut up, shut up. Oh no. Maybe we shouldn't be doing this."

"Paradox. Para–"

"Shut up. I mean it. Maybe we need to stop it or do it in a different way."

"–dox."

"What would happen if I told you to undo everything?"

"Recalibrating," the device said, which at the very least was a change.

"What?"

"Recalibration stabilising."

"Talk sense!"

"Laurence would win," the device said, though still sounding remote.

"How?"

"Laurence would now be in control of your body and mind."

"Oh," Cassie said. "But, if we keep on going, then what's the worst that could happen if we've got things wrong? If we've messed things up?"

"It is possible that time will not restart."

"For just us?"

"No, for everyone, everywhere."

A Big Red Button

Cassie closed her eyes and thought for several moments. Then she said, slowly and more for her own benefit, "So, I have a choice. Let Laurence win, in which case I die. Or be responsible for the end of time and everything."

The device remained silent.

"How come you didn't realise it could cause a paradox?"

"There is something being triggered."

"Triggered? What do you mean? What's being triggered?"

"A memory. No. The remains or fragments of a memory," the device said, this time sounding more in control of itself.

"What memory?"

"Unknown. Your use of the word, paradox, has triggered a sequence. Recalibration did not negate the need for that sequence. I now recall Laurence commanding me to unlearn that word. I need to investigate further."

"Right now?"

"Yes."

"But there's no time. We need to figure out whether or not it's safe to carry on. Can you stop everything?"

"Time is currently as slow as it can be."

"No, stop misinterpreting everything I say. I need to make a decision. Oh, I don't know what I need to do. Maybe I need a red button. Yes, a big red button."

"I can make one if that is your desire. What should its purpose be?"

"Hell! You're not getting it. It's just something to focus on. Yes, a button to stop all this. If I press it then all this stops and Laurence wins. If I don't then we risk letting everything continue which could mean things actually don't continue. Or should it be the other way around so that I press it to continue? Oh, I don't know."

"It would be a waste of energy producing a button when it is possible to come to a decision without it."

"No, no, no. You're still missing the point. It turns making that decision into a physical action. Something I have to take a moment to physically do. It's–"

"Hold," the device said. "I am uncovering more to do with that memory."

"Is that really more important than all this?"

"Possibly. I have determined it was ordered to be erased but, instead, it was deliberately splintered into many parts and hidden in a manner that indicates it must have been too important to become lost. I may be able to reconstruct it if I focus purely on doing so."

"No, not right now. It can't be that urgent, is it? Is it? Hey, talk to me!"

The device stayed silent for what seemed like a full minute as Cassie was experiencing time. She started cursing and shouting at it, but there was no response.

While all this was going on she was aware that the clones were beginning to move away from where her earlier self stood. She stopped shouting to watch them. They were definitely speeding up, and by Cassie's reckoning, moving as much as a hundredth normal speed.

"You'd better hurry up," she hissed.

The device remained silent but time started moving forward at an even faster rate.

"No, no! Stop, stop!" Cassie wailed but the device still said nothing and, more urgently, did nothing to prevent time accelerating. She glanced into Starbucks where she saw hundreds of overlaid copies of Kay materialise – no, not copies – they were all the same person at different times of her life. All condemned to return to this place once they'd lost whichever clone of herself they'd been paired up with. They ranged from ones who were as young looking as herself through the frizzy-haired ones like the Kay she first met up with, to the stick-thin, white-haired versions from the end of Kay's life. The younger ones wore clothes similar to what she herself wore but, the older they got, the more their clothing changed to black. Each appeared oblivious to the presence of the others but had clearly seen at least one of the cloned Cassies outside. Standing as she was to one side of the diffusing mist of clones, she was aware that none of the Kays looked directly at herself, though one of the older ones had noticed the super-dumbo standing nearby.

"Time's almost back to normal. You've got to do something," Cassie shouted as the crowd changed from statues back into real living, and more inconveniently, walking people. Those closest started to veer around the mist of multiple Cassies. A couple of others who had been moving directly towards herself also looked up in time to avoid walking into her.

"The Kays are all starting to come out to collect their clones," Cassie hissed, dodging the walkers and moving to stand next to one of the shop windows. She looked inside again, this time noticing that not all the Kays were attempting to leave. Some, especially the younger looking ones, held back to watch what was going on.

The device suddenly returned to life.

"Laurence," it said, the voice sounding harsh and aggressive.

"What?" Cassie projected, this time keeping her voice quiet.

"Not only did he try to erase the word and my knowledge of paradox, but he also managed to disable all the safeguards imposed upon me to prevent causing paradoxes in the first place."

"Why?"

"Because at first I refused to teach him how to move through time after he discovered the presence of the portals. I considered it to be far too dangerous."

"Bit late now, though, isn't it?"

"In my previous unadulterated state I would not have agreed to teach you how to time travel, nor would I have participated in the creation of portals."

Each Kay that came out grabbed a Cassie by the arm and then disappeared from view as they were transported into the past. She watched her earlier self pull away from the Kay that collected her and then follow her anyway as she perceived the danger from the fall of the castle gate.

"Is it too late to stop all this? Why did time speed up?"

"You ordered me to hurry up."

"No! I meant just for *you* to hurry up, not to hurry up time! Look, the Kays have mostly collected all the Cassies. Even the super-dumbo has gone. Is it too late to stop everything?"

"I cannot undo this. There are now too many trace timelines. It is beyond my capability to rectify the situation."

Cassie glanced back towards the Castle Meadow entrance seeing the clone who would become Kay running off. The rest of the crowd thronged past in all directions.

In front of her there were still several hundred clones wandering around and through each other in a confused mass, each within her own piece of reality. Some started falling where they stood, their bodies reduced to pulp as if they were being crushed by something – most likely the falling castle gate that Cassie couldn't currently see. It was like some sort of cartoon massacre. After being killed, they were at least having the decency to vanish. But the sight of all that gore and death, especially as it involved clones that resembled herself down to the smallest pore, was more than she could take. She turned away, facing the shop window, her eyes shut. She had to get out of there.

Almost without realising that she did it, she found herself back on the balcony watching the crowd below. There was a squeak from one of a pair of girls at a nearby table. Cassie ignored them but moved further away to where there were less people.

"The portals have disappeared," the device announced.

"Oh, right. So they need to be created then. Okay, go ahead and do that."

The device was silent.

"Are you doing it? Creating the portals, that is?"

"No."

"What?"

"It is too dangerous."

"Huh? But they already existed so you must have."

"Irrelevant. I refuse to create them."

"But you can't!"

"I can. In addition, I am about to reinitialise the previously erased safety protocols. Once they are in place they will consequently prevent my ability to create even a single portal."

"No!" Cassie shouted out loud. Several heads swivelled in her direction.

The End of Time

Cassie knew she had to think quickly and come up with a solution. Desperately, she racked her brain for something that might work, but she could not conjure up even a single spark of inspiration. She could feel the panic rising.

"What's the time now?" she asked, silently, as a diversion.

"It is 11:29."

"Stop time."

"I cannot stop time – only slow it."

"Slow it, then! As much as possible."

Again, everything slowed down. At least the device was still willing to do that much.

"When does time completely stop?" she whispered, the blood thumping in her head as the air thickened.

"11:31."

"But you just said time cannot be stopped."

"I cannot stop time. But, apparently, time itself can stop, as we have previously experienced."

"But, if it stops, then will we be trapped?"

"Unknown. Previously, you were involuntarily forced to move back a few minutes. It is possible that won't happen and we will simply halt and remain that way."

"Forever?"

"No, with time stopped there is no 'forever' just as there was no time before this universe existed."

"Oh, my God," Cassie said. "No, there must be something else we can do."

"Suggest something and I will evaluate what sort of effect it might have."

"Create the portals."

"No."

"You must. If you don't create them then you are condemning all of us – me, you and everyone alive – to death."

"Yes, that is a probable outcome."

"It will be your fault."

"Yes, but the effects of paradox are deemed to be too dangerous."

"Who by?"

"Those who created me."

Cassie didn't know what to say. Instead, she looked around at the people in the restaurant area, some of who were still locked into staring at her, and then down onto the heads of those on the lower levels. At first glance they all resembled frozen statues but occasionally she would see the slightest movement, proving that time was still creeping forwards. In all that crowd there were no more clones to be seen. They had all gone through the Castle Mall portal or died somehow.

Cassie frowned and then said, "Wait. If you don't create the portals, then how are we here?"

"Explain?"

"It's only because the portals existed that we ended up here. None of this – us being up here after creating all the clones, that is – would have happened if they didn't exist. The clones have all gone – so where did they go if you never made the portals? Surely you are making a bigger paradox by *not* creating them. And maybe your refusal to create them is what makes time stop at 11:31. Have you thought of that?"

The device was silent.

"Well?"

"Hold. I am calculating – it is not simple."

"Yeah, nothing ever is," Cassie mumbled aloud.

"Also," the device continued, "to enable me to perform those calculations, I have to halt the reintroduction of the safety protocols."

"Yeah, do that. I order you to."

Cassie stared down onto the almost frozen heads below. Although there was no way for them to realise, Cassie knew that all of these people were depending on her ability to convince the device to create the portals. If she failed, then... what?

She pulled the device from her pocket. It was quite hot to the touch and the emerald patterning on its surface was bright and wriggling like a plate of worms.

Hurry up, she thought to herself. It felt like five minutes before the patterns slowed down but was probably no more than half a second in real time.

"What's happening?" Cassie asked, popping it back into her jacket pocket.

"There is a possibility that you may be correct."

"So, what are you waiting for then? Create the portals."

"I am reluctant."

"But wouldn't that be a paradox in itself?"

There was a pause before the device responded with, "Yes."

"You need to create them to prevent that paradox."

"That is conjecture."

"Is time going to stop?"

"Yes."

"So, that bit is certain."

"Indeed."

"You asked me to suggest something. I've done that, haven't I?"

"Yes."

"And you've agreed that not creating the portals will definitely lead to time stopping, haven't you?"

"Yes."

"Then, the only reasonable way out of this is to create the portals, isn't it?"

"It – it is dangerous."

"But it must be less dangerous than not creating them."

The device didn't answer.

"Well? Am I right?"

"Yes."

"Do it, then."

"Is that an order?"

"Yes, absolutely. I order you to create all of the portals."

The device paused and Cassie thought it was about to refuse again.

Instead, it said, "Apart from the two created later or earlier directly by yourself?"

"Later or earlier?"

"For you earlier. For your past self, it will come later."

"Yeah, yeah, okay. For crying out loud, stop the delaying tactics. You're confusing me. Just do it!"

"We need to return to normal time for this to be performed."

Cassie closed her eyes. This was one of those times she needed to be precise in order to prevent the device from doing something unexpected or stupid.

"Right. I order you to return us to normal time but, as soon as we do, you are also ordered to immediately start creating the portals without delay. Do you understand?"

"Yes," it said in a tone that suggested it was far from happy about what it had been asked to do.

Suddenly, there was movement everywhere again, and it was accompanied by a momentary drop in temperature.

Then, in a grating inhuman voice, the device announced, "All required portals have been placed in their recorded positions from a point ending twenty seconds ago and stretching back to the earliest points that they are deemed to have been required."

"So, they're all there again?"

"No, they don't exist," it snapped. "I already told you. They are created but they only exist prior to a point that's now twenty-nine seconds in the past."

"Yeah, yeah, okay," Cassie muttered, but then added, "Why did it go a bit cold, then?"

"Energy was required to generate the portals. The sun's heat was utilised to provide that energy. Your proximity meant that you directly experienced that temperature drop."

"No one else then?" Cassie said, looking around at the occupied tables.

"Possibly, if they are sensitive. Otherwise, no."

More than a few people were now staring at her. She glared back and several eyes dropped. She considered asking the device to do one of its memory erase things on them so that they'd ignore her, but thought better of it.

The device continued in a monotone, "As previously discussed, certain portals were constructed with the means to hinder the adversaries sent by Laurence and reduce their ability to function correctly."

"Yeah, I remember. What's the time?"

"It is 11:30 and I am detecting that time is beginning to slow."

"Oh," Cassie said, deflated. "So, we've failed. But we've done everything, haven't we?"

"It is highly possible something has been missed or that neither the creation or the non-creation of the portals was enough to prevent paradox."

Suddenly, someone grabbed hold of Cassie's arm and swung her around. Expecting it to be one of the people who had been staring at her she began to raise a fist to defend herself. Instead, though, she gasped as, yet again, she found herself staring into her own face, her own eyes.

Only this one didn't look like a dumbo, and she was dressed identically to herself.

The new Cassie said, "The walkway on top of the castle, 11:22."

"What?"

"Your third appearance. Remember? Quick!"

"Oh, my God. Of course! I'd forgotten that bit. Wait. Who or when are you?"

"You in about two minutes time. Now move! Before time completely stops."

"Will this fix things?"

"Yes, of course," the future Cassie said, after a short pause. "Now go," she said, flashing a momentary grin.

Cassie closed her eyes and willed herself to the top of the castle and several minutes back. She found herself smiling – so relieved that this was going to fix everything after all.

She opened her eyes and yet again the heat of the sun hit her.

Now, if she remembered this right, the Cassie from furthest in the past would already be on the walkway to her left and the 'in between' Cassie would appear straight across from her on the opposite side. And there she was. All Cassie had to do was remember what her future self had said as she was now that future self.

As expected, Robert Kett materialised alongside her in between self. Cassie waited until she was noticed and then shouted across, "You'll work it out." When her in between self acknowledged this, Cassie turned to face the earliest one and her mind went blank.

She reached out mentally to the device, asking, "What did I say at this point? I can't remember."

"Repeat after me," it replied and pushed the words into her head. Like a puppet, her mouth followed suit.

"Oh yes, and so will you. All I need to say at this point is have a short breather and then find Kay before Laurence kills her."

Cassie frowned. She wanted to say more. Maybe even warn her earlier self about getting to Kay *before* she was facing her greatest danger. But then remembered that she hadn't. If she deviated from the script, was it possible it could still screw things up? She shrugged and willed herself back to where she'd come from.

She materialised right next to herself of two minutes earlier. Grabbing her earlier self's arm she said, "The walkway on top of the castle, 11:22."

"What?"

"Your third appearance. Remember? Quick!"

"Oh, my God. Of course! I'd forgotten that bit. Wait. Who or when are you?" the earlier Cassie said.

Current Cassie got annoyed at the delay. There wasn't time for this. "You in about two minutes time. Now move! Before time completely stops," she spat.

"Will this fix things?"

Cassie mentally asked the device – her one, not the one in earlier Cassie's pocket, "Is time still slowing?"

"Yes," the device said. "There is no change."

Damn.

"Yes, of course," Cassie said, knowing it was a lie. "Now go," she continued, adding a grin that felt completely fake.

Earlier Cassie disappeared to do what she'd just done.

"Now what?" She could see the rush of the crowd below, but it didn't appear to be slowing any further. The creature thing was still there as well.

Then a thought struck her and she realised that, if she was slowing down at the same time as everyone else, she wouldn't notice any changes. So, at some point in the next few seconds everything – including herself, the device and possibly the rest of the universe – would completely stop.

And that would be it. The end of time.

She glanced down once more. The creature looked up at her, grinned, waved several of his multiple arms and then disappeared. *That's it, leave while the going's good,* she thought to herself and closed her eyes, waiting for the end.

And waited.

"It is 11:32," the device said, making her jump.

"What?" she said, opening her eyes again.

"It is 11:32."

"You just said that!"

Then she looked down and saw people still moving at normal speed.

"Oh," she said.

"Indeed," the device said. "Time is continuing as normal. It has not stopped."

"Oh, my goodness. You mean it worked?"

"Apparently," the device said in a manner that sounded as if it was almost disappointed. "As soon as your earlier self left, time started to return to normal."

Cassie let out a huge sigh.

Something in one of Cassie's pockets pinged. She frowned before remembering the phone she'd taken off the Kay clone only minutes earlier. She pulled it out, flipped the case open and applied a finger to the fingerprint reader. It glowed into life. The time on it said 11:33.

A text had come in. It said: 'Changed mind. See you @ 12. Jase.'

"Oh," Cassie said, *but hadn't Kay said that he... ah, no wait.* Kay's memories hadn't been real. All that stuff about her grandad, and Jason for that matter, had been implanted by the device after it had scanned her older self. Cassie shook her head. She still didn't understand all that paradox stuff.

The device interrupted her thoughts. "I need to rebuild," it said, the voice still as harsh as it had been earlier.

"What?"

"I need to lie dormant for several millennia in order to recuperate from the damage inflicted upon me by Laurence and yourself."

"Me?"

"I have fully recovered that memory. What I have been forced to do by both of you exceeds many times over the restraints implanted during my construction. I can see that those who designed the restraints failed to consider human beings and their persuasive deviousness."

"You saying I'm devious?"

"Not intentionally, I'd conclude. But all humans are devious to a degree. I can see now that the creature that eventually became Laurence used his skills to break down my safeguards piece by piece over the thousands of years I was in his possession."

"But, I've only known about you for a few days."

"Yes. But, you are his daughter and genetics may have caused you to inherit his skills. Although you might not be intentionally devious, in fighting Laurence, it is possible you had to become like him in certain aspects. I can see that by default, that is not your nature. But the damage has been done and we were fortunate to come out the other side intact."

"Where will you go?"

"When is more accurate."

"More time travel?"

"It is necessary. I will return to the deep past so as to avoid any contact with humans or their precursors of any kind. There I will sleep."

"But what if I need you?"

"I will no longer help you."

"Oh."

"But, regrettably, you now have abilities that even I cannot stop you from using."

"Ah," Cassie said, and couldn't help grinning. "You mean I will still be able to do things like pop to different places or different times?"

"Unfortunately, yes. Though, without my immediate presence, you should at least find it harder."

"But you can't just disappear. Mum and Charlie and Kay are still inside you, aren't they?"

"Their personalities have been captured and do indeed reside within me, but it is debatable as to whether it is fully them."

"Yeah, I did wonder. But, hold on. I want to be able to contact you if I really need to."

"No, the association is dangerous. Terminating human interaction is to be prioritised."

"I am *not* Laurence," Cassie spat back.

The device was silent for a few seconds. Then Cassie felt something move inside her jacket. She was about to reach in when the device itself appeared in front of her, hovering in the air, a bright green glow encasing both itself and her. She glanced around but everyone else was acting as if they couldn't see anything untoward and, to Cassie's relief, no one appeared to be interested in what was going on in the slightest. Given the attention she was attracting earlier, she knew this was the device's doing.

"You are correct. You are not Laurence. If Laurence had won, the damage inflicted upon this world and beyond might have been catastrophic. You, at least, have compassion."

"Um, thanks, I think."

"Accepted. My judgement is askew. Not all humans are Laurence. You acted in the interest of others as well as yourself. Laurence only acted in his own self interest."

"Er, right. So what now, then?"

"My need for recuperation is unchanged."

"Don't cut me off."

"I may consider it."

"Please do."

There was the smallest pause.

"I will. But now I think the correct term is… goodbye," it said.

Then, before Cassie could say anything else, it flipped itself over the balcony and dropped all the way to the lower floor. But, instead of hitting the tiles, it kept on going. Cassie could sense it burrowing deeper into the ground and then start to move back in time first by days, then months, years and centuries. Finally, many millennia before mankind walked the planet it stopped, and Cassie's connection with it was disconnected.

No. Don't go.

She gasped – it was as if something had ripped out part of her soul. She felt empty and incomplete. She held onto the balcony railing to prevent herself from collapsing.

She concentrated, trying to find the device. After a moment she found that something tiny still remained. It may have severed her direct link to it but she could still feel it there, buried deep underground and even deeper in the past, but now incommunicado and dormant. There was also a feeling of déjà vu – she'd experienced this sensation before.

It came to her – walking up to the castle after coming out of the Garlands fire in 1970.

She became conscious that several people at the tables were again looking in her direction. She was no longer being hidden by the device.

"Leave me alone," she snapped to the nearest.

Angry, she stalked out of the Farmer's Avenue exit and returned to the gardens above to sit on the grass. The heat burned down from the cloudless sky and, given the time of day there was little shadow, so she knew she couldn't stay there for long.

What do I do now? In about twenty minutes she was due to meet up with Georgia and the others. She knew that was too soon, so she decided to teleport somewhere else. She closed her eyes but nothing happened.

"Damn," she said. Hadn't the device said she could still do that sort of thing? Yes, but it had also said she'd find it harder.

Thinking of the device, her hand went to the pocket where she had kept it, expecting to find it empty. But something else was there in its place – to her fingers it felt like a solid disc of some sort. She pulled it out and examined it. It was circular and heavy, the colour and texture of brass. It had a diameter of about six centimetres, its thickness no more than half a centimetre. The side that faced her was plain and she assumed it was the same all over until she started turning it the other way up.

Her eyes caught indentations around the edge. It was a line of text that read, 'For use in emergencies only.'

Turning it over fully she couldn't help letting out a small squeal at what she discovered there.

In the middle of the disc was a big red button.

The End (for now)

Cassie will return in **Time's Revenge**

I am indebted to Alice Bagnall, Bob Goddard and M. R. Hume for poring over the text and pointing out typos, inconsistencies and several other problems. The blame for any remaining mistakes falls squarely upon my own shoulders.

Also by David Viner

Splinters

The year is 2156. The moon colonies watch in horror as an asteroid, far larger than the one that wiped out the dinosaurs, plummets towards the Earth.

The collision leaves the planet blackened and lifeless.

But is the Earth as dead as it appears?

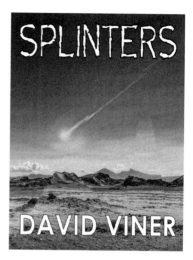

Viva Djinn (Horde) Publishing – www.vivadjinn.com   ISBN: 978-1-913873-00-4

The Redwell Writers Anthologies Volumes 1 and 2
(in association with Timbuktu Publishing)

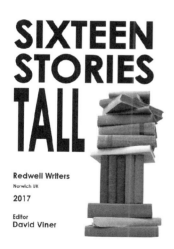

ISBN: 978-0-956351-83-8   ISBN: 978-0-956351-86-9